Praise fo

"I had almost give. _____ ___ _____ ___ ____ picked up *Creature of the Cascades*. Here is something you don't see every day. Rob Phillips writes real places into this page-turner, and he is not averse to taking risks with humor, suspense and wordplay. I was hooked from the first jump."

—Gary Lewis, TV host and author of *Fishing Central Oregon*, *Fishing Mount Hood Country*, and *John Nosler Going Ballistic*

"Rob Phillips takes you on another fun romp into the wilds of Washington State as Luke McCain works ... to figure out who or what is killing pets, livestock, and wild game in the South Cascades. Is it Sasquatch as some believe or is it something else?"

—John Kruse, host of *Northwestern Outdoors* and *America Outdoors Radio*

"*Cascade Manhunt* is the fifth book of Rob Phillips' Luke McCain series, and I believe it to be his best work . . . . As a retired Washington State undercover Fish and Wildlife detective, I found Rob's book to be spot-on. I simply couldn't put *Cascade Manhunt* down and am already thirsting for Rob's next book."

—Todd Vandivert, retired Washington State Fish and Wildlife detective and author of the Wildlife Justice series

"Poaching big game . . . check. A loveable yellow Lab . . . double check. Computer hackers from India . . . WHAT! That last item is the big checklist twist in outdoor writer Rob Phillips' latest novel, *Cascade Kidnapping*, the fourth in his Luke McCain series. As in all of Phillips' books, *Cascade Kidnapping* reinforces healthy respect for the outdoors and laws that protect it."

—Bob Crider, retired editor and publisher, *Yakima Herald-Republic*

"*Cascade Kidnapping* has Washington State game warden Luke McCain and his yellow Lab, Jack, arresting salmon poachers, investigating a serial elk killer, and dealing with administrative duties.

. . . Phillips' writing displays a real knowledge of the outdoors, as well as the duties and responsibilities of game wardens. A very enjoyable book!!"
    −Rich Phillips, book reviewer for the *International Game Warden Magazine*

"*Cascade Predator* is a well-blended stew of Northwest icons, a reflection of Rob's intimate knowledge of wildlife, outdoor realism, and page-turning curveballs that is just flat tough to put down. This latest edition to the Luke McCain series confirms Rob Phillips' standing as a skilled mystery writer. Already I want to read another."
    −Terry W. Sheely, northwest author and writer

"This is crime fiction at its finest−the perfect blend of a compelling mystery, a fabulous setting, the best dog ever, and a very likeable hero you won't forget."
    −Christine Carbo, award-winning author of the Glacier Mystery Series

"*Cascade Vengeance* takes readers on a thrill ride through the dual worlds of drug dealing and big-game hunting deep in Washington's Cascade mountains. Rob Phillips uses his extensive knowledge of the region to tell the fast-moving tale . . . on the way to the story's harrowing and heartbreaking conclusion."
    −Scott Graham, National Outdoor Book Award-winning author of *Mesa Verde Victim*

"*Cascade Vengeance*, the second book in the Luke McCain series, is another hang-onto-your-hat, nonstop action episode with Luke, a Washington State Fish and Wildlife officer, his FBI girlfriend Sara, and Jack, his loyal yellow Lab. I felt like I was riding shotgun in Luke's Ford pickup, bouncing along forest service roads where very bad guys might be lurking."
    −Susan Richmond, owner of Inklings Bookshop

CREATURE OF THE CASCADES

Book and cover design by Kevin Breen

ISBN: 978-1-957607-29-0
Cataloging-in-Publication Data is available upon request

Manufactured in the United States of America

Published by
Latah Books, Spokane, Washington
www.latahbooks.com

The author may be contacted at yakimahunter@yahoo.com

CREATURE
OF THE
CASCADES

A LUKE MCCAIN NOVEL

ROB PHILLIPS

LATAH
BOOKS

Also by Rob Phillips

THE CASCADE KILLER

CASCADE VENGEANCE

CASCADE PREDATOR

CASCADE KIDNAPPING

CASCADE MANHUNT

A DOG LIFE WELL LIVED

DEDICATION

Although all my Luke McCain novels are works of fiction, I work
hard to make them as realistic as possible in showing the often
thankless, and always tireless, work of the underappreciated real-
life men and women who risk their lives to protect our wildlife
and wildlands. To all of them, all of you, I dedicate this book.

CHAPTER 1

Bill Hoyt was awakened by the barking. Again. Almost every night, or more accurately, early morning for a week now, the two big German shepherds owned by the neighbor just up the road would start barking uncontrollably. Something would set the dogs off around three o'clock, awakening Hoyt right in the middle of REM sleep, and it was starting to piss him off.

After what seemed like an hour, but was realistically more like ten or fifteen minutes, Hoyt would hear the neighbor screaming at the dogs to shut up, and eventually they would.

This time was different. Hoyt listened as the dogs barked like they usually did, then they became almost hysterical. He could hear them growling as their barking came faster. Normally, the barking was just that, barking. Now they were getting serious. Like they were ready to attack someone. Or something.

Why, Hoyt thought, wasn't Martin hollering at the dogs to shut up? He sat up, running his hands through what little hair he had left on the top of his head and listened for a few seconds.

Finally, Hoyt stumbled through the dark to the window to see what might be creating the commotion. Which was stupid, he thought, because it was nighttime and pitch black out there, and the trees between his place and the neighbors were so thick you couldn't see anything through them.

Just as he got to the window, which was raised to let the cool morning air in, Hoyt heard one of the dogs, or maybe it was both, let out a loud yelp. And then there was dead silence. It was like someone flipped a switch and turned the dogs off.

Hoyt had been around dogs of various types all his life, and almost always when a dog gets hurt, it will yelp and yelp and yelp. He thought it was weird to hear just one yelp. He thought about it for a second, scratched his head again, stumbled into the bathroom, peed, and wandered back toward his bed.

As he passed the window, Hoyt stopped to listen again. Nothing. Then he heard footsteps. Heavy footsteps. Running through the trees between his place and Martin's. It wasn't the dogs running—he knew that for sure. And he didn't think it was any other four-legged creature. The steps were wrong.

Thud . . . thud . . . thud . . . thud. The sound of the steps disappeared off into the distance.

Hoyt had heard big mule deer bucks bouncing through the trees a few times before. Maybe that was what it was, he thought. It sounded something like what he had just heard. But the steps still didn't sound quite right.

"Whatever," Hoyt mumbled to himself and lay back down on his bed. Then as he thought about it, if there was someone out there running around, maybe he should be prepared. He went to his gun safe, pulled out his loaded revolver, and placed it on the nightstand.

With no more dogs barking, he thought if he could get back to sleep right away, he would be able to get two more hours of much-needed rest before the alarm woke him to get ready for work.

The phone on his bedside table beat the alarm by half an hour.

"Hulloo," Hoyt grumbled into the phone after fumbling for it on the table and trying to slide the button on the screen about five times.

"Hey, Bill. Sorry to wake you. This is Jerome."

Jerome Martin had purchased the place next to Hoyt's almost a year ago, and not long after he moved into the house on the property, he had bought two German shepherd pups. He'd told Hoyt that he wanted the dogs for security to help keep any unwanted visitors, human or not, off his property.

The problem was, Martin had never really worked with the dogs. He spent no time with them and did little to no training. The two pups grew quickly, and while they were friendly enough when Hoyt was near them at the fence between his property and Martin's, they would bark at damn near everything, and everyone else.

Hoyt had talked with his neighbor about the nighttime barking, and Martin had said he would keep the dogs in at night, but for the last week, the dogs had been outside day and night.

"What's up?" Hoyt asked groggily.

"Well, I just got home, and I don't see my dogs. You haven't seen or heard them, have you?"

"I heard them," Hoyt said, trying to focus on the digital clock on his dresser. "That was about an hour and a half ago. They got pretty riled up."

"Well, they're gone. And it looks like someone, or something, tore the gate out of my back fence."

"Tore it out?"

"Yeah, like right off the hinges. And dragged it or threw it ten yards out into the trees."

Hoyt told Martin what he had heard, how the dogs had sounded, the yelp, and the heavy footsteps.

"The house wasn't broken into," Martin said. "Nothing else seems out of place. Just the gate. And Brutus and Buster are gone. They've never run off like that before."

He wanted to tell his neighbor that it didn't surprise him that the dogs had run off, taking the chance to enjoy some freedom from

3

the fenced backyard where they had spent ninety-nine percent of their time since they had arrived as puppies, but he didn't.

"Well, they probably chased whatever that was I heard running away and are now having fun running around out there. I'm guessing they'll show up soon."

"I hope so. Ron Elmore told me he has seen cougars on his place twice in the last few days, and there was that bear everyone was seeing over by the highway."

"I don't think a cougar or a bear would take on a big dog like a shepherd. But you probably don't want the dogs near the highway. That's a recipe for an accident."

"Yeah, you're right. Well, if you see them, will you give me a call? I'm going to go looking for them."

"Will do," Hoyt said. He empathized with his neighbor, but on the other hand if he had done more training with them, this might have been avoided.

It was too late to try to get back to sleep, so Hoyt got dressed and went to the kitchen to fire up the coffeemaker and fry some eggs.

As he stood over the three extra-large eggs crackling in the cast iron pan, Hoyt thought about the dogs barking and the thumping footsteps he had heard. Whatever he had heard running through the night had to be something big.

He had been thinking about putting up some trail cameras around his ten acres, just to see what wildlife was wandering through. But he hadn't done it. Now he wished he had.

Hoyt made a mental note to stop by Cabela's the next time he was in town to pick some up. He would also buy some ear plugs. When Martin's dogs returned, he was sure they'd be barking again while he was trying to sleep.

*

Luke McCain was chatting with a couple of fly fishermen on the Tieton River when his cell phone started buzzing. He looked at the screen, told the two anglers he needed to take the call, and excused himself.

"McCain," he said after he slid the button on the phone's screen.

"Hey, Luke," Yakima County Sheriff's Deputy Paul Garcia said. "Any chance you're anywhere near Bumping Lake?"

"I'm on Highway 12 just above the elk feeding station, why?"

"We have a strange one up here. We could use some expertise from the state's most famous game warden."

It had been almost a year since Luke had tracked down the mass murderer Claude Rakes—a man who had been called the most wanted man in America—as he was running loose in northcentral Washington. The manhunt had caught the attention of the national news media, and Luke had been interviewed by dozens of papers and all the TV networks after the killer had been caught.

It hadn't helped that Luke had been put on the case by the governor of Washington. After that, most of the folks in local law enforcement thought of Luke as the golden boy. Most everyone, except those who were closest to Luke, was more than a little envious of the notoriety.

Those who were closest to Luke, though, knew he hated all that stuff. He was just doing his job. Garcia knew Luke disliked all the publicity, but he still didn't pass on the chance to razz him.

Luke had learned to just ignore the jabs and said, "What you got?"

"It's hard to explain," Garcia said. "You really need to see it."

"Okay, shoot me your location, and I'll be there as quickly as I can."

Luke ended the call, walked back over to the two anglers he had been checking, and handed their fishing licenses back to them.

"Sorry about that. Everything looks good here. Thanks and good luck to you guys."

Luke climbed up the riverbank, jumped into his pickup truck, radioed in to dispatch to let them know where he was headed, and pulled the Chevy onto the highway.

For the past decade, Luke had been driving a state-issued 2012

Ford F-150. He really liked that truck. But with over 250,000 miles on the engine and transmission, someone over in Olympia decided it was time for him to have a new truck. Luke and the other Region 3 Fish and Wildlife enforcement officers received new Chevy 1500 four-wheel drive pickups loaded with all the latest bells and whistles. The truck's color had been described by one of the locals as "shit-knuckle brown," which made Luke laugh. The rig still had that new car smell, which Luke figured might last another week if he kept letting a wet yellow Labrador retriever ride in the back seat.

Luke's Lab, Jack, had been an on-again, off-again passenger on patrols over the years. While the Department had rules against officers traveling with their personal dogs, Jack had been unofficially signed in as a K-9 officer and was allowed to ride with Luke. The higher-ups were more than willing to allow Jack's presence because the big yellow dog had saved Luke's life a couple of times and had been essential in tracking down more than one poaching suspect.

Over the years, Luke had been called by the sheriff's office to dozens of different crime scenes. He and Jack had once been called in to find what turned out to be a dead woman after they'd backtracked a black bear that had been killed by a young hunter. The bear had some of the woman's body parts in its stomach, and Jack led Luke to the dead body.

Luke had also been called occasionally by state patrol officers to come deal with a deer or elk or bear that had been hit by a vehicle as it was trying to cross the road. Sometimes the animals were dead when he arrived, so he would load them into his truck for disposal. Other times, when the animal was still alive and suffering, Luke would have to put it down.

He thought about the many different assistance calls he had received over the years and wondered what this one might be. Little did he know it would be the strangest call of his professional career.

CHAPTER 2

As it turned out, the location Garcia gave him was just short of Bumping Lake in a group of private homes, which some people called cabins. Luke turned up a gravel road and soon found Garcia's Yakima Sheriff's Office rig parked in the driveway.

Garcia, a longtime deputy, was short and stout. Luke had once been invited to a birthday party at Garcia's house, and after consuming a dozen handmade tamales Mrs. Garcia made, along with the best refried beans Luke had ever eaten, he wondered how the deputy didn't weigh a hundred pounds more.

When he saw Luke driving up, Garcia, who was talking with a couple of men in their late 30s or early 40s, turned and walked over to his truck.

"Whoa. When did you get the new rig?" Garcia asked.

"A couple weeks ago. I'm still getting used to it."

"Nice. No other colors available? That brown is ugly."

"I drive what the boss tells me to drive," Luke said.

"Did you bring Jack?"

"No. You think we might need him?"

"I'm not sure what we are going to need. This is a weird one."

"So, what's the deal?"

"Like I said on the phone, it is best you see it first. Then we can talk."

"Alright. Lead the way."

Garcia first walked back over to the two men in the driveway of a small, older house painted blue with white trim around the windows. Three concrete steps led up to the front door which sat to the right of a largish picture window. He introduced Luke to the two men who Luke thought must be related. They were the same medium height and build with brown, curly hair popping out from under trucker-style caps.

"Luke, this is Jerome Martin. This is his place."

Luke shook Martin's hand and then the other man's.

"I'm Jerome's cousin, Jason Ball."

"Nice to meet you," Luke said.

"Jason came over to help me find my dogs," Martin said.

As all four men walked toward the back of the yard, Martin told them what he'd found.

"I was gone until early this morning. When I got home, my two dogs were missing and the back gate was gone."

"What time was this?" Luke asked as he wondered why law enforcement would be called in just because a couple of dogs were missing.

"I don't know—about four, four-thirty."

They walked through the opening in the back fence to where a gate was lying in the grass.

"Looks like it was ripped from the hinges," Ball said. "Who has the strength to do something like that?"

Luke looked at the gate, searching for claw marks. A black bear could certainly rip a gate off a wood post. But from what he could see, there were no marks of any kind.

"Was it rickety? Like loose?" Luke asked.

"No, sir. I replaced the hardware earlier this spring. I didn't want the dogs pushing through and running off," Martin said.

"So, did the dogs come back?" Luke asked.

"No, sir. But we found one of them."

"Where?"

"Up here," Garcia said. "You'll see."

The group of men walked another forty yards up a gradual incline into some taller coniferous trees. As they walked, Luke looked for tracks. It had to be a bear that ripped the fence apart. He was still looking around on the ground when the group stopped.

Martin said, "There he is."

Luke looked around. Seeing nothing, he then noticed the men were all looking up in a big fir tree.

When Luke finally saw the dog, he was perplexed. The German shepherd was upside down, his ears and tongue hanging down, and it was like he was suspended in air.

As he moved around to get a better look, Luke could see the dog had been impaled on an eighteen-inch dead broken branch that had grown out of the trunk of the big fir tree. The poor dog, obviously dead, was suspended about fifteen feet off the ground.

Luke just about said, well, you don't see that every day, but thought better of it. Martin was obviously upset about finding his dog like that.

Then Luke asked the obvious question.

"Anyone have any idea how this might have happened?"

"That's why you're here," Garcia said. "What do you think?"

"Well, I thought it was a good possibility a black bear tore the gate out, but a bear couldn't do this. Hell, I don't know if a man could do this."

As he was talking, Luke was looking for any clues that a ladder had been placed next to the tree where someone might have carried the dog up and stuck it on the broken branch.

"Well, we need to get the dog's body down to get a better look at it. And I want to spend some time checking around the area for any tracks, but right now I have no clue what happened here."

"I might," Ball said.

All three men stopped and looked at him.

"When I was a kid, my grandpa used to tell all us kids a story about a creature that lived in this area," Ball began. "He called it a sasquatch. Said the thing was twelve feet tall, covered in dark brown hair, and it lived in caves high up in the mountains."

"I don't remember Papa telling us anything about that," Martin said.

"It was my other grandpa, on my old man's side," Ball said. "He said that when he worked felling trees for the lumber company, he and some of the guys he worked with would sometimes find animals skewered on limbs here and there. Deer, young elk, even a bear or two. The animals would have a hindquarter gone or some chunk of meat torn out of it, and the rest would be left stuck up in the tree."

"How did he know it was a sasquatch?" Garcia asked.

"He said one morning when he was driving up to work, he caught movement in the headlights of his old truck on a logging road. Something big and brown had crossed the road. At first, he thought it was just a brown phase black bear, but when he caught movement in the trees, the creature he saw was moving fast, and it was walking upright, on two legs."

Garcia had a grin on his face.

"Okay, we've all heard the sasquatch stories," he said. "I'm sure your old granddaddy was just joshing you."

"If you heard him tell the story, you'd believe every word of it," Ball said. "Until his dying day, he swore he saw what he saw and believed that was the beast that was killing animals and sticking them up in the trees."

Everyone stood and thought about that for a minute, then Luke said to Martin, "You got a ladder so we can get your dog down?"

As Martin went to retrieve the ladder, Luke took some photos with his phone of the dead dog stuck to the side of the tree.

Martin climbed the ladder and pulled the big German

shepherd off the limb. He lost the grip on the dog, and it tumbled to the ground, hitting with a thud.

"Crap. Sorry, Buster," Martin said and then climbed back down the ladder.

Luke did a quick check on the dog and thought the animal's neck had been broken. And, from what he could tell, the dog had been forced onto the sharp branch with brute strength.

"I sure hope Brutus is okay," Martin said to no one in particular.

"You should put something on Facebook about the dog, show a photo and let people know he is missing," Garcia said. "I'm guessing he'll show up at someone's place before too long."

"Yeah, unless he's stuck in another tree around here," Martin said.

"We'll go do some looking around," Ball said to his cousin. "I'm sure we'll find him."

"Have you had any other issues with the dogs, or heard of any problems with other animals around here?" Luke asked.

"Well, for the last week or so the dogs have been pretty restless in the middle of the night. They'll start barking and won't shut up until I get up and holler at them. Pisses my neighbor off to no end. He's called me a couple of times complaining that the dogs are waking him."

"Which neighbor is that?" Luke asked.

"His name is Bill Hoyt. Lives over there," Martin said, pointing back down the hill. "I called him when I saw that the dogs were gone. Woke him up, which didn't make him very happy, and he said he heard them barking around three o'clock and then they just shut up."

"Hmmm," Luke hummed. "Is Mr. Hoyt home?"

"I don't think so," Martin said. "He works down in Naches. Probably won't be home until later this afternoon."

"Okay, well, I'll try to talk to him later. I'm going to take a look around for a few minutes. Here's my card. If you find your other dog, or think of anything else I might need to know, give me a call."

With that, Luke shook the two cousins' hands and walked back to the vehicles with Garcia.

"What do you think of all this?" Garcia asked.

"I don't know what to make of it," Luke said. "If the neighbor was pissed enough that the dogs were waking him every night, it could have been him. Otherwise, we might have some sicko out there killing people's pets."

"So, you're not buying the whole sasquatch thing?"

"Are you?" Luke asked.

"Kind of. But my people are the ones who will find an image of the Virgin Mary on the back of a road sign or in a potato chip, so I'm a little more susceptible to this kind of stuff."

Luke didn't know if Garcia was being funny or what, and then the deputy let out a big laugh and said, "Gotcha!"

"Yeah, well, if this story gets out, we're going to find out there are plenty of people who are believers."

"So, let's not tell anyone."

"I have to fill out a report. And we should let people know to be aware. If there is a bear or cougar killing people's pets and we don't let the residents in the area know, I'd be in hot water," Luke said. "But maybe we leave out a few of the details."

"You really think a bear did that to the dog?" Garcia asked.

"No, I don't. A cougar might drag a kill up in a tree to keep it away from coyotes, but how did it get skewered perfectly on the branch? And I saw no signs that an animal of any kind had attacked the dog. There were no scratch marks or bite marks. Just the puncture wound on the side."

"And then there's the whole broken neck thing," Garcia said.

"Well, yeah, there is that."

"Since this is most likely a wildlife issue, I am going to leave this in your capable hands," Garcia said and turned to get in his SUV. "Good luck with whatever the hell this is."

Luke gave the deputy a sideways head nod and turned to go back to check around the area. Whatever did that to the gate and to the dog had to have some size and strength to it. There had to be some tracks left behind. He just had to find them.

*

Two hours later, Luke had found nothing. Or, nothing that would explain what had happened to Buster the German shepherd. Luke had seen deer tracks, elk tracks, coyote tracks, cougar tracks, and even a really big bear track. But all the tracks were old. The only fresh tracks he found were human tracks, and those had been made by Martin and his cousin as they'd searched for the missing dog.

As Luke walked back to his truck, Martin came out of the house onto the front step.

"Sorry about your dog," Luke said. "I'll talk to your neighbor later today, but for now I don't know what else I can do."

"Thanks, officer," Martin said. "I appreciate your help."

Luke hopped into his truck, fired it up, and headed back toward Yakima. As he drove, he thought about the dog in the tree. Luke was a big man. He stood close to six foot five inches tall and weighed 225 pounds. His morning routine included lifting weights and a cardio workout that kept him as fit as men half his forty-two years of age.

He estimated the shepherd had weighed at least ninety pounds. Could he have carried the dead weight of the dog up a ladder and have the strength to push it onto the dead branch of the tree? Probably, Luke thought, if he had to, but it would be a struggle.

But there were no scuffle marks around the tree or any other evidence that someone, or something, had killed the dog and put it in the tree. It was like Buster had flown up there, or been thrown up there. Who, or what, would have the strength to do that?

CHAPTER 3

"Do you believe in bigfoot?" Luke asked fellow wildlife enforcement officer Stan Hargraves as they were eating lunch at a little Korean barbecue place in Yakima. Hargraves had called Luke as he was driving back to town and asked if they could meet.

"Naw," Hargraves said between bites of his chicken teriyaki. "I've spent about a million hours in these mountains over the years. If there was a sasquatch or some other similar creature out there, I would have seen it . . . him . . . them."

Hargraves was a thirty-year veteran of the Department of Fish and Wildlife, and most all of his service time had been spent in Region 3, patrolling hundreds of thousands of acres from the Pacific Coast Trail in the Cascade Mountains to the Columbia River.

"That's kind of what I think too," Luke said. "Wouldn't some hunter have shot one accidentally, thinking it was a bear?"

"Yeah, or every other species of animal that lives in the woods at one time or another gets hit by a vehicle. Nobody has ever smucked a sasquatch," Hargraves said as he chewed. "At least not that we know of."

"And think about all the game cameras in the woods now," Luke said. "Certainly, someone would have captured a decent photo of bigfoot if there was one running around out there."

"Why do you ask?" Hargraves asked.

Luke told Hargraves about the German shepherd skewered in the tree up by Bumping Lake. He showed Hargraves the photo he'd taken of the dog and told him about the gate that had been ripped from the fence.

"You don't see that every day," Hargraves, who had stopped chewing to examine the photo, said.

"My thoughts exactly. I couldn't reach the dog from the ground. It was a good fifteen feet up the tree."

"Isn't this something for the sheriff's office to handle?" Hargraves asked. "Someone killing pets isn't something we normally investigate."

"Garcia handed it off to me, saying it was most likely a bear or mountain lion that did this. Although I found no evidence at all that the dog was killed by any kind of animal."

"What are you going to do?"

"I'm going back up this afternoon to chat with a neighbor who heard the dogs barking, evidently right before the one was killed. He seemed to have a beef with the owner of the dogs and had complained a few times that their barking was keeping him up at night. Maybe he had something to do with it."

"Again, that would be a YSO problem."

"Yeah, I'll call Garcia if I think the neighbor is involved somehow, but this thing is really intriguing. I'd like to figure it out."

Hargraves took one last bite of chicken slathered in gooey brown teriyaki sauce and said, "Well, good luck with that. Now, I might need your help with something else—that is if you can pull yourself away from the search for bigfoot."

"Sure, what's up?"

Hargraves pulled a toothpick out of a shirt pocket and picked at a couple of stray pieces of chicken caught in his front teeth.

"Where were you raised, in Buena?" Luke asked after watching Hargraves dig at his teeth. "The lady at the next table just gave you a look of disgust."

"Hey, I got gaps. If I don't get the debris out of them, my gums will go bad and my teeth will fall out."

"Who told you that?" Luke asked, laughing.

"Nobody," Hargraves said. "But you can't be too careful. Have you seen how much those damn implants cost? I'd rather eat soup."

"So, what is it you need my help with?"

Hargraves told Luke there had been an anonymous tip called in to the Region 3 office about some men who might be taking young falcons out of nests around eastern Washington and shipping them to Russia, where some oligarchs were having them trained to hunt rabbits and other small game. The caller, who Hargraves said had a heavy accent, probably Russian, mentioned that the men were also looking to secure some young golden eagles that would be trained to hunt deer and sheep.

"The caller said the oligarchs are offering big bucks for the young raptors," Hargraves said.

"This is the time of year when the young birds would just about be ready to fly," Luke said. "But it's been quite a while since I've seen a golden eagle nest. And I don't know if I have ever seen a falcon nest."

"That's probably because they nest on sheer rock faces," Hargraves said. "It would take some work to get to them."

"Surely one of the biologists in the Department is an expert on falcons and knows where they nest."

"I've already checked. There is a guy. Name is Barrett Lemon. Young, only been with us for a year, but he seems to know everything there is to know about falcons and other birds of prey, or so I'm told."

"So, what do you need from me?" Luke asked.

"I want to set up a meeting with Lemon, and then we need to go try to find some nests to check on."

"You know I hate heights," Luke said. "I'm not going to be rappelling down some granite cliff on a tip from a Russian caller."

"I don't think we'll need to do that, but we will need to watch them. Let's talk to the biologist first and figure out where we go from there."

"Okay, let me know about the meeting," Luke said as he slid the check to Hargraves. "Thanks for lunch, and by the way, you still have a piece of chicken in your teeth."

*

After spending some time in the office taking care of emails and other tedious stuff, including writing up a short report on the call he'd made with Deputy Garcia to Martin's residence, Luke headed for his truck to drive back up to Bumping Lake to talk with Bill Hoyt.

"How's it going, Luke?" Captain Bob Davis asked just as Luke was standing to leave.

Davis was a big man, a former college football player, now pushing sixty. The man wore his thinning hair very short and sported a bushy mustache. Both the mustache and his hair had gone from mostly black when Luke first met him to mostly gray now. In an earlier time, Davis's mustache would have been called a "cookie duster."

"Going good, Cap. Did Hargraves tell you about the falcon nest deal?"

"Yes, he did. I told him to get some help from you if you have the time."

"I should have the time, but I'm also following up on a strange call I took this morning. Not sure where it is going to go."

Luke recapped his morning up near Bumping Lake and showed Davis the photo of the dog stuck to the tree.

"There's something you don't see every day," Davis said as he studied the photo.

"No, you don't," Luke said. "I'm having trouble figuring it out."

Luke then told his captain about the story Jason Ball had shared about his grandfather and the sasquatch. Davis listened intently.

"I've heard something similar before," Davis said when Luke was done. "But it had to be thirty, forty years ago. Not long after, that Yakima guy claimed to have taken film of a bigfoot walking up in the mountains of northern California."

Known as the Patterson film, the 16 mm movie was a minute long and showed a big, hairy creature walking along through some rocky terrain. The film was scratchy and slightly out of focus, but viewers could certainly make out this being, walking upright, long arms swinging as it takes big strides. The beast even turns and looks at the camera for a few seconds.

The film was shot in 1967 by Roger Patterson and Bob Gimlin. Patterson died of cancer in 1972 but maintained right up to his death that the creature on the film was real. Patterson's friend, Gimlin, always denied even being involved in creating the film with Patterson.

Patterson and Gimlin even made plaster casts of footprints they claimed came from the creature.

In 1999, a Yakima man hired a local attorney after someone had tracked him down as a contributor to the movie. The man claimed, according to the attorney, he had been the person in the bigfoot suit that Patterson filmed.

Still, there are plenty of people who believe the Patterson film is real, and there are those, including bigfoot believers, who claim the film was a hoax.

"Well, I'd like to get to the bottom of it," Luke said. "I was just on my way up to talk to Martin's neighbor, who supposedly heard what happened."

"Okay. That dog didn't just fly up there, so there has to be an explanation. I guess in this crazy world, there could actually be a bigfoot."

"I'm not ready to go that far," Luke said.

"Listen," Davis said. "We were told over and over again by the leading experts that all the big mountains in the Cascades, including Rainier, Adams, and St. Helens were dead. May 18 of 1980 proved that scientists aren't always right."

Luke thought about that for a minute, then turned and headed for the door.

"I'll let you know what I find out," he said with a wave.

*

On his way back up into the mountains, Luke called his wife. Sara was a special agent with the FBI, stationed out of the Yakima office. Most of her work was done in conjunction with the Yakama Nation, and she worked closely with tribal officials and other law enforcement agencies on the growing number of murdered and missing indigenous peoples.

Sara was a tall, slender, beautiful woman with hair that was as shiny and black as a raven's wing. Her dark eyes were warm and full of life, but they would cut right through you if she had a mind for it. Luke thanked his lucky stars every day since Sara had come into his life, and somehow, she had fallen in love with him.

It didn't hurt that he had rescued her from possible death at the hands of a serial killer. They'd been married for five years, and Luke figured at some point the potion would wear off and she'd tell him that she'd made a huge mistake. They say most marriages end around year seven. He figured he had a couple more years to go. Maybe.

"Hey there, handsome," Sara said by way of answering the phone. "Wanna play around tonight?"

"What, hey, I have you on speaker phone with about six guys standing around," Luke fibbed.

There was a long silence, then Sara said, "You're kidding, right?"

"Yeah, but what if I was with some other folks?"

"I guess they'd know that you might be getting lucky tonight."

"Might?"

"We'll see. That wasn't funny, your little joke."

"Listen, I may be home late. I'm running up to Bumping Lake to talk to a guy. Long story, but I need to find out what he knows about a dog that ending up skewered on a limb fifteen feet up in a tree."

"There's something you don't hear every day," Sara said. "Well, hurry home. You can tell me all about it when you get there. I'm late for a meeting."

Then, she was gone.

"You are one lucky man," Luke muttered to himself as he pushed the new Chevy on up the highway.

CHAPTER 4

Bill Hoyt wasn't home when Luke arrived, so he pulled into Martin's driveway. Martin stepped out on the porch when Luke pulled up to the house. Luke looked to see if a German shepherd might be accompanying the man out of the house, but Martin came out alone.

"No luck finding your other dog?" Luke asked.

"No, sir. My cousin and I looked for six hours today, and nothing."

"Well, he was probably scared off by whoever killed Buster."

"Or, *what*ever killed him," Martin said.

Luke didn't respond to that but did ask if the men had found any unusual tracks or anything else out of the ordinary while they were out looking around.

"No, nothing that we noticed. But you know, I didn't think about this until I came home and sat down. While we were out there, it was eerily quiet. No birds chirping. No squirrels chattering.

That never happens. There is always something in the woods making noise. Any idea what might cause that?"

Luke thought about it and then said, "No, I can't say that I do. You think your neighbor will be home soon?"

Martin turned and looked inside his house. Luke saw a clock on the wall.

"Should be home any time. But who knows. If he stopped at the tavern for a beer or met someone for dinner, he might not get here for a couple of hours."

"Okay, I'll go sit in his driveway for a bit. But if I miss him, would you give him my card?" Luke said as he handed Martin the card.

"Sure," Martin said. "Officer McCain? Do you have any idea what happened here last night? I'm feeling so guilty about being gone. Yes, the dogs barked sometimes at night, but I was okay with that. They told me if something or someone was out there. And they are . . . or were really nice dogs. They were like family to me."

"I totally understand," Luke said. "I have a yellow Lab at home that is like a child to my wife and me. If something happened to him, I don't know what I would do." Luke paused for a second and then said, "And no, I have no clue what happened here last night. It's the most perplexing thing I have ever seen. But I am going to figure it out, and we'll catch whoever, or whatever, killed Buster."

Martin hung his head and said "thanks" before turning and going back into the house.

✳

Bill Hoyt arrived ten minutes after Luke parked in his driveway. He pulled around Luke's truck and looked at him as he moved by. Hoyt parked and got out of his truck, carrying a small bag of groceries and an old-fashioned lunch pail. Luke saw he was a man of around fifty, with salt-and-pepper-colored hair that desperately needed a trim. Hoyt was of average height, maybe five-ten, and weighed around a hundred and seventy pounds if Luke had to guess. Probably not fit or strong enough to break a big dog's neck and skewer it onto a broken limb fifteen feet off the ground.

"Is this about the neighbor's shepherds?" Hoyt asked.

"Yes, it is," Luke said. "Can we chat for a minute?"

"Sure, c'mon in. Can I get you a beer?"

"No thanks. I'm on duty. But go ahead if you'd like."

"Don't mind if I do," Hoyt said. "I like to have one after work. It kind of settles me down."

"So, tell me what you heard last night. Martin told me what you told him on the phone, but I'd like to hear it from you."

"Sure," Hoyt said. "But first, don't think I don't like those dogs because I do. They seem really nice and have always been friendly to me whenever I've been around them. But for the last week or so, they will start barking at something in the middle of the night. I don't know if it's coyotes or a cougar or a bear, but they start barking and won't stop until Martin yells at them. I asked him to keep them in at night, but for some reason he has had them out the last several nights."

Luke said, "But last night was different?"

"Yeah, it started out the same, but after ten or fifteen minutes, Martin still hadn't yelled at them. I was getting pissed. I have to get up early to make it down to Naches by seven. Being awakened night after night at two or three in the morning is pretty aggravating."

"I bet it is," Luke said.

"So anyway, I was sitting on the edge of the bed, getting madder and madder, then I heard the dogs get really wound up. You know how it is when dogs are fighting. They were growling and snarling and then all of a sudden I heard one yelp, and it all went silent. I thought that was kind of weird, but hey, they had stopped barking, so I laid back down. That's when I heard the footsteps. Heavy footsteps, running through the back of my place."

"Could it have been an elk?" Luke asked. "One elk can sound like a herd of elephants when it runs."

"Nope. Elk have four legs. They sound sort of like a horse. Whatever was running was on two legs. No animals run like that, so I assumed it was a person. A big person!"

"What did you do next?"

"I tried to see out the window, but it was blacker than an Angus's ass out there. I couldn't see anything. So, I grabbed my pistol, put it on the nightstand, and went to sleep. An hour or so later, Martin was calling me, upset that his dogs were gone."

"Did he tell you what happened to one of his dogs?"

"No, I haven't talked to him since his call in the middle of the night. What happened?"

Luke opened his phone and brought up the photo of Buster hanging from the branch in the tree.

"This is what happened," Luke said.

"Wow. You don't see that every day."

"The dog's neck was broken, and he was stuck on a branch fifteen feet up in the tree."

"Now that is weird," Hoyt said. "There's some sick bastards out there, isn't there?"

"The funny thing is, there were no tracks around the tree or around the back fence. Something also ripped the gate out of the fence in Martin's backyard."

"Whatever was running out there had to leave tracks," Hoyt said. "It was someone heavy. The footsteps were loud—thud, thud, thud, thud—like a fat guy running on stilts."

"You mind if I go out into the back and see if I can find any tracks?"

"Not at all. I'll come with you."

The two men wandered around in the back of Hoyt's place for half an hour. Luke asked Hoyt to try to point out where he thought the footsteps had come from, but the backyard was mostly long wild grass, and they found no tracks of any kind.

"I swear, whatever or whoever it was, ran right through here," Hoyt said, pointing back toward his back fence.

"I believe you," Luke said. "But I sure can't find the tracks."

"Maybe you should get the sheriff's tracking hounds. They might be able to follow a scent."

"I thought of that," Luke said. "Actually, my dog is a pretty good tracker. But I think it's too late. The area is so dry, the scent would be difficult to pick up."

The two men chatted for a few more minutes. Luke told Hoyt that the other shepherd of Martin's was still out there somewhere, and he might keep an eye out for it. Hoyt said he would. And he said he was going to drop over and visit with his neighbor to offer a hand fixing the gate.

Luke thanked Hoyt for his time and went out to his truck. Before he started the engine, he sat and thought about everything. How could something that heavy not make any tracks anywhere? It went against the laws of physics.

About then his stomach rumbled. He started his truck, looked at the clock on the dash, and saw it was way past his normal dinner time. He was frustrated and hungry. And, as he remembered the quick call with Sara, for whatever reason, she was eager for him to get home.

But Luke didn't hurry driving home. As he drove, he looked at the country on both sides of the road. Normally, he would see deer and elk this time of night. Tonight, there was nothing.

He stopped the truck in the middle of the road and rolled the window down. He listened and heard nothing. No birds, no frogs, no crickets, nothing. What had Martin said? Eerily silent? Luke might have described it as deadly silent. Whatever it was, it was weird.

Later that evening, as he was describing everything he had experienced during his day to Sara, she listened intently, without asking any questions. She was a law enforcement officer. An investigator. But she knew this was not the right time to be asking questions. Her husband had probably asked all the questions she might come up with to himself a dozen times, and still he couldn't come up with any answers.

Finally, she did ask, "Do you think there could be a creature—a sasquatch, or something like that—out there that did this?"

"Twenty-four hours ago, I would have laughed at you and said no way, but now I am starting to wonder."

"Well, enough of this," Sara said with a coy grin as she grabbed his hand and started pulling him out of the kitchen chair in which he sat. "I think I have something that might take your mind off of all this stuff."

CHAPTER 5

As Luke drove into the office the next morning, his phone started ringing. On the heads-up Bluetooth display on his truck dash, he saw the caller was Hargraves. Luke pushed the button on the steering wheel to answer the call and said, "Hey, Stan."

"I've set up a meeting with Barrett Lemon to discuss the nesting habits of the peregrine falcon. Our office conference room at ten. Can you be there?"

"Sounds enlightening," Luke said. "Can't wait."

As he drove, he thought about the number of times he had seen falcons in the wild. He could recall a few, but even though he was out in nature for work and recreation most of the time, the little birds of prey were remarkably unnoticeable.

Over the years, bald eagles had become much more prolific in the area, and Luke saw them frequently. During the winter months, it was nothing to see fifteen or twenty of the majestic birds along the Yakima River. And he had seen several golden eagles over the years, but they were not nearly as plentiful as the bald eagles.

If the person calling in the tip was right, and someone was planning to rob fledglings from eagle and falcon nests, it was going to be a challenge to catch them. Hopefully, Lemon could shed some light on where they might start looking.

Luke wandered into the conference room a few minutes before ten and found a young man sitting at the table. Dressed all in tan, the man looked a bit like John Lennon, circa 1969, around the time Yoko Ono broke up the band. The young man's long brown hair was parted in the middle. Round, wire-rimmed glasses were perched on Lemon's nose.

As Luke walked in, the young man, who was tall and had the physique of a triathlete, stood and offered his hand.

"Officer McCain, I'm Barrett Lemon."

"Nice to meet you, Barrett, and please call me Luke," Luke said, wondering how Lemon knew who he was.

"I watched you on TV when you were bringing that serial killer down the hill on those horses," Lemon said. "That was quite an ordeal."

"Yes, it was. How long have you been with the Department?" Luke asked, changing subjects. He really didn't like talking about Claude Rakes.

"About two years," Barrett said. "I'm over in the Ridgefield office. That's why you haven't seen me around. I'm working on my doctorate on Washington State's birds of prey and have studied peregrine falcons for several years. When I saw you were looking for someone who might be able to help figure out where someone might find their nests, I called Officer Hargraves and volunteered to come over to assist."

"Well, we certainly appreciate it. I don't know much about the investigation, or even if you could call it an investigation yet, but Stan... er... Officer Hargraves will bring us both up to speed."

"Cool, so, what was it like capturing the most wanted man in America?"

"I was just doing my—" Luke started to say as Hargraves walked in.

"Hey, Barrett. I'm Stan Hargraves. Thanks for coming over this morning. Luke and I have no idea what might become of this, but we need your help in figuring out where we might find some falcon nests, and maybe a golden eagle nest or two."

Lemon gave the two officers a quick tutorial on falcons and their nesting habits.

"They will even nest on the ledges of skyscrapers in the bigger cities. They prey on the pigeons that have become pests just about everywhere in the United States."

"So," Luke asked. "We should have some nesting in the cliffs in the Cascades?"

"Most assuredly," Lemon said. "Back in 1987, a biologist named Jennifer Simmons did a lengthy study—"

Hargraves stopped him mid-sentence. "Sorry, Barrett. We don't really need that much history and detail. What we need is for you to ride with us and look at some country and tell us if you think there may be some falcons nesting there."

"Oh sure, sorry," Lemon said. "I just really get into this stuff. But going into the field and looking for nests will be great. Let me get my equipment, and we can go right away."

Hargraves raised an eyebrow at Luke.

"It's your case," Luke said. "Why don't you go with Barrett, and if you guys spot some nests, I'll help with surveillance or whatever you want me to do."

Lemon had left the room by then, and Hargraves said, "Wonder what kind of equipment he's talking about."

"If it's ropes and helmets and other climbing equipment, I'm out," Luke said.

Hargraves laughed.

"Yeah, we'll leave that to young Mr. Lemon," Hargraves said. "He looks like he could run to the top of Mount Adams this afternoon if we asked him to."

"Ah, youth," Luke said. "I remember those days."

"Let me tell you something," Hargraves said. "You're in way better shape and younger than me, so if there is any rappelling down a mountainside to check on a nest, it'll be your ass strapped into the gear, not mine."

"We'll cross that bridge if we come to it," Luke said as he headed for the door. "I have to go find a sasquatch. Have fun birdwatching."

Luke headed out to his truck, fired it up, and started to drive. He wasn't sure where he was going but he felt like he needed to be in the mountains. If nothing else, he wanted to check the road up by Bumping Lake to see if the birds and animals were acting normal again. Last night had been very eerie.

*

On his way through Naches, headed west on Highway 12, Luke spotted a familiar pickup truck in the parking lot at the diner. He decided to pull in and chat with the owner of the truck.

"Hey, Luke," Jim Kingsbury said when he saw him coming through the door. "What's going on with you today?"

Kingsbury was a well-known character around town who always wore t-shirts with funny or poignant sayings on them. In the time Luke had known him, he had never seen the man wear the same t-shirt twice. Today's shirt was a light purple-colored, short-sleeve shirt with a drawing of a black cat with a deadly serious face holding a long white bone. "I Found This Humerous" was written under the cat.

Sitting across from Kingsbury was his friend with three first names, Frank Dugdale. The men wore hats, Kingsbury an Australian-style leather hat, Dugdale a Seattle Mariners ball cap. Dugdale also had a safari-style vest over a yellow t-shirt. Both men were just finishing up a piece of apple pie à la mode.

"How's the pie?" Luke asked.

"Not as good as my grandma's," Dugdale said. "But it's not bad."

"I have a question for you guys," Luke said. "You ever hear any of the old tales about a sasquatch in the mountains west of here?"

Both men smiled as they thought about it for a bit.

"Didn't I ever tell you the story about the time bigfoot came into our hunting camp and had a hamburger with us?" Kingsbury said.

"About a hundred times," Dugdale said. "And it is pure fabrication."

"Now..." Kingsbury said. "Luke hasn't heard it. Let me tell it."

"Better sit down," Dugdale said to Luke. "You're gunna be here a while."

Luke sat down in the booth next to Dugdale to get a better view of Kingsbury's face as he told the story.

"We were hunting elk up by Kloochman Rock," Kingsbury started. "This was back when we could shoot any bull, before your genius employers totally screwed up the hunting around here. Anyway, we were back at our camp, inside the wall tent that was our cook tent. Old Duke Anderson was on the grill, cooking up some burgers from the spike he killed the previous year, and we hear this funny grunting outside the tent. Tuffy Spellman takes a look out the tent flap and lets out a scream. Not a blood-curdling scream, but you know, more like a you-scared-the-shit-out-of-me scream. I say, 'What's out there, Tuffy,' and he doesn't say a word—he just points, his eyes as big as goose eggs. So, I go to take a look, and there's nothing there. 'There's nothing there,' I say to Tuffy, and he slowly comes up behind me and looks out the tent flap. 'It was right there,' Tuffy says and then slowly goes out and starts looking around. I follow him out the door and start looking around too. Now, I'm thinking there musta been a bear sniffing around the tent, so I ask Tuffy, 'What was right there?' His eyes are still about as big as golf balls, and he says, 'I think I just saw bigfoot.'"

"Here's the good part," Dugdale said with a big grin on his face.

"After looking around and not seeing anything, I say to Tuffy, 'You sure you didn't just see a bear,' and he says, 'I know what a bear looks like—I've seen a thousand of them. This was a bigfoot, and it was eating the hamburger I just set down out there before coming in here to get the ketchup.'"

Luke chuckled at the thought of the bigfoot eating a hamburger.

"We looked around, and sure enough Tuffy's hamburger was gone, but we never saw the thing going through the trees. After dinner, I went out and looked for tracks but never found a thing. Tuffy swore to his dying day that it was a bigfoot he saw that day up there in the mountains, eating his burger."

"Have you ever heard such a thing?" Dugdale asked with a laugh.

"Everyone thought Tuffy had been drinking his bathwater or something," Kingsbury said. "But he said he knew what he saw, and what he saw could only be described as a bigfoot—big, tall, hairy, standing on two feet, taking a bite out of his hamburger."

"I forgot to ask," Dugdale said. "Did old Duke cook up another burger for Tuffy, or did he have to go to bed hungry?"

Then he laughed.

"Very funny," said Kingsbury. "So, why do you ask, Luke?"

"Oh, one of the residents up by Bumping had a strange deal happen the night before last with his dogs. His cousin thinks it might be a bigfoot that caused the trouble."

"What would his cousin know about bigfoot?" Dugdale asked.

"He doesn't really. He just shared a story his grandfather told from back in the day when he was a tree faller for the lumber company. Claims he saw a sasquatch."

"I bet he did," Kingsbury said. "If you saw Tuffy's face that night, you would believe it when he said he saw bigfoot. After a while, folks were making so much fun of him, Tuffy stopped telling the story and never said another word about it. Right before he died, I went to visit Tuffy, and he said to me, 'You know, Jim, that day up by Kloochman Rock, I really did see bigfoot.' So, I believed him."

"Well, thanks, fellas," Luke said as he stood to leave.

"You should try the apple pie before you go," Dugdale said. "Not as good as my grandma's, but it's pretty darned good."

"Next time," Luke said. "See you guys around."

As he drove on up the highway, Luke thought about the story Kingsbury had just told him, and he started to chuckle. Bigfoot stealing a hamburger. That was a good one.

CHAPTER 6

Desdemona Sands was trudging along with her Monday morning hiking-slash-birdwatching group when she stopped to take a quick look in the trees. A notification on the local Audubon Society's Facebook page said that a rare male red-naped sapsucker had been seen off the Bethel Ridge trail, so the all-woman group, known as the Weekly Walking Warblers, set off to try to find the oddity.

Given that the average age of the members in the hiking group was around seventy-three, the ladies would often refer to their club as the W-E-A-K-L-Y Walking Warblers, and after they told someone that, they would all titter, sounding like a banditry of mountain chickadees.

When she finally caught her breath from hiking up the hill, Sands focused her 10x45 Zeiss binoculars into a stand of fir trees and spotted something. After trying to make sense of what she was seeing, she let out a shriek.

"Ladies, ladies, look at this!" Sands exclaimed.

Thinking that the lucky Sands, called Mona by the group, had been the first to spot the sapsucker, thus winning her a dollar from each of the other members and possibly getting her name in their monthly newsletter, they all turned and looked.

"What is it, Mona?" asked Ruth Rogstad, the self-imposed leader of the group who none of the other ladies really liked but put up with because she had a Chevy Suburban that could shuttle them all to their weekly excursions.

"Up there in the fir tree, see it?" Sands said.

The other ladies, all with matching binoculars, looked up and focused on the tree.

"All I see is a dead deer stuck on a branch," said Doris Engle, whose low, gravelly voice sounded like she had just inhaled a lungful of exhaust from a school bus. "Where's the sapsucker?"

"That's what I see," Mona said. "The deer skewered on the branch. You just don't see that every day."

The ladies talked about the deer in the tree and what, if anything, they should do about it. Finally, thinking that someone might have poached the deer, they decided they should call it in to the authorities.

"The man at the Department of Wildlife office said they'd send someone up as soon as possible," said Rogstad, who had given her name and cell number to the gentleman on the phone.

"So, what are we supposed to do now?" croaked Engle.

"I say we keep hiking and looking," said Betty Harris, a fit octogenarian with short white hair who really didn't care much about the birdwatching. She liked to hike, but all the other hiking groups around town were made up of what she believed to be a bunch of male chauvinists. So, she became a Weekly Warbler.

"Okay," said Rogstad. "We'll keep hiking and looking for the sapsucker. If we hear from the game warden, we can meet him back here."

"Or her," said Harris. "The game warden could be a her."

"Yes, Betty. Of course, he could be a woman, but he's a man, because the man I just talked with on the phone said the game warden would be a man. His name is Lucas McCain."

"Like the character from the old TV show *The Rifleman?*" Engle growled.

"I guess so," said Rogstad. "Now, let's go see if we can find that damned sapsucker."

"I wonder if he looks like Chuck Conners?" Mona Sands said as they started back up the trail.

"That would be okay with me," Doris Engle said and tittered.

Off in the distance a mountain chickadee tittered back.

*

Luke took the call about the possible poaching case and headed to the Bethel Ridge trailhead. He knew the trail well, as he often checked on elk hunters in the area during the fall.

He was told some ladies had found a dead deer, and they thought someone should take a look at it. Before he got out of cell service range, he tried to call the woman who had made the report, but it just rang four times and went to voicemail.

When he arrived at the trailhead, he found a black and dust-covered Suburban parked there. He got out and looked at the tracks around the rig and on the trail. Several different sets of smallish hiking boot tracks were headed up the trail. The group of women, for sure.

Luke grabbed his daypack out of the back of the truck and pulled it over his shoulders. The pack contained some water, some basic survival gear, and some items that could help him collect any evidence around the poached deer.

He took off up the trail, hiking at a brisk pace, his steps covering twice the ground the steps the ladies' bootprints took. After walking at that pace for just fifteen minutes, he heard some women talking in the distance.

"I'm sure that's an ash-throated flycatcher," one of the women said.

"I beg to differ with you, Ruth," another woman's voice said.

"That's a black-capped chickadee."

Luke walked up to the group of women and said, "Good afternoon, ladies."

The four women all turned in unison and looked at Luke. They saw the badge on his shirt and a taller woman, with hair dyed as red as a scarlet tanager said, "Hello, officer. I'm Ruth Rogstad, leader of this little band of birdwatchers."

One of the women in the back of the group coughed. Luke thought he heard her say something inside the cough but didn't catch it.

"Yes, Ms. Rogstad, you were the one who called in the poached deer. I hate to interrupt your discussion here, but could you show me the deer?"

"Of course," Rogstad said. "It's back down the trail a ways."

She turned and started marching back toward the trailhead, and the other women fell in behind her. As the ladies walked, Rogstad said, "So you are Officer Lucas McCain?"

"Yes, ma'am, but please just call me Luke."

One of the women, Luke couldn't tell who, whispered, "He's much better looking than Chuck Conners." The other ladies tittered.

About four hundred yards down the trail, the group all came to a halt. Rogstad pointed to some trees and said, "There it is."

Luke looked down around the trees and saw nothing.

"Are you sure it was here?" Luke asked.

"Yes," said Rogstad. "And it is still here. See it up there, stuck in that tree?"

Luke looked up, and sure enough, there was a mule deer doe, impaled on a branch, eerily like the German shepherd had been just two days before.

"We were talking, and we can't quite figure out how someone could get the deer up that high," Rogstad said.

"Or why," growled Doris Engle.

"Stay here," Luke said as he walked down to get a closer look at the deer in the tree.

Closer examination showed that the left hindquarter of the deer was missing but was hard to see because that side of the deer was up against the tree trunk. He looked around the tree to see if there were any tracks but found none. He searched farther away from the tree, walking around it in circles. He still found no tracks.

As Luke stood and looked up, he tried to reach the doe. It was just out of his reach. Similar to the dog, the deer was roughly fifteen feet above the ground and had been forcefully stuck on a broken branch on the fir tree.

After taking some photos of the deer in the tree, Luke looked around and found a solid dead branch on the ground that was six feet in length. He used it to pry the doe off the branch. It was a bit of a struggle, but the animal finally slid off and flopped to the ground. As it did, Luke heard some groans from the ladies on the trail.

"Sorry," Luke said to his small audience. "But I need to take the deer back to the office to have a better look at it. We'll determine how it died, which might give us a better idea as to how it ended up in the tree."

"Maybe a bear dragged it up there, and it got stuck," said Betty Harris. "Or a cougar."

"That's a possibility," Luke said. "But I found no bear or cougar tracks under the tree."

"How about a golden eagle?" Mona Sands offered. "We've all seen videos of goldens attacking young deer and antelope and bighorn sheep."

The ladies murmured and nodded their heads in agreement. They had all seen the videos on the internet.

"Could be," Luke said. "If that's what happened, I will find evidence on the deer's back or neck where the eagle grabbed it with its talons."

He didn't want to tell the ladies it wasn't an eagle, though, because an eagle wouldn't have so cleanly taken the hindquarter off the dead deer. It would have torn a hole in the belly of the animal and eaten the organs.

Luke dragged the deer up a slight incline to the trail as the ladies all watched.

"Oh, it's missing a back leg," Sands said. "That's weird."

"This whole thing is weird," Harris said.

"Yes, it is," Luke said. "Listen, I want to thank you ladies for calling this in. Sorry that I interrupted your hike. Just a couple more quick questions. Was there anyone else parked at the trailhead when you arrived this morning?"

"No," the ladies said in unison.

"Did you happen to see anyone hiking on the trail or in the surrounding area today?"

Again, the ladies responded with a "no."

"Okay, thanks again. Enjoy the rest of your hike and be safe. Oh, and keep your eyes open. There's a rumor that a red-naped sapsucker has been seen around these parts."

Luke hefted the doe onto his shoulder, resting it the best he could on his backpack, and started down the trail to his truck. It was only a short hike, mostly downhill. It would be quicker carrying it this way versus taking the time to lash it to his pack. As he left, he heard the woman with the gravelly voice say something he couldn't understand, and the other women all tittered.

*

When Luke got back to his truck, he swung the carcass off his shoulder and put it on the tailgate of the pickup. He looked the deer over and could find no wounds or any other sign that something wild had attacked the deer. He could tell, though, that the animal had a broken neck.

He pushed the deer into the bed of his truck, pulled his daypack off, placed it in the back seat, and climbed into the driver's seat. Before he fired up the truck, he sat and thought. Who could be doing this? It had to be a who, not a what, right? Someone was playing a strange little game.

Luke figured the dog that was killed up near Bumping was roughly eleven or twelve miles from where the deer had been impaled in the tree. That was as the crow flew. If the crow was driving an ATV, it would be closer to twenty miles. Could some kind of an animal cover that amount of country in two days? It was rough country, but yes, it probably could. Biologists had tracked bears that would cover ten miles in a day. And wolves regularly traveled fifteen or twenty miles in a day.

He was convinced, though—it wasn't an animal that was doing this. There would be tracks somewhere around the site.

But wouldn't there be tracks if a human were doing this? And how could someone get the animals up in the tree without a ladder or some other climbing aid? They would have to be fairly strong too. Both the shepherd and the doe weighed around ninety pounds. Very few people would be capable of hoisting that amount of weight up a ladder and then, with the force needed, stick the animal on a sharp branch.

The biggest conundrum was why. Why would someone, or some*thing*, be doing this? Were they saving the animals as food, to be collected later? Placing an animal in a tree would certainly keep the coyotes and badgers from scavenging the meat. The crows and magpies could still get at it, but surprisingly, none had bothered either animal.

Luke had no answers, so he started thinking about other things, like what Hargraves and Lemon might have found in their search for falcon nests. And he thought about the ladies who were hiking the trail looking for birds.

He enjoyed watching birds too and could identify many of the different birds that made the Cascade Mountains their home. But to just go out and see how many different varieties you could see— that didn't interest Luke. Not that he thought it was bad. In fact, he thought it was great. It got people outdoors and moving around.

The ladies had been very observant to spot that doe in the tree. Ninety-five percent of the hikers on that trail, maybe more, would have walked right by it. Luke wondered why he hadn't crossed paths with the lady birdwatchers prior to this. He had seen two or three other groups of birders here and there and was familiar with most of the regular hiking groups in the area. He was glad the ladies had called in the report of the deer in the tree. But it sure made things more confusing.

CHAPTER 7

Sergi Petrov knew a good thing when he heard it. And when his cousin in Russia told him about one of the richest men in the old country's search for falcons and eagles, he figured he and his brother had hit the jackpot.

Gregorio Petrov, Sergi's younger brother by fourteen months, wasn't quite as enthusiastic.

The brothers, who were in their mid-thirties, had immigrated to the United States nine years earlier, with plans to work in the oil fields of North Dakota. They had been working in the oil fields in Russia for a decade, with little to show for it. They were tired of barely making enough to pay rent and put crappy food on the table. One of their friends had moved to the U.S. two years before and told them about the great money he was making.

"There are restaurants on every corner and easy women in every town," their friend had told them. "The pay is good, and the work is easier than in Russia."

After hearing that, the Petrov brothers packed up and headed to the U.S. Actually, the two men arrived in Vancouver, Canada first. They then worked their way to Saskatchewan, where, in the cover of darkness, they crossed the border into North Dakota and soon found their way to Minot.

After securing the necessary green cards and identification, all fake, the brothers were quickly hired. Anyone with a pulse and half a brain got jobs, and because the brothers had experience working in the fields of the motherland, they became well-liked by the foremen on the jobs. Even when the boom died down around 2015, the brothers were able to stay on as part of the smaller crews still working to get the black gold out of the ground.

The other advantage Sergi and Gregorio had was they were used to working in harsh conditions. North Dakota received a couple of blizzards each winter and one or two in the fall and spring. They had worked in almost constant bad weather in Siberia, and the few days of snow and wind on their new jobs were nothing to them.

Then one day the foreman came up to them and handed them pink slips.

"What does this mean?" Sergi asked the foreman.

"Sorry, fellas," the man said. "It was a good run, but the Feds are shutting us down."

The brothers were drowning their sorrows in a bottle of vodka a couple of days later when their cousin called from Moscow.

"A very rich man," their cousin, Maxim Volkov, said, speaking Russian over the phone, "is looking for some birds. Did I say he was rich? This man is extremely rich. One of the richest in all the country."

"What kind of birds?" Gregorio asked.

The older Petrov stood five-foot-eleven, an inch taller than his brother. He had the identical gray-blue eyes and black hair as his brother, and both men were slim and very fit from working in the oil fields. Gregorio sported a thick black mustache; Sergi did not.

"Birds of prey," Volkov said. "He wants to hunt rabbits and

grouse with a falcon. And deer with an eagle. He is willing to pay very big money for these birds. He is very, very rich. Did I tell you that?"

"How would we do this?" Sergi asked.

"I don't know, but he wants the birds soon. He has done some research, which means he probably saw a show on America's cable television networks, about falcons and eagles in the western part of the country. He believes they are there for the taking."

"Like how much money are we talking?" Gregorio asked. "This sounds like it is probably illegal and possibly dangerous."

"I don't know how much, but I tell you, the man is rich," Volkov repeated. "And he REALLY wants these birds. I think his mistress believes it would make him more powerful and sexy if he were to hunt with a bird on his arm like they used to do back in the days of the czars."

"Okay," Sergi said. "We will start doing some research on where to find these birds. You find out how much this man is willing to pay."

After hanging up the phone, the brothers talked.

"What else do we have to do?" Sergi asked. "I am not going to work at McDonald's for minimum wage. This might be good."

"I don't know," Gregorio said. "I am sure we can find a construction job somewhere."

"I am sure we can too," Sergi said. "But if this were to pay really big money, we could start our own business and make our own money."

"Let's find out more," Gregorio said and changed the channel on the TV to watch Jerry Springer reruns. He and his brother thought it was amazing that they would put such stupid stuff on TV and wondered why anyone would watch it. It was so stupid, people fighting and cussing and slapping each other. They never missed an episode.

*

"I believe that's a falcon nest right there," Barrett Lemon said with his right eye glued to the eyepiece of a spotting scope.

The scope, sitting on a sturdy tripod, was roughly the size of a large man's leg and seemed powerful enough to spot the flag that Buzz Aldrin had planted on the moon.

"Yep," Lemon confirmed. "There's the female falcon. At least I think it's the female. All I can see is an eyeball."

"Lemme see," Hargraves said, stepping over to the giant spotting scope. "I see the eye, but how do you know it's a falcon? Can we back this thing off just a tad?"

Lemon turned a ring on the scope, and Hargraves got a better look at the bird's head. He kind of knew his birds, and it looked like a falcon to him. As he watched, he saw two little falcon heads bob up and down.

"There are chicks in the nest," Hargraves said. "Are they called chicks?"

"A baby falcon is called an eyas," Lemon said. "Until they are forty days old or so, then they are fledglings."

"Okay, whatever," Hargraves said. "Let's mark the nest on our GPS and go look for more."

"Should we put a camera up there to keep an eye on them?" Lemon asked.

"You brought some?" Hargraves asked.

"Yeah, I have several. I can run one up there and place it. Won't take but a few minutes."

Hargraves looked at the columns of basalt, which seemed straight up and down, and wondered how anyone could 'run up there.'

"Go for it," Hargraves said. "What do you want me to do?"

"Just hang here for a bit," Lemon said as he was grabbing his gear. "I'll be back in forty-five minutes."

Hargraves watched as the young biologist threw a backpack over his shoulders and headed through the brush along the Tieton River, toward the rock columns. A short time later, he watched Lemon, now outfitted in a bright red helmet and a harness of some kind, skillfully climb up the side of the rocks, placing anchors in the cracks as he moved up the wall to attach a safety rope.

"Geez," Hargraves muttered to himself as he watched Lemon scale the column next to the one where the falcon nest sat neatly on a shelf about three hundred feet up. The kid was climbing the column like it was nothing. Hargraves couldn't have done that if someone had offered him ten million dollars to do so.

Lemon got just above the level of the nest, and Hargraves watched him secure a mount into a crack and then place a small camera, about the size of a pack of cigarettes, on the mount. He checked the camera's view, pushed a couple of buttons, and then, without seemingly giving it a second thought, started effortlessly rappelling down the rock face.

Ten minutes later, Lemon was hurrying through the brush along the river headed back to the truck.

"Okay," Lemon said as he took his backpack off and threw it into the back of Hargraves' truck. "Let's go find another one." The young man was barely breathing hard.

"That was amazing," Hargraves said to Lemon. "You did that like it was nothing."

"It's what I do on the weekends for fun," Lemon said as he opened a bottle of water and took a big swig. "That was an easy one."

"So how will you know what is on the camera?" Hargraves asked.

"Oh, I'll climb up and check the SIM cards every couple of days. I left the anchors in so I can get up there to check it out."

The duo spent the rest of the day checking for likely falcon nests up Highway 12, traveling all the way to the White Pass ski lodge. They found two more nests. Lemon set a camera in some rocks near the second nest. On the third, he climbed a huge pine tree and set the camera there. He told Hargraves that the camera didn't have a great view of the nest, but they would easily be able to see if anyone pilfered the nest, taking one of the three eyas there.

As they were headed back toward the office in Yakima,

Hargraves said, "It would seem to me those falcons wouldn't just sit by and let something take their babies. Don't you think they would attack someone?"

"I don't know," Lemon said. "Maybe if it were a bobcat or a raven that was robbing the nest, but something the size of a man, they may not."

"Those things fly really fast," Hargraves said. "Like two hundred miles an hour. If they wanted to hit a person, it would definitely hurt and might knock them right off the cliff."

"If a person were smart, they would be in a safety harness to avoid just such a thing," Lemon said.

"I don't think we're dealing with brain surgeons here," Hargraves said. "Someone stupid enough to try it deserves whatever Mother Nature pours out."

*

Back at the office, Luke was just shutting down his computer for the day when Hargraves and Lemon came in.

"How'd it go, fellas?" Luke asked.

"Really well," Lemon offered before Hargraves could speak. "Three falcon nests, and we have eyes on all three."

Luke gave Hargraves a questioning look.

"Our boy here is something of an accomplished rock climber," Hargraves said. "He scaled sheer cliffs and a giant pine tree to get cameras on all three nests."

"Who is going to check those when Barrett goes back to Ridgefield?" Luke asked.

"Not me," Hargraves said. "Let's hope if someone is coming for the eyas, they'll come soon."

"For the what?" Luke asked.

"Eyas. Baby falcons. Come on, Luke. Everyone knows that," Hargraves said with a poor attempt at a British accent.

"Is that what they call them in New Zealand?" Luke asked.

"What?" Hargraves asked.

"You pronounced that like a Kiwi."

"Baby kiwis are called chicks," Lemon said.

"What?" Hargraves asked.

"You asked what baby kiwis are called. They are called chicks."

Hargraves just shook his head and asked, "How'd it go in your search for bigfoot?"

"Weird," Luke said. "It went weird."

He told Hargraves and Lemon, who had scootched his chair over to listen in, about his call from the birdwatcher ladies and the deer they had discovered impaled on the branch of a tree near the Bethel Ridge trail.

"Just like the shepherd?" Hargraves asked.

"Exactly," Luke said.

"What's that?" Lemon asked.

So, Luke explained the situation with the dog in the tree from two days before and showed him the photos of the dog and the deer.

"Boy, you sure don't see that every day," Lemon said.

"Any tracks around the deer tree?" Hargraves asked.

"Not a one. Like I said, it was weird. I brought the deer down and am sending it to the lab in Oregon so they can go over it with a fine-toothed comb. Maybe they can find something that will tell us how the deer died and how it got stuck on that branch in the tree."

"I heard Stan jokingly suggest bigfoot, but that may be what you're dealing with here," Lemon said matter-of-factly.

"Why would you think that?" Hargraves asked.

"The indigenous people around here all believe in bigfoot," Lemon said. "They call him sasquatch and believe it is a creature that can become invisible."

He went on to tell them that sasquatch is common in the folklore of most Northwest Native American tribes. Their legends usually describe the creatures as around six to nine feet tall, very strong, hairy, uncivilized, and often foul-smelling, usually living in the woods and often foraging at night. These creatures, according to legend, are almost always said to be unable to speak human languages, using whistles, grunts, and gestures to communicate with each other. In some stories, male sasquatches are said to be able to mate with human women.

After hearing this, Luke thought about the story Jim Kingsbury had told at the diner, about the creature that was grunting outside of their wall tent. And he thought about the size of the creature that Lemon said the indigenous people described. Something nine feet tall could certainly place an animal fifteen feet up into a tree, probably standing flat-footed doing so.

"Invisible?" Luke asked. "That's a bit hard to swallow."

"It's what they believe," Lemon said. "But maybe the creature can move so quietly, and quickly, that they just seem to disappear."

Luke would have to think about that a bit.

"Okay," Hargraves said as he headed toward the back door. "Enough fairy tales. I have a pot roast waiting for me at home. See you guys tomorrow."

CHAPTER 8

Ten thousand dollars a bird. That's what the oligarch in Russia was offering to pay for each young falcon they could ship to him in Moscow. And he would pay twenty-five thousand for each young golden eagle.

"Did he say how many he wants?" Sergi Petrov, speaking his native tongue, asked his cousin Maxim Volkov after he was told the price the rich Russian was willing to pay. "Because we could probably supply several."

"He did not say," Volkov said. "But they must arrive in good condition. He will not pay for a sick or dead bird."

"That is certainly understandable," Sergi said. "We have done some research and believe we have found an area that is rich with falcons. We will be moving there tomorrow to start searching for nests. We could have birds for him possibly by next week."

"I will let my contact know this," Volkov said. "Stay in touch."

"We will," Sergi said and hung up.

"So, is it a go?" Sergi's brother Gregorio asked.

"I believe so. We will be paid ten thousand dollars for each live and healthy falcon and twenty-five thousand for each young eagle. Five falcons and two eagles, and we will have one hundred thousand dollars."

"We have to catch them first," Gregorio reminded his brother. "And we must locate them before that. Do you still want to go to Washington State?"

The Petrov brothers had a friend who lived in Seattle, and during his travels through eastern Washington, he had spotted three peregrine falcons along the rivers that ran to the east out of the Cascade Mountains.

"Demetri says there are many rock cliffs and canyons along the rivers where the falcons surely nest. They should not be that hard to find."

"Finding them is one thing," Gregorio said. "I am worried about getting to them. It may be more difficult than we imagine."

"We used to climb the cliffs in the Urals when we were boys," Sergi said. "It will most likely be similar to that."

"We were much more agile and stupid back then," Gregorio said.

"And we were poor," Sergi said. "We do this now for money. Money is a great motivator."

Gregorio stopped and thought about it for a minute. "And what do you think the mother birds will do when they see us stealing their babies? It is my guess they will not just sit idly by and watch it happen."

"Falcons are small," Sergi said. "It will be like swatting bees."

"It is not the falcons that worry me," Gregorio said. "Although they might be fiercer than you give them credit. It is a mad mother eagle that I worry about. They have been known to carry off deer and sheep. A protective mother eagle will not be swatted like an insect."

Sergi waved his hand and made a "pffft" sound with his mouth, like it was nothing. Inside, though, he also worried about what a mother eagle might be willing to do to a person who was trying to snatch one of her babies. He decided to concentrate on the hundred thousand dollars and went to get ready for a move to Washington State.

*

Hargraves and Lemon spent another day looking for nests, this time up Highway 410 toward Chinook Pass. They located two falcon nests, and one was so far across the Naches River they decided not to put a camera on it.

"I know where it is now," Hargraves said to Lemon when they decided not to place the camera. "I'll show it to McCain too, and we can keep an eye on it from the highway on our patrols up here."

After Lemon placed a camera at the more accessible nest, the men went in search of a golden eagle eyrie.

"This will be more difficult," Lemon said about locating the eagle nest. "They're much larger, so they'll be easier to see, but they usually are well away from any human activity. We'll probably have to do some hiking."

Hargraves thought about that for a second and said, "I have no problem hiking through these mountains—I do it all the time. But it would be best if we had some idea what kind of terrain we are looking for."

"Their nests can be in trees," Lemon said. "Like bald eagles. But they can also be on the ground or on cliffs. Sometimes they'll actually nest on man-made structures such as observation towers or power poles."

"Well, that helps," Hargraves said sarcastically. "There are only about ten bazillion acres up here, and in all my years I have never seen a golden eagle nest. Not that I was looking for one."

"How about the Goat Rocks?" Lemon asked. "That might be a good place to start."

"Did you just see that name on a map or something?"

"No, I did some climbing with a couple of college buddies up that way a few years ago. We didn't see any golden eagle nests, but

I did see a golden eagle."

"That's a bit of a drive from here, on the other side of White Pass," Hargraves said. "I know where there are some steep rock faces up near Norse Peak, which is much closer. Let's go give that a look."

The drive up the forest service road that led into the Norse Peak country was rough and dusty. Any time they could see some craggy ridges or cliffs from the road, they would stop and look, first with binoculars and then, if something looked like it might be a nest, Lemon would break out his powerful spotting scope and they would check it out.

They saw several elk, a few mule deer, a small flock of turkeys, and they even found a nanny mountain goat with two kids in a spot on a sheer rock cliff that looked like if the baby goats made one slight misstep, they would fall hundreds of feet to almost certain death.

But they found no eagle nests.

"I don't know how anyone is going to be collecting any eaglets in this country," Hargraves said after searching another group of rock bluffs.

"Me neither," said Lemon. "I think we should concentrate our time watching the falcon nests and see what happens."

"I concur," Hargraves said. "We're going to be out of daylight before long. Let's head back to town and figure out what to do from here. Heck, we're not positive there is anyone looking to poach some of these birds anyway."

"The captain told me it was a pretty credible tip," Lemon said. "I'd like to catch him if it is true."

✳

There was, in fact, someone looking to grab some falcon and eagle chicks. Two someones. The Petrov brothers had arrived in Yakima three days before the tip came into the Fish and Wildlife office. They had driven Sergi's Jeep Cherokee from Minot, across the unbelievably massive state of Montana, then through the panhandle of Idaho before traveling to central Washington. Their Jeep only broke down twice.

Luckily, the first time it broke down, they were just outside of Butte, Montana. A water pump went out, and after hitching a ride into town, finding a NAPA store that had a replacement, and then hitchhiking back to the rig, the brothers replaced the part.

They were just about to the state line between Montana and Idaho when a fan belt broke.

"Why did we bring this piece of junk?" Gregorio Petrov asked.

"Because your piece of junk wouldn't even start," his brother said.

"Oh yeah. Well, when we get paid for these birds, the first thing we are going to do is buy a dependable mode of transportation. I hate hitchhiking. The people around here don't seem overly friendly when they learn we are from Russia."

"It is because that idiot Putin has given us all a bad name. They think all Russians are bullies and criminals."

"You mean like criminals who would steal baby birds from their nests to sell for large amounts of dollars?"

"Americans admire entrepreneurs. That is all we are. We are using our skills to make money. It is what this great country is all about."

"We have never found a falcon's nest or stolen a baby bird in our life, so there might be a question about our skills."

"We will soon find out," Sergi said.

"Yes, if we could ever get there," Gregorio said, sticking out his thumb as another vehicle zoomed by them.

CHAPTER 9

"So, what are you going to do?" Sara McCain asked her husband at dinner after Luke told her the story of the birdwatching hikers finding the deer in the tree.

"I'm not sure," Luke said. "Technically, no laws have been broken, or at least none that I am aware of. Killing someone's dog will get you in hot water, but we don't know if it was even a person who did that. And the deer could have been poached, but with no bullet or arrow holes, it could have died of natural causes and then an animal or bird placed it there."

"Do you really believe that?" Sara asked.

"I don't know what to believe. The kid who is helping us locate falcon nests told how the local natives believe in the beast they call sasquatch. The thing is big, hairy, smelly, and can disappear into thin air."

"You really think something like that is involved?"

"Logically, no. But I can't find any evidence that anything, or anyone, was involved. All I have is two dead animals impaled on branches."

"Well, maybe the techs at the lab will find something that helps point you in the right direction," Sara said. "It's a strange one, for sure."

That told Luke that his wife was done discussing this subject for the time being.

"Now, about that new couch and loveseat," she said. "You ready to go look at some?"

Luke was not ready to go look at furniture. The couch and loveseat in their living room had been there long before they'd first met five years before, and frankly, they still looked good to him. They were comfortable, and even though the arms on the loveseat had a couple of areas where the threads had worn down to nothing, some kitchen towels covered those nicely. And the spot where he had accidentally spilled some salmon egg dye on the middle cushion of the couch, well, you had to look hard to see it.

"Why don't you go and pick out what you like," Luke said. "I'll be happy with whatever."

"Oh, no you don't," she said sharply.

Luke rarely saw Sara get angry, but when she gave him that look with her dark, almost black eyes and had that tone in her voice, he knew she meant business.

"If I picked something out you didn't like, and you said something about it a year later, I would have to shoot you. I wouldn't kill you, but I would maim you."

Luke thought about that for a second. It had been years since he had heard anyone use the word "maim." Coming from his wife's lips, it did not sound good.

"Could you describe the maiming?" Luke asked with a smile.

Sara just continued to give him that stare. She meant business.

"I'll start the truck," Luke said.

*

Barrett Lemon spent three more days working out of the Yakima office. He rode with Hargraves two of those days, and with Luke the third day. They checked the falcon nests and looked, without any luck, for a golden eagle nest.

Lemon scaled the different spires and columns each day and found absolutely nothing on his cameras. The same number of eyas were in the nests, and even though it had been just days, the young birds were growing fast.

"If someone is going to grab those chicks," Luke said on the day Lemon rode with him, "they better do it fast. It looks like those birds will be flying in a week."

Each passing day with no activity made the two game wardens believe the call about someone stealing the baby birds might very well be a hoax.

Still, because young Lemon was willing to gear up and climb to check on the cameras and nests, they went through with the surveillance.

"What are you guys going to do when I leave tomorrow?" Lemon asked Luke after checking on the one nest up Chinook Pass where they had a camera.

"We'll check on them," Luke said. "But neither of us is comfortable with climbing up there like you do. We'll check on them from the rig with binoculars."

"What if someone comes in and gets them while you are off on some other calls?"

"I guess we'll just have to cross that bridge when we come to it."

"But you might not know," Lemon said and then sat quietly.

Luke could see him thinking.

"Here's what I will do," Lemon finally said. "I don't think my boss will let me spend more time up here during work hours, but I will come back this weekend and check the cameras. Like you said, those eyas will be leaving the nest sometime in the next couple weeks probably. I'd only have to come up maybe two more times."

Luke appreciated the young biologist's dedication.

"That's up to you," Luke said. "But I promise we'll check on them the best we can too."

Luke and Lemon were about three miles back down the highway headed to Yakima when they passed a red Jeep Cherokee coming up the highway, traveling at about twenty miles an hour.

The two men in the Jeep were looking off toward the river, but as soon as they saw Luke's truck and recognized it as a law enforcement vehicle, they sped up.

"That was weird," Luke said to Lemon.

"What was weird?"

"Those guys in that Jeep. Normally, when someone recognizes my rig as law enforcement, they slow down. Those guys sped up."

"Should we go run them down?" Lemon asked. "I've never been on a stop before."

"Naw, we really have no reason to stop them, but maybe we should go get their license plate just for the heck of it. There have been some burglaries up here. It might be good just to have it for the record."

Luke spun his truck around and headed back up the highway.

"Where are they?" Lemon asked after they drove for a few minutes.

"I don't know. We should've caught up to them by now."

"They must have pulled into one of these private drives," Lemon said.

"That's probably what they were looking for, one of these cabin driveways. That's why they were going so slow."

Both men looked up the few driveways they passed going back down the highway, but most were heavily lined with trees, and they couldn't see much past the mailboxes.

"Oh well," Luke said. "I'll watch for them, and if I see them again, I'll check 'em out."

*

The rest of Luke's week went by without much happening. Well, that is, until his last angler check of the day on Saturday.

Luke had spent the afternoon checking a few anglers who were fishing on the local rivers. The different streams had different rules.

Some allowed fish to be kept, while others were all catch-and-release. Some had other restrictions on the use of bait and barbed hooks. Frankly, it was hard for the average Joe to keep up on all of it.

Luke was pretty lenient with most of the people who were breaking the laws when it came to those varying rules. He would ask them a few questions, and if it looked like they had read the rules and regulations and were simply confused about them, he would give them a warning, take their names and fishing license numbers, and put them in a notebook. If he caught them again, well, then he would give them a citation.

The majority of anglers on the streams knew the rules about keeping, or rather, not keeping, bull trout. For years, anglers could catch and keep the fish, then called Dolly Varden, but at some point, twenty-five years before, it was determined that the bull trout were endangered and keeping one was a definite no-no. Because that law had been in effect for so long, Luke wasn't normally in a warning mood when he caught someone who had kept a bull trout.

Unfortunately, there were some people who had no clue. Or there were people who just didn't care. Plenty of people fished for something to eat while they were camping in the mountains, and they wouldn't know a bull trout from a bulimic bass, so Luke would have to try to explain why the angler was getting a hundred-and-sixty-dollar citation for catching the wrong fish.

Sometimes the anglers got more than a little belligerent about receiving the citation. Luke had run into one of those guys on his last contact of the week.

"What the hell!" the guy, named Darin Goff, screamed after looking at the ticket. "I'm not paying that for some damn fish I can't even eat."

"That's your prerogative, Mr. Goff," Luke said, wondering if the guy would know what "prerogative" meant.

Goff was roughly five foot ten, barrel-chested with thick arms and legs, and wore a purple bandana tied around his head. He wore cut-off jeans and a tie-dyed t-shirt. Long stringy brown hair ran down to the man's shoulders.

Luke had taken the now dead bull trout, a nice one of about two pounds, from the man and was putting it in a cooler in his pickup.

"You're damn right it is. And don't give me that Mr. Goff shit! I paid good money for my fishing license and when I finally do catch something that is worth eating, you take it from me and give me a ticket. That's horseshit!"

"I understand," Luke said. And he meant it.

He could see Goff wasn't having any of it though. The fireplug of a man was getting wound up. His face was getting red, and his large arms were starting to flail about. Luke reached around and made sure his Taser was ready to go if he needed it.

"What are you gunna do with that fish?" Goff asked. "Take it home and eat it?"

"No, I am not," Luke said.

Goff started slowly moving toward Luke as he yelled. "Then I'll have it back!"

"I can't do that," Luke said. "Turn around and head back to your truck."

"You ain't gunna eat it," Goff said, still coming at Luke. "I want my fish!"

Luke could see the fire in Goff's eyes and noticed that the man's hands were now balled up in fists.

"That's far enough," Luke said, holding his left hand up while placing his right hand on the Taser on his belt.

Goff did stop when he saw Luke reaching around his back. "What? Are you gunna shoot me? Over a damn fish?"

"This isn't a gun," Luke said as he pulled the Taser. "It is a Taser. If you want to tell all your buddies what it feels like to have five thousand volts running through your body, just keep coming."

Luke could see the man thinking about it.

"I mean it," Luke said. "You'll be flopping around in the dirt and will probably piss your pants."

Goff slowly started to turn back to his truck, but Luke could see his face had gone a deeper shade of red.

"All I want is my damn fish," Goff said as he turned and came at Luke with amazing quickness.

Goff's roundhouse swing came fast and hard, but Luke was able to sidestep it and duck just enough so that the blow glanced off his left shoulder. Goff's momentum took him a step past Luke, and that's all he needed.

SNAP!

The two barbed darts from the Taser hit Goff in the back, and the man took one more labored step and went down, shaking and shuddering.

Luke stepped over to the man and took his finger off the trigger, stopping the electricity that was running down the wires into Goff's back. The second the electricity was turned off, Goff tried to get up, muttering something about the "damn fish."

Luke hit him with another 5,000 volts, and Goff went face first into the dirt and gravel again.

"Stay down," Luke said as he pulled handcuffs from his utility belt.

Goff did stay down. Luke put his knee in the man's back and pulled one thick arm around, stuck a cuff on his wrist and reached around, got the other wrist, and cuffed it behind Goff's back. Then he helped the man stand up and plucked the two darts out of his shoulder. He checked Goff's pockets for weapons, grabbed his wallet, keys, and an Old Timer folding pocketknife, and put them in a bag.

"All I wanted was my damn fish," Goff mumbled as Luke walked him to his truck.

He helped Goff into the back seat and went back to make sure nothing had fallen out of the man's pockets. He grabbed up Goff's fishing rod and gear, took them back to the man's truck, and locked the stuff in the front seat.

When he climbed into his truck, Goff said to Luke, "You're an asshole. But you were right about one thing."

"What's that?" Luke asked.

"I pissed myself."

CHAPTER 10

The Petrov brothers spent three days searching along the Yakima, Naches, and Tieton Rivers for nests that might hold young falcons or eagles. They preferred to find an eagle's nest, as the wealthy man in Russia was willing to pay $25,000 for each eaglet they sent him. But they would happily send little falcons too. A few of those, maybe four or five, would be well worth the effort.

Finally, after spotting a falcon flying along next to the highway they had traveled about twenty times and watching it fly up onto a shelf on some rocky columns across the Tieton River, they found the nest.

"Now we must get across the river, climb that rock wall, and get the birds," Sergi Petrov said as they sat in the Jeep next to the highway watching the nest with binoculars.

"That will not be easy," Gregorio Petrov said. "We will need some equipment. Ropes and anchors and some chest waders to get across that river."

After sitting and watching and discussing the situation, the brothers developed a plan. They would go get the equipment they needed, and then Gregorio would climb the rock wall. He had always been more agile and athletic than his older brother.

Sergi would be Gregorio's spotter, tending the safety rope and keeping his brother secure if he were to slip and fall at some point during the climb.

"There are not as many vehicles traveling this road early in the morning," Sergi said after thinking about the times they had driven along the highway. "We will secure our gear tomorrow and come get the birds at daybreak the following morning."

The men had not actually seen baby birds in the nest but assumed that since there was an adult flying back and forth from the nest, there was at least one young falcon there.

"I hope there are many babies," Sergi said.

"Don't count on it," Gregorio said. "I have done some research on peregrine falcons. They normally have one or two babies, and many times only one survives during the time in the nest."

"Well, I guess we had better go find some more nests," Sergi said. "We are not going to risk our life for ten thousand dollars. We need to find an eagle nest."

*

A few days after Barrett Lemon had returned to his job at the Department of Fish and Wildlife's Region 5 office in Ridgefield, he was back in Yakima County, checking on the cameras he had placed near the falcon nests. The young man skillfully climbed to each camera, removed a small SIM card, and put a new card in. When he returned to his truck, he fired up his laptop, placed the card into the reader, and looked at the photos.

Each of the four cameras showed the young falcons getting bigger every day, with adult birds coming and going regularly to feed the eyas pieces and parts of a variety of different birds and animals.

In one of the nests, where there had been three young falcons, now there were only two. Lemon wondered what had happened to the baby, knowing that stuff happens in the wild. Most likely, the baby fell, maybe being bumped from the nest by one of the other eyas.

"I haven't seen any evidence that someone is tampering with the nests," Lemon said to Luke over the phone after he had done his checks.

"We've been keeping an eye on them," Luke said. "But we're not watching them all the time."

"I'll come back and check the cameras next weekend. The eyas should be flying soon, then we won't have to worry about them."

Luke didn't want to tell the biologist that he and Hargraves weren't really all that worried about the baby falcons now. At least not as worried as the young biologist was.

"Sounds good," Luke said. "Stan and I will keep watching the best we can until then."

*

The Petrov brothers were not totally stupid. They were smart enough not to speak Russian in the store, which they figured would create some unwanted attention. But they spoke loud enough that the kid behind the counter at the climbing supply store could hear them. The kid wasn't listening on purpose but heard what they said anyway, and it made him wonder just what the two men with the foreign accents might be up to.

After the men left the building, the clerk called the sheriff's office.

"What now?" was the response from the deputy who came on the line after the kid sat and listened to two minutes of a really bad Muzak on-hold version of The Doors song "Light My Fire."

"These two foreign dudes, maybe Russians, were just in the store, and they mentioned something about grabbing some baby birds."

"What kind of store do you have?"

"Well, it's not mine. I just work here. I'm a student at YVC, but I've done some climbing, so I know the equipment and—"

The deputy interrupted. "What kind of store do you work at?"

"We sell climbing supplies. And winter camping supplies. And we can get you scuba gear if you need it. But mostly we sell climbing supplies. Climbing is the second-fastest growing segment of the extreme outdoor sports category. Right behind sail surfing. Oh yeah, we can get you some sail surfing stuff too."

"So, what about the baby birds?" the deputy asked.

"Well, these two guys, brothers I think, were buying some ropes and anchors and carabiners, and they wanted to buy some chest waders, but we don't sell those. I told them they'd have to go to a fishing supply store for those. Anyway, after I showed them where some of that stuff was, the one guy, probably the younger brother, said to the other guy, 'This stuff is costing us a fortune. Those baby birds better be in that nest.' I wasn't trying to listen to them, but they said it loud enough so I heard. So, I'm thinking to myself, they are going to go try to climb some rock cliffs and capture some baby birds."

"Okay," the deputy said. "What did these guys look like?"

"They looked like brothers. And Russian. Is it racist to think someone looks like a Russian? Maybe they were Albanian or Yugoslavian. Somewhere from over that way. You know. They had that look."

"No, I mean, how tall were they? I need their age and hair color. And if they had any facial hair or tattoos."

"Oooo, oooo," oooed the clerk excitedly. "The one guy had a dark mustache, and if he shaved the outsides just a quarter-inch or so, it would look like a Hitler."

"A what?" the deputy asked.

"A Hitler. Some guys are starting to grow them. Mustaches like Hitler, the German Nazi leader, you know, the type of little square mustache like he always had."

"I know who Hitler was," the deputy said, now with some tension in his voice. "So, one of the guys had a mustache like Hitler?"

"Well, no," the clerk said. "But if he shaved a quarter-inch off of each end of his, it would look just like a Hitler."

After a few more minutes of going down another rabbit hole or two, the deputy finally got a decent description of the two men, who, if the clerk was right, were going to climb some rocks and steal some baby birds.

"Maybe pigeons," the clerk said. "But they wouldn't be worth anything, and you can find them anywhere, right? Could be some hawks or something. They'd be more valuable, wouldn't they? But who would buy any kind of bird. Maybe it is for a zoo or something."

The deputy cut him off, thanked him for the call, and took a breath. Then he called over to the Fish and Wildlife office and asked for an officer.

He got Hargraves.

"So, is that all?" Hargraves asked after the deputy gave him the information he'd gleaned from the clerk at the climbing store.

"No, the kid told me fifty other things, but none of it really got us to where we needed to go. I left that out. His name is Emery Hart if you want to talk to him. Give yourself a little time, though, because the kid can talk."

"Emery, like one of those fingernail boards?" Hargraves asked.

"I guess," the deputy said. "Why don't people name their kids Dave or Greg or Jim or Doug anymore. Now they're all named Jaiden and Laiden and Kaiden and Braiden."

"And Emery," Hargraves said. "Thanks for the information. We'll definitely follow up."

As soon as he hung up, Hargraves called Luke.

"Looks like the tip we got earlier about someone wanting to grab some young falcons and eagles was right. YSO just called me to say they received a call from a clerk at the climbing supply store that overheard two guys he thought might be Russian who were buying climbing gear, and he overheard them talking about grabbing some young birds."

"Hmmm," Luke hummed. "Maybe we need to pay a little more attention to those nests."

"Probably," Hargraves said. "But how would we know which ones to watch? And maybe they found some nests we didn't."

"I don't know, but let's try a little harder. Sounds like these guys are going to be doing something fairly soon."

"The deputy said the kid said the two guys were asking about chest waders, so they must be going across one of the rivers. That might eliminate the one nest that's next to the highway."

Hargraves agreed to go up the Naches River and watch the nests there. Luke would patrol the nests up the Tieton River.

"The kid at the climbing store didn't happen to see what kind of rig they were driving?" Luke asked.

"I don't know. The deputy didn't say anything about it, so I guess not."

"Maybe I'll run by and talk to the kid. What's his name?"

"Erby," Hargraves said. "No, that's not right. Emery. Yeah, that's it. Emery."

"You mean like the cloth?" Luke asked.

"Geez, how do I know? Just go talk to him. But be forewarned—the deputy said the kid can talk."

Luke found the climbing supply store, parked his truck, and walked in. The place looked like a climber's fantasy dream. Every wall but one was loaded from floor to ceiling with climbing gear. The wall without the gear was an actual climbing wall. Two twenty-something blondes in skin-tight yoga pants were all harnessed up and working their way up the wall. A thirty-something guy was paying particular attention to the girls, standing by like he was there as a spotter for their safety.

Luke had no idea that so many people were into rock climbing. He thought he might come down to try the climbing wall some time.

The young kid behind the counter turned out to be Emery Hart. He was tall and thin, probably six-two and a hundred forty pounds with a couple rocks in his pockets—one of those kids who looked like if he stood sideways, he could hide behind a flagpole. But Luke could tell there was some strength in Hart's long, thin arms. He wore his light brown hair long but unkempt, like it hadn't been brushed in a week, with bangs almost touching his dark brown eyes. Hart wore a t-shirt with the word Mammut on the front and safari-style short pants. Luke assumed Mammut was some kind of climbing gear.

Hart told Luke he hadn't seen the vehicle the two men had driven, but he did remember a couple of things that he hadn't told the sheriff's deputy.

"They were kind of rough looking," Hart said. "Not mean, just, you know, rough, like they worked in construction or something. They had those yellow boots on that a lot of construction guys wear, and the boots were pretty beat up and stained, like they'd been around building sites or something."

"Okay," Luke said. "Anything else?"

"Actually, now that I think about it, they kind of smelled a bit oily," Hart said. "Maybe like they were car mechanics or something."

Luke thanked the kid for calling the report in and headed back to his truck. As he walked out the door, he looked back at the two women on the climbing wall. One had almost made it back to the bottom of the wall, and the spotter dude was right there to help, with his hand noticeably close to her butt.

CHAPTER 11

Luke most likely would have caught the Petrov brothers at the falcon nest they had found if it wasn't for the call he received from dispatch telling him a woman up in the north fork of the Ahtanum was having some issues with a critter, or critters, getting into her small herd of goats.

"She'd like you to call her right away," the dispatcher said.

So, Luke took the number and dialed it up.

"It could have been a cougar, or a bear, or maybe a wolf," April Sommers said into the phone. "Someone needs to get up here and take care of this issue."

Evidently, the woman had called once before, but this time she thought a couple of her goats were missing and she was tired of having to deal with the predators going after her livestock.

Luke felt like telling her that putting a herd of goats in the middle of the mountains, where all the predators lived, was maybe not the best idea, but he didn't.

"I'll be up there as quick as I can," Luke said after getting her address and clicked off.

On his way out to April Sommers' place, Luke called Hargraves. First, he told Hargraves how Emery Hart had described the two men, including their boots, their smell, and the dark mustache on one. Then, Luke told him that he probably wouldn't make it to the falcon nests until sometime later in the day.

"I have to see a goat lady out in the north fork," Luke explained.

"Okay, well, if I get a chance, I'll go over and see what I can see," Hargraves said.

Over the years, Luke had taken hundreds of these calls about wildlife doing damage to livestock or crops. It was inevitable that there would be conflicts between humans and wild animals. The calls were multiplying every year now that the laws had done away with many hunts that helped control the populations of cougars and bears. The calls that really astounded Luke were the ones from the people who would complain about the deer eating their flowers or blueberry bushes.

"I can't keep a garden," one distressed woman had said after Luke had driven up to her place in the Nile. "Those damn deer, excuse my French, come in here every night. If it's not my petunias, it's my chrysanthemums. I planned on entering them in the fair and now look at them."

Luke had glanced over at the flower patch, and it looked like someone had gone through it with a weed-whacker. He'd almost laughed.

"There's not much I can do about that, ma'am," Luke had said. "You are out here where the deer live, and they eat what they like. The best thing to do is put up a ten-foot-tall deer fence. That should keep them out."

"Can't you shoot them?" the woman asked. "If it was a racoon or a skunk, you'd shoot them wouldn't you, if they were being a pest?"

"No, I probably wouldn't," Luke said. "Only if there was a chance they are going to cause harm to people. Then we might take permanent measures."

When Luke had left the woman, he was only about fifty percent sure she wasn't going to get a rifle and take things into her own hands. People loved to look at the pretty deer, and some were totally against hunting the poor, innocent creatures, but as soon as the animals started munching on the marigolds, it was war.

Luke pulled up to April Sommers' residence and parked. April was a pretty woman, but she looked hard. She was petite, in her mid-forties, with dishwater blonde hair braided into a pigtail that wound its way out of the back of a baseball hat with a Justin Boots logo on the front. Only about five-foot-two and maybe a hundred and ten pounds, Sommers was fit and possibly a little tightly strung, Luke thought.

"Thanks for coming," Sommers said as she started walking back behind her small house even before Luke was totally out of his truck. "The goats started raising a ruckus around three o'clock this morning, and I figured it was a coyote or maybe a cougar. We've had some cougar sightings recently. Anyway, I grabbed my shotgun and turned on the outside lights, but I couldn't see anything."

"So, you think a couple of your goats are missing?" Luke asked. "Was the pen gate open?"

"Only one is missing," Sommers said. "I was in a bit of a panic when I first called, but now that I've had a chance to check, I'm missing just one. A tan Boer named Sam. And no, the gate wasn't open, so how did it get out of the pen—fly?"

"Have you looked around for your goat?" Luke asked. The second he saw Sommers' face, he realized it was a stupid question.

"Yes, officer, I have," she said curtly.

Luke thought about asking if she had looked in any trees, but thought better of it.

"Well, you mind if I take a look around? I might be able to find some prints that would point us at what was creating all the commotion during the night. And I might find your goat's prints."

"Be my guest," Sommers said as she grabbed a big scoop shovel to go do something, anything, away from Luke.

The area out behind the goat pen was grassy with some young

pine trees popping up here and there. Farther back, a group of larger fir trees grew. Trails led here and there, and after looking for a minute, Luke could see that at some point Sommers must have let the goats out to wander around. Goat tracks were pretty much everywhere.

As he looked for cougar or bear tracks, Luke thought about the woman's name. He wondered if Sommers was a married name, or if her parents had given her the first name of April to go along with Sommers. A month and a season. Kind of weird, but kind of cool, Luke thought.

He was joking, sort of, when he thought about asking the woman if she had looked in the trees, but now, as he was entering the stand of taller fir trees, he did exactly that. It only took a minute of looking, and there it was—a tan-colored goat, impaled on a branch, hanging upside down, right against the tree trunk.

"Well, hell," Luke muttered to himself as he started to search around the tree for anything that would tell him who, or what, skewered the goat on the branch.

Fifteen minutes later, after looking thoroughly, on his hands and knees even, Luke had found nothing. He walked back to the house, where Sommers was raking the front yard.

"Anything?" she asked, without even looking at him.

"Yes," he said. "I found your goat."

She turned with a smile, then she saw the serious look on Luke's face and realized it was not good news.

"Sam's dead?"

"Yes, ma'am. And it is an unusual circumstance."

"What's that supposed to mean?"

"Best you come and take a look," Luke said and turned to walk back to the tree.

"What is it? Did the cougar half eat him or something? I've seen most everything, so it won't bother me."

"No, a cougar didn't get him."

"So, what is it?" she said as she walked quickly alongside Luke and looked up at him.

"He's impaled on a limb in one of the big fir trees in the back."

"What?" she yelled in disbelief. And then quieter, "What?"

Luke didn't say anything else, just walked her to the tree. Sommers looked up and started to sniff, holding back tears. She was tough, but not that tough, Luke thought.

Finally, she said, "What in the hell did this?"

Luke noted that she didn't say 'who in the hell did this.'

"I don't know, Ms. Sommers. I've looked all around, and I can't find a track or anything else that might tell me how Sam got up there. I will tell you that this isn't the first we've seen of this. A guy's dog was found like this up near Bumping Lake, and some ladies walking a trail up off Highway 12 found a deer impaled on a branch just like this as well."

"What kind of a sick bastard would do this?" Sommers asked.

Now she was thinking it was a who and not a what.

"We have no idea. It's absolutely baffling."

Sommers looked at Luke like he was insufficient in some way, then her face changed.

"Wait a minute. You're the game warden who tracked down that guy who was killing women and dumping their bodies in the mountains around here. And you caught that mass murderer up near Canada last year."

"Yes, ma'am."

"So, you know how to find criminals?"

"Sometimes. But seriously, I have no clue who, or what, is doing this. We have the deer carcass down at the crime lab in Oregon being checked out, but just like here, there were no tracks, no ladder marks, and frankly, there haven't been any marks on the animals other than the puncture wounds from being impaled on the branches."

"Sounds like aliens maybe, huh?"

Luke looked at her and could tell she was being facetious. She was pissed.

"Actually, some people have mentioned bigfoot."

Sommers laughed. "Yeah, right."

Luke then told her about the tales of sasquatch that Native Americans had passed down through generations, and the story Jason Ball shared about his grandpa with the logging crew.

"So, you believe all that?" Sommers asked.

"No, I don't. But the more I hear, and the more I look at these dead animals and have no clue how they are ending up in the trees, the more I start to wonder."

"I think I'd keep that to myself," Sommers said. "You don't want people thinking you're losing your marbles."

"Thanks. I'll do that."

She smiled at Luke and said, "So what do we do from here?"

"You have a ladder?" Luke asked as he pulled his phone out to take some photos.

When he got the goat down out of the tree, Luke could tell immediately the animal had a broken neck. But, like the dog and the deer, there were no other marks on the body. No bite marks. No claw marks. Nothing.

"Do you need the goat?" Sommers asked after Luke packed it down to her house.

"No, I don't think so."

"I sell most of my goats for meat. But Sam was one of my first. Can't let him become taco meat. I'm going to bury him."

"I can help you with that if you'd like," Luke offered.

"Naw, I want to do it," Sommers said. "It'll help to wear off a little of this anger."

"Okay, well, sorry about Sam. I'll let you know if we figure this thing out."

"You mean *when* you figure this thing out," she said.

Luke smiled and said, "I'll let you know."

As Luke was backing out of the driveway, he could see Sommers talking to her dead goat, Sam, lying in the grass in the shade next to the house. He got a little lump in his throat and had to swallow about five times and blow his nose twice before it went away.

CHAPTER 12

"Looks like there are two babies," Gregorio Petrov said as he dangled from the climbing rope.

"Grab them, and let's get the hell out of here," Sergi said as he held the end of a rope that was attached to Gregorio's climbing harness.

As he was climbing the rock face to where the falcon's nest was perched, an adult falcon flew off the nest and landed on a rocky point not far away. When Gregorio reached for the babies, they started to squawk and flap their wings wildly. The young falcons were growing their flight feathers but still were unable to fly.

The commotion in the nest was all the adult falcon needed to come in for an aerial attack on the threat to her young. The bird buzzed so close to Petrov's face, he could feel the wind created by the bird's wings.

"Damn thing," Gregorio said as he flailed at the bird.

"Just get the babies and come on!" Sergi yelled.

Gregorio reached into the nest and grabbed the closest falcon. The thing squawked even louder, which made the adult falcon turn and come back at Petrov like a rocket. As it whizzed by, it actually ticked the top of Petrov's helmet with its talons.

Petrov ducked, put the chick into a cloth bag, and then stuffed it into a larger bag attached to the belt on his climbing harness. He did the same with the second young falcon.

"I've got them and I'm coming down," Gregorio yelled to his brother.

It was a clumsy descent, but he rappelled down without issue. Sergi helped him unhook from the rope, and as soon as he was loose, Gregorio turned for the highway.

"Wait, are we just going to leave the rope here?" Sergi asked.

"Yes, we can buy more rope. I need to get away from that bird, and we need to get to the Jeep."

The two men hurried back to the spot next to the river where they had left their chest waders. They climbed back into the waders, carefully crossed the river, and hustled to the turnout on the highway where they had parked the rig.

"This is good," Sergi said as they drove back toward Yakima. "We have just made twenty thousand dollars."

"We have not made one cent yet," Gregorio said. "All we have done is captured two young falcons."

"Yes, but the hard part is over," Sergi said.

"It wasn't hard for you. That bird wasn't trying to take your head off."

Sergi laughed.

When they were closer to civilization, Sergi looked at his phone. He had enough bars to call his cousin Maxim Volkov in Russia.

"Maxim, this is Sergi. Good news. We have secured two young falcons to send to Moscow. Let us know where they need to be shipped."

"That is good news," Volkov said. "Mr. Sokolov will be pleased, as will his mistress. Here is the address."

After giving his cousin the shipping information for the oligarch in Moscow, Volkov said, "The birds must be shipped in the most expedient way possible. They need to arrive in Russia tomorrow."

"We are headed to Federal Express now," Sergi said.

"Good. This is very important. Pay extra if you have to. I will cover the extra expense."

"Yes, Maxim," Sergi said. "He will be very happy with these falcons."

"Good. On their arrival, I will wire the money to you. Now, what about an eagle? Mr. Sokolov desperately wants an eagle."

"As soon as we get the falcons shipped, we will go in search of a baby eagle. And we will find some more falcons to send."

"That is good," Volkov said. "You have done well, cousin."

And with that, he was gone.

"Do you have any idea where we might find an eagle's nest?" Gregorio asked his brother after listening to half of the phone conversation. "Because I don't. And if an eagle is anything like a falcon in protecting their nest, I might very well lose my head."

Sergi laughed again.

"You worry too much brother," Sergi said. "Besides, where else can we find twenty-five thousand dollars so easily?"

"Easy for who?" Gregorio said.

*

There was some unwanted discussion at the Federal Express office about just what the men were shipping to Russia. They told the clerk there were extremely valuable racing pigeons in the box, and they needed to arrive in Moscow within twenty-four hours.

"Can't they just fly back there themselves?" the woman at the counter said as she took the box and put it on a scale.

About that time, one of the baby falcons squawked, and the woman looked at the Petrovs.

"Doesn't sound like any pigeon I ever heard," the counter lady said. "I thought pigeons cooed."

"They're probably just hungry," Sergi said. "That is why they need to get to Russia overnight."

"Okay, okay," the lady said and started printing out stickers that read: LIVE ANIMALS. FRAGILE. HANDLE WITH CARE.

She had seen some boxes arrive that looked like the baggage handlers at the airport had played soccer with them and hoped the dolts could read well enough to not crush this box with whatever kind of bird was in there. She was positive they weren't pigeons.

"That's the best I can do," she said after she'd put the last bright red sticker on the box and put it on the conveyor belt to be driven to the airport.

As the Petrovs were walking out the door, the woman hollered after them, "You guys were just pulling my leg about the pigeons, right?"

The men left the building and jumped into their Jeep. Somewhere in the mountains to the west were some birds worth twenty-five thousand dollars apiece. They needed to go find one.

*

It was after lunch before Luke got out to check on the falcon nests along the Tieton River. The first nest he got to looked just fine. He spent half an hour watching the nest through his binoculars before he finally saw an adult falcon arrive with something in its talons. Luke thought it might be a valley quail, as he watched the falcon start pulling pieces and parts off the bird and feeding it to some open beaks just visible over the edge of the nest.

So far so good, Luke thought as he headed up Highway 12 to the next nest.

It only took about twenty seconds of looking to spot a green rope dangling off the side of the nest sitting on a shelf on the face of a basalt column. The rope hadn't been there the day before.

"Crap!" Luke hollered. He called Hargraves, and after he answered, Luke told him, "I'm pretty sure the bird bandits struck this morning."

"What? How can you tell?"

"Well, there is a rope hanging from the nest. I don't think the baby's mama hauled it up there. And I've been watching the nest for a bit now, and there is no activity."

"Is the camera still up there?"

Luke hadn't looked for that.

"Let me check," he said and moved his binoculars to the right of the nest. "Yep, it's still there. So we should at least have photo evidence of what happened."

"If we can't get Lemon up here, we'll need to find a rock climber."

"I could check with that kid at the climbing store—Ebert something," Luke said. "I remember he said he did some climbing."

"Emery," Hargraves said. "Like the cloth."

"That's right. Let's try for Lemon first, and then try Emery."

"I'm still up 410," Hargraves said. "I think I'll stay here in case they come for one of these nests. What are you going to do?"

"I figure those guys are going to have to get the birds shipped quickly to wherever they are sending them. They aren't driving them to Russia. So, I'll go check with the shipping companies. See if any men that fit the description of our guys shipped anything overseas in the last few hours."

"Let me know if you find anything," Hargraves said, then clicked off.

When Luke pulled into the Federal Express shipping center out by the airport forty-five minutes later, he spotted a woman standing at the corner of the building, smoking a cigarette. She was a tall woman with auburn hair that looked like it had just survived a hurricane. The woman was slightly overweight, wearing a purple FedEx shirt that was about a size too small, showing off two extra rolls over the top of her dark blue short pants.

When she saw Luke's truck with the star on the door, she dropped the cigarette on the ground, and while exhaling a lungful of white smoke, she crushed the butt with her foot and started walking over to him.

"You here about those two Russian dudes shipping some birds to Moscow?" she said in a deepish, cigarette smoke-altered voice.

Luke was amazed.

"As a matter of fact, I am."

The woman, whose name badge read Brenda, told Luke the whole story, about them lying about what kind of birds were in the box and how they were concerned that they needed to get to Moscow within twenty-four hours.

"Racing pigeons, my fat ass," Brenda said. "I knew there weren't no pigeons in that box."

"So, what happened to the birds?"

"We shipped them. They went out on the noon plane. The damn things are probably over Canada or Alaska or somewhere— whichever way they fly to Russia."

Luke got a description of the men, which matched the description Emery Hart had given him, and asked to look at the shipping label and receipt the men had filled out.

"The one guy—they looked like brothers—but the one guy did all the talking. He paid cash."

Luke looked at the name on the receipt. Supposedly, the guy who was shipping the birds was Boris Yeltsin.

"Did you look at the name here on the receipt?" Luke asked Brenda.

"Yep," she said confidently. "He sounded like a Boris to me. Had the accent and everything."

"You didn't recognize the name?"

"No. Why should I? I've never seen either of those dudes before."

Luke had Brenda make copies of the shipping label and the receipt and then thanked her for her help, handing her his card.

"If Boris and his brother show up again wanting to ship more birds, will you give me a call? And whatever you do, DO NOT ship the birds. They're probably breaking about eleven federal laws, and you and your employer don't want any part of that."

An overconfident look quickly disappeared from Brenda's face, and she said, "Yes, sir. I will do that."

*

About the time Luke was chatting with Brenda, the Petrov brothers were heading toward the mountains. They drove up Highway 410 right by Stan Hargraves, who was sitting back off the highway watching the falcon nest across the Naches River.

Hargraves saw the older red Jeep Cherokee go by but didn't think much about it.

"Was that a police officer?" Gregorio asked after they got past Hargraves' brown WDFW Chevy pickup.

"Yes, I believe so," Sergi said.

"You think they are looking for us?"

"How would they know to look for us?"

"I don't know. Maybe that woman at the shipping place called them. She seemed very suspicious."

"I gave her a false name, address, and phone number. I am not worried. But I am hungry. Let's pull in up here. I see a small café ahead."

The brothers ate hamburgers with French fries. Sergi had a Pepsi, and Gregorio washed his burger down with an iced tea. When they were done, they paid their bill, tipped the waitress a whole two dollars, and went back to their truck.

"That was pretty good," Gregorio said. "I'd eat there again."

"Hopefully, we can find an eagle, and maybe a couple more falcons, and get back to North Dakota," Sergi said.

After a minute, Gregorio said, "Why would we go back to North Dakota?"

"That's where we live."

"We've only been here for a few days, but this place is so much nicer. There are rivers and mountains and trees. That big river we crossed coming here, the Columbia, has hundred-year-old sturgeon to be caught. Imagine the caviar in those fish."

"I would like to catch another sturgeon someday," Sergi said. "Let's find an eagle to send to the rich man in Moscow and then figure out where we are going to live."

CHAPTER 13

Luke decided he would run over to the climbing store and see if Emery Hart was around. As he drove, his phone started buzzing. He looked at the screen and saw it was the local ABC television station calling, and that could only mean one thing. Crack reporter Simon Erickson, the eager young man with a slight speech impediment, was most likely on the other end. Erickson had covered several of the stories Luke had been involved with, and Luke liked the kid.

"Hello, Simon," Luke said, assuming it was him.

"This is Amber Knight," a young female voice said. "Simon no longer works for our TV station." The woman's voice was professional and curt.

"Oh, sorry to hear that," Luke said. "Where did he go?"

"He went to Rapid City, South Dakota to be their morning anchor," Knight replied in a tone that said, 'not that it is any of your business.'

"How can I help you, Ms. Knight?"

"It's Mrs. Knight."

Here we go, Luke thought.

"Okay, how can I help you, Mrs. Knight?"

"We received a call at the station that said you were working on a case about some animals being killed in an unusual way, and some people believe it may be the work of bigfoot."

"Oh boy," Luke said.

"So, it's true then, Officer McCain?"

"Part of it is true. Yes, there have been two domestic animals and a deer that have been killed and left in trees. I do not believe it is the work of bigfoot."

"So, how do you explain it?"

"We're still working on that, but it could be an animal like a cougar that is killing the animals and dragging them into the trees, or it could be a person who is doing it. We are having the animals tested to see how they died."

"Do you have any photos of the animals?" Knight asked.

"Yes, but right now I can't release them to the media," Luke lied.

"I'm going to talk to your supervisor, and if I have to, I will file a public records request to get those photos."

Luke was getting pissed. Now he really missed good old Simon.

"You do what you have to do," Luke said. "But I would go easy on the whole bigfoot deal. You might just come out looking, should we say, unprofessional."

"You just watch what I do," Knight said and hung up.

I bet she's a blast at a party, Luke thought. Just what he needed was having to deal with a reporter who had landed in the 112th largest TV market in the country and thinks she's going to be the next Barbara Walters.

As he drove back to town, he thought about the call, and it made him even madder. He was hoping to have some more time to investigate the dead animals without having to deal with any disruptions. Chasing down baby bird poachers wasn't helping.

And, he thought, if the bigfoot idea got out there, who knows what could happen.

He hadn't paid that much attention to the people who believed in bigfoot, but he knew they were around. Just like the folks who believed in UFOs crashing in New Mexico, or those who thought the landing on the moon back in 1969 was all a hoax. The possibility that bigfoot was involved in these weird killings just might bring all kinds of people out of the bushes.

Not much he could do about that now, so he thought about something else, like where he might find the two men who had just shipped two young falcons to Russia.

*

When he walked into the climbing store, Luke spotted Emery Hart right away. He was over at some shelves loaded with helmets and helping another young man who was trying them on. Luke decided to give him a minute to help the customer while he wandered around the store.

He spotted another woman all geared up in a climbing harness with ropes attached getting ready to ascend the climbing wall. Like the women he had seen on the wall the other day, this woman was wearing skin-tight yoga pants. Luke wondered if that was what every rock climber wore.

The man who was spotting the two women the last time Luke had been in the store was again working with this young lady. Luke watched as the woman started to climb the wall, helped by the man's hand on her right rear cheek.

"The pay is not great, but the benefits are pretty good," Luke mumbled to himself.

"Officer McCain," Hart said from halfway across the store. "Did you catch those guys you were looking for? The brothers, you know, the one with the mustache who wanted to buy chest waders? Did you go to Cabela's to see if they went in there too, to buy the waders? That's what I would have done. They seem to have the best selection in town for waders, although I don't know that for sure because I don't fish. I like to climb."

About then the kid took a breath, and Luke took the opportunity to say, "That's what I'm here about. I was wondering if we might get you to do a little climbing for us."

Hart's eyes got big as he grinned. "Really? I could work a case with you? That would be so cool. I need to text my mom right now."

Luke watched the kid draw his phone from his back pocket and start poking letters with his thumbs so fast he believed it was as quick as the fast draw artist that had been at the sportsman show.

"We just need someone to go up a rope that was used to climb a rock face where there were some baby falcons."

"Really?" Hart asked and again started pounding letters into his phone. "Cool. When do you want me to go do this?"

"We have a camera set up near the nest and would like to get it down to check the photos as soon as we can."

"Really! Cool."

Again, he tapped out a message with his thumbs on his phone and pushed send.

A second later, his phone burped, and Hart read it.

"My mom thinks it's cool too, but she asked if you are going to pay me. Not that I care about that, because I think this is really cool. But I do have some expenses as I am still taking classes at YVC, and what with gas going sky high, and I'm only getting seventeen hours a week here." Hart took a breath and then said, pointing to the guy spotting the yoga-pants-clad climber on the wall, "Dave over there, he's the manager, and he likes to have me here at the register when he is doing climbing lessons on the wall. I could be a spotter, but Dave, he likes to do it."

"No problem," Luke said. "I'm sure we can cover your gas and pay for your time."

"Okay, cool," Hart said. "What equipment am I going to need? I have everything, you know, a harness, helmet, shoes."

"Whatever you normally use to climb," Luke said. "Our guy put some anchors in, and they are still on the wall, and the dudes we think stole the baby falcons left a rope."

"First rule of climbing," Hart said. "Never trust anyone else's equipment. But I could talk to the guy that mounted the camera and get an idea how good he is. My mom would kill me if I got killed."

Luke chuckled at that.

"No seriously," Hart said. "She would be really pissed if something happened. So, when do you want to go?"

"As soon as you can," Luke said.

"I'll ask Dave if I can leave after he is done with his climbing lesson."

Both men looked over at Dave, who had somehow fenagled his way under the climber and was looking straight up at her tightly clad bottom, which was only two feet from his face and getting closer as the gal inched down the rope.

"Looks like he's about done," Luke said.

"Yeah, I think so. Although sometimes he practices with them on their rappelling and descent work several times."

They looked at Dave again, and he had both hands on the woman's buttocks, taking the weight off the rope so she could disconnect.

"Couldn't he just let the lady get down to the ground and get out of the harness there?" Luke asked.

"Dave has his own techniques," Hart said naively. "Especially with the girls."

"I'll bet he does," Luke said, handing Hart his card. "Call me as soon as you are off work, and we'll meet to go climb that rock. Oh, and grab some waders. The nest is on the other side of the river."

*

Two hours later, Luke and Hart were parked in the pullout near the nest that had been pilfered.

"I had to borrow my friend's boots," Hart said as he was pulling climbing gear out of the trunk of his 1997 Chevy Blazer. "I don't fish, but he does, and so he had these waders. I might like to fish, but my dad, well, my dad isn't around, and my mom knows nothing about fishing, so I've never gone before."

"Fishing is fun," Luke said. "But it looks like rock climbing is fun too."

"Yeah, it is really fun. My sister's boyfriend Nick started me climbing. He's really good. But he goes to college now, over in Pullman. And he's no longer my sister's boyfriend. That kind of bummed me out because he was a cool guy, but for some reason my sister didn't like him anymore. She's gone through about five other guys since Nick. I really liked Nick."

While Hart talked, they walked down to the river. Luke was only half listening as he looked at the ground for any clues that may have been left behind by the bird burglars. He also watched the nest. Still no bird activity that he could see.

When they got to the wall, Hart checked out the rope the poachers had left behind. He pulled on it, then held onto it and stepped up on a rock and leaned against it using all his weight.

"Feels like it is secured pretty well," Hart said. "But I am still going to run a second rope to my harness and use the anchors that your guy put in. Can you spot me? The first rule of climbing is always have a spotter."

Luke thought about the other first rule of climbing Hart had told him—something about never trusting someone else's equipment—but didn't say anything.

"I can spot you," Luke said. "Just tell me what to do."

Hart showed Luke how to wrap the rope around his waist and hang on to it so that if he did slip, Luke would be able to stop him from falling.

"If I fall, my mom is really going to be mad," Hart repeated from their earlier conversation. "So, don't let me fall."

"I won't," Luke assured. "Now, see that little square black box?"

Hart looked up and said, "Yep."

"That's a camera. All I need you to do is get it off that anchor and bring it down."

"Got it," Hart said and started climbing the wall—the whole time talking. "It looks like your guy set the anchors perfectly. It took me a while to learn how to really get them secured in the clevises. That's pretty important, you know. Especially if you are going to sleep on the side of a rock face. Have you seen those TV commercials where those people are camping on the side of this huge rock face. I think it might be Red Rock Canyon in Utah. I've never been there, but I want to climb there some day. Right now, my mom won't let me. She's worried I might fall and kill myself. She's a worrier, my mom."

Luke watched as the kid skillfully made his way up the face of the wall to the camera, detached it, and put it in a pocket of his pants.

"Got the camera," Hart said. "You want me to get this other rope down while I'm up here?"

"That'd be great," Luke said.

The young man worked to his left, detached the rope, and sent it dropping to the ground after hollering "heads up."

Then, Luke watched as Hart rappelled down the wall, hitting the face of the rock with his feet, pushing off, sliding down the rope, hitting the wall and pushing off again. He landed next to Luke in about twenty seconds.

"That's the funnest part of climbing," Hart said. "The going up is fun because it is challenging, but coming down, that's exhilarating."

"I bet it is," Luke said as he dropped the rope from around his waist and grabbed the camera from Hart.

They gathered up the extra rope, hiked back to the river, put on their waders, crossed back to the highway side, and headed to their rigs. The whole time, Hart jabbered.

As they loaded Hart's climbing gear back into the trunk of the Blazer, Luke said, "I sure appreciate you doing this today, Emery. Seeing what is on this camera could help us catch these guys, for sure."

"No problem," Hart said. "I can't wait to tell my mom what

happened. And if you need any more help, just let me know. I think I can get off from the store if Dave doesn't have a climbing lesson on the wall."

CHAPTER 14

Luke was thinking about the camera and what might be on it as he drove back to town. He wanted to get a look at the photos but figured it could wait until the morning. He was just back into decent cell service when his phone rang. A quick look at the screen showed it was Sara calling.

"How can I help you, my beautiful wife?" Luke said happily.

Sara noted his happiness and said, "You may not be quite this happy when you find out what was on the TV news at six."

Luke thought immediately of the call he had received from Amber Knight.

"Let me guess—it has to do with bigfoot?"

"Yep. They're spreading the word that the local wildlife department is investigating some problems with dead animals around the area, and they've been told that it possibly could be bigfoot who is killing them and leaving them in trees."

"Great," Luke said sarcastically. "I hope they didn't show any photos."

"No, but they ran the old Patterson footage of the bigfoot walking through the rocks, and the reporter, Amber somebody, said that on tomorrow night's news they would have photos of the dead animals stuck in the trees."

About that time, Luke's phone buzzed showing another call coming in. It was his boss, Bob Davis.

"Captain Davis is calling, I'll call you back," Luke said to Sara and clicked the button to switch the call to Davis.

"Hi, Cap. What's up?"

"The bigfoot shit has hit the fan," Davis said. "After that report on the local ABC station tonight, my phone could only be described as ringing off the hook—if phones still sat on hooks."

"Aw, geez," Luke said. "I was hoping this wouldn't happen. I really needed some more time to figure out what was going on."

"Well, that isn't going to happen now. Somehow, the president of some bigfoot institute got my phone number and wanted all the details. Evidently, he's been contacted by one of the Seattle TV stations, and they are going to do a report on what's happening over here."

"Great," Luke said again. He wondered who had told Amber Knight about what was going on and why someone would do that.

"If the media stuff isn't bad enough," Davis said, "we're getting calls from all around the Northwest from folks who have either seen bigfoot or who have lost animals in the woods."

"The office is closed, right?" Luke asked.

"Yeah, but we have that emergency number that comes on with our recorded message," Davis said. "Everyone is calling that number and leaving their messages. The message box is already full. And that's just from Yakima and the Tri-Cities. Wait till Seattle TV puts it out there to half the state."

"And if Seattle runs the story, we'll be hearing from every newspaper and television station from here to New York."

"I'm afraid so," Davis agreed.

"Do you know what that will do?" Luke asked.

"Yeah, we'll have ten million bigfoot hunters crawling around here like fleas on a desert dog."

There was a long pause, then Luke said, "There is some good news."

"Oh, what's that?"

"We retrieved the camera at the nest that was pilfered by those Russian guys."

"Wait, what?" Davis said. He hadn't heard about the falcons being grabbed and shipped to Russia.

Luke apologized for not keeping the captain up to speed on the bird burglary.

"Don't apologize," Davis said. "I kind of thought that was going to be a false tip."

"So did Hargraves. And me too. But it's a real deal. Two falcon chicks—eyas they're called—were taken this morning from a nest up off Highway 12, and they were shipped to Russia."

Luke told the captain the rest of the story, about going to FedEx and then getting Emery Hart from the climbing store to come help retrieve the camera.

"I'd like to get him paid for his time this afternoon," Luke said. "He's a college kid and could use a few extra bucks."

"No problem," Davis said. "Put in the request. I'll approve it."

"Anyway," Luke said. "We have a pretty good description of the guys who were shipping the birds, and now, hopefully, we should have some good photographic evidence on the camera."

"Good work," Davis said. "Better get some rest. I think this bigfoot thing is about to explode and unfortunately, you're at the epicenter of the whole deal."

"Thanks, Cap. I'll see you in the morning," Luke said and clicked off.

Just what he needed was a media firestorm, and who-knows-how-many people showing up to search for sasquatch. As Luke drove, he wondered if there were any other animals impaled on branches out there. And, he wondered, who was doing it. He had pretty much ruled out any predators putting the animals in the trees. And unless there really was some creature out there doing it—a sasquatch, bigfoot, or whatever you called it—which he seriously doubted, it had to be a person or persons killing the animals and skewering them on the tree branches. But why would they be doing that?

*

When he got home, his yellow Lab, Jack, greeted Luke at the door. The big dog was now seven years old, and even though he could still run all day chasing pheasants or swim halfway across the Columbia River to retrieve a duck, Jack was spending more time napping around the house. He still liked to ride with Luke as he patrolled the mountains, but many times now if Luke asked Jack if he would like to go along, Jack would raise his head off his bed, look at Luke, and then drop his head back down and close his eyes.

Come hunting season, Luke was sure Jack would be as eager as ever to go if he saw the hunting boots, shell vest, and shotgun come out. But during the warm days of early summer, Jack now seemed to prefer the cool house and his soft dog bed over riding around in the back seat of Luke's truck.

"Hey, boy," Luke said to Jack as he gave the dog a good scratch behind his ears.

Jack sniffed Luke's pant legs to get an accurate reading on where he'd been during the day.

"I'm here too," Sara said from the kitchen. "I guess I should come running to the door when you get home so that you'll say hello to me too."

"Do you want me to scratch your ears?" Luke asked.

"What did Captain Davis say?" she asked, ignoring his question.

Luke could smell something really good coming from the kitchen. He'd been so busy during the day, he hadn't eaten anything since breakfast.

"He said we need to prepare for the craziness that is about to engulf us because of the bigfoot rumors. His words were, 'It is going to explode.' What do you have cooking in there? I am famished."

"I threw together a meat loaf," Sara said as she stood on her tippy-toes and gave her husband a quick kiss on the lips.

As she turned to go back to the kitchen, Luke grabbed her, spun her around, and gave her a better kiss.

"Did I ever tell you, you are the best wife ever?"

"I've heard it once or twice."

"Well, you are. Now, let me at that meatloaf."

After dinner, which Luke ate in about four minutes, they sat at the table and talked.

"So, what are you going to do?" Sara asked.

"I'm not sure," Luke said. "There are just so few clues. No tracks, nothing. I guess I'll just keep thinking about it and see what happens. Maybe another dead animal will turn up."

"That might help," Sara said. "But it will only add fuel to the bigfoot fire."

"I know," Luke said. "I just need to think. In the meantime, we know who took those two falcons. That gives us someone to look for. My guess is they aren't done stealing young birds, so we need to try to get them corralled before they do it again."

A minute later, Luke's phone rang. He looked at his phone and saw it was a *Yakima Herald-Republic* number. Only a few media folks had his personal phone number, and there was just one writer for the paper who had it. The reporter's name was James Dover, and Luke had given the young man his number because Dover had always done an excellent job keeping his stories to the facts without any dramatic or sensational information.

"This is Luke," he said after sliding the answer button on the phone.

"Hey, Luke. This is James Dover calling from *The Herald*."

"Hi, James. What's up?" Luke asked, but he knew why the reporter was calling.

"I saw that story on ABC this evening about a situation that might include a bigfoot sighting or something. It said the Fish and

Wildlife Department was investigating. Can you tell me anything about it?"

"I'd be happy to tell you everything I know," Luke said and went on to tell him the whole story, from being called to Jerome Martin's house and the dog in the tree, to the lady bird watchers finding the mule deer doe, and then the dead goat of April Sommers'. He didn't give Dover the names of the people but did describe what he had seen and the general area where the dead animals were found.

"The fact is," Luke continued, "that we have no real clues yet as to how the animals died or how they ended up in the trees. But we do not believe it is the work of some mystical creature. Our investigation continues."

"Do you think this will spur on all the believers in bigfoot?"

"Unfortunately, it probably will. And having a bunch of people out in the woods looking for bigfoot will most likely hinder our investigation. But we can't really control that."

"Okay, well, my editors want something, so I need to write a story. I'll keep it to the facts, for sure."

"I'd appreciate that," Luke said. "And could you keep my name out of it? Just say the information came from a Fish and Wildlife official or something?"

"I can do that," Dover said. "Thanks, Luke. And if you hear anything else, would you mind giving me a call?"

"I'll do what I can," Luke said and rang off.

"The cat's out of the bag," Sara, who had been listening to the phone conversation, said. "I think Bob is right. This bigfoot thing is about to explode. Better keep your head down."

"Dealing with the media is one thing, but he said our voicemail box is already full of people who called in to say they had recently seen bigfoot or they were missing animals that they feared were victims of bigfoot."

"Great," Sara said.

"My thoughts exactly," Luke said. "Thanks for a perfect dinner. Now, I'm going to bed. It's been a long day."

"Tomorrow may be longer," Sara said and kissed him goodnight.

CHAPTER 15

The Petrov brothers had also seen the bigfoot story on the TV news. They had discussed it a bit after they watched it, but as soon as they found a repeat of *The Jerry Springer Show* on the TV, they forgot about the bigfoot report and watched as two women started fighting over a guy that had to weigh four hundred pounds.

"Who watches this stuff?" Sergi said.

"I don't know," Gregorio said. "But that woman with the red hair got in a good one on that other woman. I'm surprised she didn't go down."

The men laughed and continued to watch.

When the show was over, Sergi said, "We need to find an eagle nest tomorrow. If we could find one nest with two young birds in it, that would be fifty thousand dollars. There must be a nest somewhere in those mountains."

Gregorio didn't say anything, but he was skeptical that such a nest existed in an area where they might find it.

*

The next morning, as the Petrov brothers drove their red Cherokee along the Naches River up into the Cascades, they again started discussing the news story they had seen on TV.

"Do you believe in the bigfoot?" Gregorio asked his brother.

"I'm not sure," Sergi said. "I worked with a man on the oilfields, before you came out there, that claimed he had seen a yeti. He was driving along the Lena River through the mountains on the road from Irkutsk to Yakutsk and he saw this large, hairy creature cross in front of him."

"Could it have been a brown bear?" Gregorio asked.

"I asked him the same thing. He said it was walking on two legs like a human, but it was very tall and covered from its head to its feet in hair."

"Sounds like a fairy tale to me."

"He said the creature walked up into the trees, then turned and looked at him as he drove by. He said the yeti's eyes were very much like a human's. They were expressive, like it was thinking about what to do if the man had stopped the car."

"Well, maybe if we are lucky, we will see this bigfoot," Gregorio said. "Then we could be famous and go on all the talk shows on TV."

"Except for *The Jerry Springer Show*," Sergi said. "That is the stupidest show I have ever seen."

"But funny, right?" Gregorio said with a laugh. "When that large man fell out of the chair when the women were fighting over him, very funny."

Sergi started laughing.

"Yes, that was funny," he said.

The men talked about several more episodes of *The Jerry Springer Show* they had seen, some more than once, and laughed at how stupid the shows were.

*

Early the next afternoon, the Petrov brothers spotted the eagle nest. It was in a large pine tree along the Little Naches River.

"This is fantastic," Sergi said. "Maxim will not believe this when we call and tell him we have young eagles for the rich man in Moscow."

"We have nothing yet," Gregorio said. "And, if I remember correctly, the rich man in Moscow wanted golden eagles. The adult eagle sitting there next to the nest is clearly a bald eagle."

"From the photos I have seen on the internet," Sergi explained, "the young eagles look almost identical. By the time the birds are old enough to tell what type of eagle they are, we will have our money."

"I don't know," Gregorio said.

"Besides, why can't bald eagles be trained to hunt? An eagle is an eagle, right?"

Gregorio thought his brother made some sense. And he certainly would like to have the money they would be paid for the young eagles.

"Okay. But now we must figure out how to get to the nest, and I really do not want to have the adults attacking me."

They talked about that for a few minutes and worked on a plan.

"We know where the nest is now," Sergi said. "We could go buy a rifle, and if they bother you, I could shoot the adults. That would ensure you would not be attacked when you got to the nest."

"Let's finalize our plan and come back here in the early morning," Gregorio said. "I am going to need some other equipment if I am going to get to that nest safely."

"Like what else do you need?"

"It would be helpful to have those spikes that the telephone pole climbers use, that fit around your boots to help get a foothold in the wood. And I need heavy gloves. Those young eagles may not be able to fly, but my guess is they have strong jaws and sharp bills from ripping meat apart to eat. I do not want to get bit. They could take a finger off."

Sergi laughed. But for only a second.

"Okay," he said. "We will find those climbing spike things, whatever they are called, and some heavy gloves and be back here at daylight."

As they were driving back down Highway 410 to Yakima, Gregorio spotted a falcon sitting on a little spire up in the rocks.

"Stop for a second," he said. "There's a falcon up there in the cliffs. If we watch, it might fly to a nest."

Sergi stopped the Jeep, and after a few seconds, he saw the falcon too. A half minute later, the bird flew a short way down the rocky hillside and landed on a shelf on a short basalt column.

"That's where the nest must be," Sergi said. "I'll watch from here while you get the gear out. Let's grab whatever is in that nest now and come back for the young eagles in the morning."

It took a few minutes for Gregorio to gather his gear from the back of the vehicle. The nest was on the highway side of the river, so no waders would be needed for a river crossing. When he was ready, the two brothers worked their way up a steep, rocky hillside to the base of the column.

"This will be a shorter climb," Gregorio said, handing Sergi the safety rope. "But still, we need to be smart and safe about this."

Even though it was a shorter climb, it took Gregorio longer to get to the falcon's nest than it had a few days before. It was more of a technical climb, for which the younger brother was not totally trained. He was having trouble finding suitable anchor points to place the carabiners on which to secure his safety rope.

"What is taking so long?" Sergi asked in a huff.

"I would prefer to not fall to my death. Or be injured doing this. So, hold on please."

"I will. Just hurry up if you can."

When Gregorio got to the top of the column, he could see a perfect nest there with three eyas. The young birds were about the same size as the ones they had shipped to Russia. Even though there were three, he decided right away he would only grab two. That might placate the adults somewhat, he thought.

As he had before, Gregorio snatched up the first young falcon, and as soon as he touched the bird, it started to screech and flap. Seeing what was happening, the adult falcons started dive bombing him. They ticked their talons off his helmet and hit him in the shoulder. The second hit he took to the shoulder tore his shirt, and even though he couldn't look at it, he was sure they had drawn blood.

He hurriedly placed the young bird in a bag and then placed that in a second bag on his climbing belt. As Gregorio reached for the next young falcon, the attack from the adults intensified. They were like a swarm of bees, buzzing around his head, hitting his helmet and his shoulder.

He had just started to grab the young bird when he was hit hard in the neck by one of the adult falcons. Gregorio flailed his arms at the bird, which caused him to lose his balance, and in an instant he began falling down the column.

His brother's scream and the safety rope buzzing through his hands brought Sergi to attention, and he grabbed the rope tighter. He looked up just in time to see his brother stop his descent and slam hard into the rock face of the column.

Gregorio just hung there for a minute and finally started to move.

"I think I've broken my shoulder," he moaned. "Damn birds."

"Did you get any of the young ones?" Sergi asked, more concerned about the ten-thousand-dollar eyas than he was for his brother's health.

Gregorio just groaned.

Finally, after dangling on the side of the rock for a minute or two, Gregorio got himself right with the world and gingerly lowered himself to the ground.

"I am serious—I think my shoulder is broken," Gregorio said to his brother as he tried to unhook from the climbing belt.

"Okay, let's get you back to the vehicle, and we'll figure out what to do from there. Do you have any birds in the bag?"

"One, but it may have been injured or killed when I smashed against the wall."

"Let me look," Sergi said as he reached over and unclipped the bag from the belt.

He looked inside and then said, "Looks like it is alright. We will take it to the shipping place and then get you to some medical attention."

The brothers carefully picked their way down the steep hill and back to the car, Gregorio holding his arm in place so the shoulder wouldn't move, which was virtually impossible. Every time he would take a step and slip in the rocks or move wrong, he would let out a groan from the pain.

Gregorio climbed into the passenger seat of the Jeep while Sergi loaded everything into the back of the vehicle.

When they were on the road headed back to town, Gregorio said, "Can we please go to the hospital first before taking the bird to the shipping place?"

"How about I drop you off at the hospital, then I will run to FedEx and come back for you after the bird is shipped."

"Whatever," Gregorio said. "As long as I get something for this pain."

When they dropped out of the mountains, Sergi grabbed his phone and dialed his cousin.

"Maxim, this is Sergi. We have great news. We will be shipping another falcon to you today, and we have located an eagle's nest, so will have young birds to send tomorrow."

He didn't tell his cousin that his brother, the man who was doing all the climbing, was injured, and they hadn't talked about how they were going to climb the tree to get the young eagles.

"That is great news," Maxim Volkov said. "The other birds arrived today in good shape, and Mr. Sokolov was very happy. I will wire the money for the two birds to you today."

"Thank you, cousin," Sergi said. "We will send you the

information on where to send the money shortly. And we will ship you the falcon to arrive tomorrow."

When he ended the call, Sergi turned to his brother and said, "Maxim is very happy with us and is wiring the twenty thousand dollars today."

Gregorio just groaned.

CHAPTER 16

Luke's day had started pretty much as he expected. His phone started ringing before he was halfway through with his morning workout.

"Are you going to answer that thing?" Sara asked from the bathroom.

"Not until I am done here," Luke grunted as he pushed two hundred pounds up the machine with his legs.

When the phone stopped chirping, and then started again, Sara said, "I'm going to put it on silent. I'm trying to listen to the news."

A few minutes later, Sara came into the spare bedroom Luke had turned into a workout area. She was drying her hair with a towel.

"The radio news is all over the bigfoot thing. My guess is they are just reading the story *The Yakima Herald* published this morning. I read it a few minutes ago online, and it was pretty much what you told the reporter last night. Your name wasn't included in the story."

"That's good," Luke said. "My phone will be going crazy as it is."

Luke finished his workout, grabbed a banana, and went to his laptop to pull up the story in the daily paper, which could only be called a paper three days a week when it was actually printed on newsprint and delivered to homes around the region. The other days, the newspaper, minus the actual paper, was available online.

Luke read the story. Just like Sara had said, Dover had included only the facts as Luke had given them to him. Luke hadn't seen the TV story that Amber Knight had produced, but he was guessing it was a bit more sensational.

After he was showered, dressed, and ready to head to work, Luke checked in with Jack. The yellow dog was sound asleep on his bed. This was probably going to be a crazy day, so he'd let the big pooch sleep. Sara had left twenty minutes earlier with a wave, a smile, and a "good luck today!"

As he was walking to his truck, Luke checked his phone. Six missed phone calls. He scrolled through the missed calls. None were urgent enough to return right away, or maybe ever. If they really wanted to talk to him, they would call back. He left the phone on silent.

After he climbed into his truck, Luke just sat there. He had no idea what he should do next to get to the bottom of this bigfoot situation. Unless another dead animal in a tree popped up, there wasn't much else he could do except join what was probably going to be a growing hoard of people scouring the woods looking for the mythical beast.

"Not going to do that," Luke mumbled to himself as he fired up the Chevy and headed to the office.

*

When Sergi Petrov returned to the hospital after shipping the falcon to Russia, he found his brother sitting in the waiting area, his arm in a sling that was secured tightly to his chest. He gave Gregorio a look of 'so?'

"I have a dislocated shoulder and a cracked clavicle. I need to stay in this contraption for two weeks."

"That's too bad," Sergi said and then dropped into a whisper. "How are we going to get those young eagles?"

If Gregorio had had the use of both arms, he would have grabbed his brother and strangled him.

"Do you not care that I am injured? And in pain? I don't care about the damn birds. I need to go to our room and rest."

"Okay. We will go rest and figure out what we do next from there."

*

"We have about three dozen calls on the phone service recorder," Bob Davis said to Luke after he had settled in at his desk. "I'm having Jessica go through them, and if there is something she thinks needs follow up, she'll relay it to me. I'll listen to it and then get it to you or Hargraves."

"Sounds good," Luke said. "Speaking of Stan, with all this bigfoot stuff, I totally forgot about the camera we retrieved from the falcon nest. We need to take a look at it."

Hargraves arrived in the office a couple minutes later, and Luke grabbed him.

"So, how did you do with chatty Mr. Emery?" Hargraves asked.

"He did great. He does talk a lot, but the kid was really good climbing up that wall."

After a few seconds, Luke asked, "You ever think about trying the wall they have at the climbing store?"

"I didn't know they had a wall at the store. Never been in it."

"Looks kinda like fun," Luke said as he was waiting for the photos to pop up on his computer screen. "But I'm not sure I'd want to climb one of those cliffs like Emery did."

The photos started appearing one by one, and they had to scroll through about two hundred different photos of falcons, both adult and young ones, moving about the nest.

"There," Hargraves said. "There's an arm."

Luke slowed the scroll and found the shot of Gregorio Petrov reaching in for the young falcons. There were several more shots of the man, but all were from behind, or three-quarters from behind. They could never see his full face.

"That's probably the best one we have of the man," Hargraves said.

Luke clicked on the photo and brought it up larger on the screen. In the photo, they could see just the side of a man's face. He had a dark mustache and dark hair protruding from a blue climbing helmet.

"Emery said one of the guys who came into the store to buy gear had a mustache," Hargraves said. "Said if he shaved the sides down, it would look like Hitler's mustache."

"That's a weird observation," Luke said.

"I got the impression some men are actually growing mustaches like Hitler's," Hargraves said. "Can you believe it?"

"No, but who would've thought putting a bull's ring through your nose would be a thing. I want to stop every girl I see with those things and tell them how stupid they look."

"I guarantee you those young girls really don't care what you or anyone else over about twenty-four thinks."

"Well, the first time I see a dude with a Hitler mustache, I may just tell him what I think."

"Good luck with that," Hargraves said. "So, what do we do with these photos?"

"I think I will run this one by the climbing store to see if Emery can I.D. this guy," Luke said. "What are you going to do?"

"I'm going to go birdwatching," Hargraves said. "Maybe I'll get lucky, and the men will show up at one of the other falcon nests."

"Watch out for bigfoot," Luke said. "And all the bigfoot hunters."

"I saw that story on TV last night," Hargraves said. "The reporter seemed kind of . . . I don't know . . . stuck up, like she is way better than us."

Luke just laughed and headed out the door.

*

Emery Hart wasn't at the climbing store. Dave, the manager, was at the register and said Hart was at class but would be in around noon.

Now that he got a good look at Dave, he was a handsome guy, Luke thought. Thick, light-brown hair was neatly combed around on his head, eyes the color of robin eggs sat perfectly placed on each side of a small nose, and bright white teeth, accentuated by unexpectedly tanned skin, flashed from his mouth when he talked. Luke was reminded of an actor—he couldn't think of the guy's name—who starred in one of those police shows on TV. No wonder the girls wanted Dave to work with them on the wall.

"I have a couple of climbing lessons, so I know he's planning to be here," the manager said, white teeth flashing out of a brown face.

Luke wondered how many yoga pants-wearing young ladies were signed up for Dave's special tutoring today.

He was on his way back to the office when Captain Davis called.

"I just got a call from Buel Stennett up in the Nile," Davis said. "You know Buel?"

"No, I don't think so," Luke said. "What's up with him?"

"I've known Buel for years. Good guy. Good hunter. Straight shooter."

"And?" Luke asked.

"He said he runs about twenty trail cameras up in the mountains to the north and west of his place. He was checking on them late yesterday, looking for a couple stray steers, and claims one of them shows what he believes to be a bigfoot."

"Okay," Luke said with more than a little skepticism in his voice.

"I know, I know," Davis said. "Anyone else, and I'd just put it in the pile with all of these other calls, but I really believe he has a photo of something he can't explain."

"So, what would you like me to do?"

"I told him I would send you up his way. You have time to do that?"

"Shoot me his address, and I'll head up there right now."

*

Knowing he was headed to the mountains, Luke decided he'd stop by the house on the way out of town and kick Jack out of bed. The exercise would do the dog good, and frankly, Luke kind of missed having his longtime riding partner along.

"Come on, boy," Luke said when he came through the front door. "You want to go for a ride?"

Jack slowly got up out of his bed, stretched for a crazy long time, and padded over to the door. Luke let the dog pee and then said, "Get up there, boy. We have to go see a man about a bigfoot."

As he drove through Naches, Luke noticed there was quite a bit more traffic in the small town than normal for this time of year. Once a shopping and farm supply center for all the fruit ranchers in the area, the little burg now also catered to the many folks driving up into the mountains to camp, fish, hike, ski, and hunt. You could reach Mount Rainier via State Route 410 and 12, both of which ran right through Naches. The highway stayed busy from Memorial Day through the last of the hunting seasons.

Several businesses had popped up along the highway over the years, including restaurants, fruit stands, an Ace Hardware, a brewery, and a couple of gas stations. One little strip mall had a grocery store, a woodworking shop, and until just recently, a small retail space that had been sitting empty.

As Luke slowly drove through town, all kinds of activity was going on at the store that used to be empty. People were hauling shelving and boxes into the store. He wondered what the new business might be.

It took him thirty-five minutes to find Buel Stennett's place. When Luke pulled up the gravel driveway, which was lined by a white two-rail fence, he could see an older gentleman mowing the lawn on a John Deere tractor mower.

The man, who Luke assumed was Stennett, was wearing a white straw cowboy hat, a blue denim shirt, Wrangler jeans, and cowboy boots. He shut down the mower, climbed off, removed his hat, and pulled a red handkerchief out of his back pocket and wiped his brow. Luke guessed the man stood about five-foot-ten but was slightly hunched over as he walked toward Luke's truck. As he got closer, Luke could see the man had a leathery face, lined by weather and age, but the look in his steel blue eyes said he was probably as sharp as a needle and could be as tough as a boiled owl.

"Mr. Stennett?" Luke asked as he stepped out of his truck.

"Yes," the man said.

"I'm Luke McCain. Bob Davis asked me to come up and see what you got going on with your game cameras."

Stennett reached a hand out to Luke and said, "Nice to meet you. And please, call me Buel. Do I see a dog in your truck?"

"Yeah, that's my lazy Lab, Jack. He rides with me sometimes."

"Well, let him out. I'd like to meet the famous dog who tracked down that killer up north last year."

"You know about that, huh?" Luke said. "Well, please don't say anything around Jack, or he'll get an even bigger head."

Stennett laughed, and when Jack climbed out of the truck, the man knelt and rubbed both of Jack's ears. Then, like David Copperfield, Stennett made a dog treat magically appear out of thin air and gave it to the dog.

"Oh no," Luke said as he watched Jack gobble the treat. "Now, he'll never leave your side."

"I'm okay with that," Stennett said. "I've had dogs my whole life. Just lost a great little heeler a couple of months ago. Haven't had the guts to get another one yet. Don't tell anyone, but I bawled like a baby when old Freckles died."

"That trick with the treat was pretty neat."

"I always carried a few biscuits for Freckles. It's a habit, I guess. I still carry a couple in my pocket."

Luke could see the man's eyes getting red around the edges, so he changed subjects.

"So, what's this I hear about a bigfoot making an appearance on one of your game cameras?"

"Come on in," Stennett said, turning toward the house. "I'll let you see it for yourself."

CHAPTER 17

Sure enough. Right there in living color was what looked to be the quintessential bigfoot. Long brown hair covering everything, including unusually long arms, and the thing was walking on two legs. The problem was, only about half of the creature appeared at the edge of the photo. Or, Luke thought, maybe only a third of the beast was visible. And it was walking away from the camera, so its face was not discernable at all.

"It's like it's avoiding the camera," Stennett said, pointing at the photo on the computer monitor. "It's off the trail by a bit. See there where the trail is?"

"That's what I thought when I first saw it," Luke said. "It seems like it knows the camera is there."

The men talked about the photo a bit more, and Luke asked the man a bunch of questions. They talked about just where this particular camera was located. Stennett showed Luke on a topo map and told him that of the thousands of photos he'd looked at from his cameras spread around his ranch, and on state and national forest lands, he had never seen anything like this.

"I've seen bears, cougars, and of course, all kinds of elk and deer," Stennett said. "And every small creature that lives in the mountains—coyotes, racoons, skunks, grouse, turkeys, you name it—I have photos of them. I've even caught a pair of wolves up in the north part of the ranch on a couple of cameras. I told your biologists about it but haven't heard back from them."

The photo of the bigfoot creature showed a time and date stamp of six days earlier, at one fifty-three in the morning. Luke thought about it. That was before Jerome Martin's dog was found in the tree.

Luke told Stennett, who was sitting in an easy chair with Jack almost in his lap, about the unusual occurrences of the dead animals in the trees.

"I hadn't heard about that," he said to Luke. "What do you think it's all about?"

"I'm not sure, but some people have suggested it might be the work of bigfoot."

Stennett sat back a little, still petting Jack, and thought about it for a few seconds.

"You know, Luke, before I saw this photo, I might be telling you that that is all a bunch of malarkey. I've lived in this house danged near all my life, and I have ridden or hiked just about every inch of these mountains. Never have I seen anything—not a track, not a hair, nothing—that would tell me there is a bigfoot roaming around this area. But now, I don't know. You might be able to put some kind of a logical spin on how the dead animals are being stuck in trees without any signs of who is doing it, but this photo, well, that would be hard to fake. I know that country up there like the back of my hand. No one is going to spot that camera and then hike in there with a bigfoot suit on. I just don't believe it."

Luke had taken a liking to Buel Stennett the second he pulled the dog treat out of his hat, or wherever it had been. But now, listening to the man speak, not only about living around here, but about the dog he'd lost and his thoughts on the photo, Luke was a fan. Stennett was genuine, and Luke believed him to be as honest as the day is long. No way had this man faked the photo. Not that Luke really thought that in the first place.

"So, Buel, do you think we could take a walk up to the camera that caught this photo?"

"You're not going to walk up there. It's about six miles from here. But there's a road that will get us close. Come on. We'll run up there in the side-by-side."

As they drove in the Polaris ATV, Luke learned from Stennett that he'd been a pro rodeo cowboy in his younger days.

"Barebacks and bulls," Stennett said.

After following the rodeo circuits for a while, he'd tired of the travel and made his way back here to the family ranch. For the past fifty years, he'd made his living as a rancher, moving cattle from his property here in the winter to some land he leased on the other side of White Pass near Packwood for summer grazing.

"That's where my cattle are now," Stennett said. "I have a man that takes care of them over there so I can stay home. I love this life, but it's definitely getting harder the older I get."

Luke was too polite to ask the man's age, but after chatting with him, he figured Stennett must be pushing eighty.

They talked about hunting and fishing too.

"I still love to hunt," Stennett said. "I could probably shoot my buck every year right out the back door if I wanted to. But that isn't hunting. So, I take a horse string up into the mountains, set up a wall tent, and do it the right way. Shot a nice three-point buck last year. I've killed my share of elk too. Just being by myself, though, I don't need all that meat, so I won't shoot an elk if I've killed a deer."

Luke wondered if there had ever been a Mrs. Stennett but didn't ask.

When they arrived at the small trail that led to the camera where the bigfoot photo was taken, Stennett parked the ATV and climbed out.

"It's only about a fifteen-minute walk from here," he said.

Luke got out, and Jack, who had ridden in the back of the Polaris all the way, bounded out and started to run around sniffing brush and trees.

"He still moves pretty good," Stennett said, nodding at Jack.

Luke watched Stennett start walking up the trail with a gait and stride of a man half his age and said, "So do you!"

When they arrived at the camera, Stennett said, "This is it."

Luke had to look closely to see the small device colored in a green and brown camo pattern and strapped to a tree just off the trail.

"Boy, I don't know how anyone would even know this is here," Luke said.

"I've never seen a person on this camera, even during hunting season," Stennett said. "Well, except for me."

"Let me take a look around a bit if you don't mind," Luke said. "I'd love to find a track or some hair caught on a bush. Anything could help."

He called Jack, and the two headed up the trail. The photo said it had been six days since whatever it was had walked through here, but maybe Jack could help find something.

Luke remembered the photo the best he could and went over to the spot off the trail where the camera had caught the creature. The area was grassy, and because it was close to nearby trees that sucked up the ground moisture quickly, the soil was as hard as concrete. Still, Luke looked.

He and Jack walked up the trail at least half a mile but could find nothing that could be identified as a bigfoot track or any other track for that matter. He did find a couple slight impressions in the soil where there was a little moisture, but they were not tracks like one might expect to see, with five toes and the certain outline of a foot.

He searched all the brush along the trail too, paying special attention to any that might be heavy enough to snag some hair. But he found nothing. Whenever Jack would stop and show some interest in a scent, Luke would go give it a good inspection, but there was never anything out of the usual there.

"It's like the thing was an aberration," Luke said when he and Jack got back to the camera, where Stennett was sitting, his back up against a fir tree. "We have photographic evidence that something walked through here six days ago, but there is nothing else that I can find that can corroborate what the camera is telling us."

They hiked back to the ATV, and Stennett took them back to his house.

"Would you mind emailing that photo of the creature to me?" Luke asked. "I'd like to have it enhanced if it can be, so we can study it more."

"Sure, anything I can do to help," Stennett said.

"And, if you don't mind, would you keep this photo and anything we have discussed under your hat for a while?" Luke asked. "I think we are on the verge of being overrun by bigfoot hunters thanks to some media reports yesterday and this morning. No need to throw more gasoline on that fire."

"Got it," Stennett said. "I don't see many people anyway, so that won't be a problem."

"Well, living up here, you could run into some bigfoot believers," Luke said. "I wouldn't laugh them off as kooks to their faces, but you might show them some skepticism. It won't bother them, is my guess—they're probably used to it."

"I'll send the photo right away," Stennett said as Luke and Jack headed to the truck. "And come by for a visit anytime. But don't come unless Jack is with you." The old gentleman chuckled and waved.

As Luke was driving down the driveway, he could still see Buel Stennett in his rear-view mirror, standing on the porch watching them go.

*

When Luke got back into town, he dropped Jack off at his house, grabbed a quick tuna salad sandwich and a diet Pepsi, and then headed to the climbing supply store. He figured Emery Hart should be out of school and at work if Dave, the handsome and handsy manager, knew what he was talking about.

Sure enough, when Luke walked through the door, he heard from somewhere in the rows of shelves, "Hi, Luke!"

Hart popped out from one of the rows and said, "That was sure fun yesterday. I told my mom all about it and my buddies at school. They can't believe I am helping with an investigation. If you catch these guys, they are probably going to prison, right? I mean, stealing wildlife for sale—that's like a federal crime, right? I hope you can catch those guys. They deserve whatever they get."

Hart took a breath, and Luke jumped in quickly.

"I need you to look at a photo that was taken on the camera you retrieved," Luke said.

"Oh cool. Is it the photo of the criminal?"

"Yes, there is a photo of a man taking one of the young falcons from the nest. I just need you to look at the photo and tell me if you recognize the man."

"Sure, I can do that. This is so cool. I can't wait to tell my mom and my friends," Hart said.

Luke pulled out the photo he had printed from the image on the camera. It was enlarged, so it wasn't quite as crisp as the photo on the camera or as it appeared on the computer screen, but it was good enough.

Hart looked at it and yelled, "Oh dude! That's him. That's the Russian guy that was in here with the other guy that looked like his brother. You know, the one I told Officer Hargraves about that if he shaved about a half inch off each side of his mustache, he would have a Hitler. That's him. I would know him anywhere."

Luke looked around and saw that Hart's loud, excited voice had caught the attention of Dave the manager and a buxom, bleach-bottle blonde who was either just about to go up the wall, or had just come down. Dave had his hand on the lady's ample derrière, which was testing the tensile strength of every thread in the yoga pants she was wearing.

"Keep it down, Emery," Dave said with a frown on his face, his hand still on the blonde's bottom.

"Yeah, yeah," Hart said, then to Luke, "This is soooo cool!"

"Okay, that's what I needed to know. Thanks, Emery. I appreciate it. And as soon as I get that expense check, I will get it right over to you."

"No problem," Hart said. "Any time. I hope you catch this guy. Do you think you will? That would be so cool. Do you think they are Russian? They sounded Russian. Why would they be stealing the birds, anyway?"

*

When Luke finally got away from the exuberant Emery Hart, he headed to the office. He wanted to download the photo that Buel Stennett had sent and get it looked at by a photographic expert. As he drove, he called Sara.

"What's up?" she asked, sounding harried.

"I can call back if this is a bad time," Luke said.

"No, no, sorry," Sara said. "They just found another dead woman out on the reservation, and it looks like she was murdered. I need to head that way."

"Oh, man," Luke said. "Sorry to hear that. I can bug you later."

"I'm okay for a minute. What's up?"

Luke told her about the photo that Buel Stennett was sending and asked if she might be able to send it to the FBI's special lab to have someone look at it to make sure it hadn't been altered in any way, and to see if they could enlarge the beast to bring it into better focus.

"I'll see what I can do," she said.

"And I have another photo of a man who we caught on another camera grabbing a young falcon. It's not a great photo—only a side view of the guy's face—but I'm wondering if you could run it through your files to see if you find a match or a name. The kid who talked to the man said he thinks they may be Russian or from one of the Eastern European countries."

"Sure, send it over. I'll get Marcy to help."

Marcy was Sara's assistant in the small FBI office in Yakima.

"Great, thanks," Luke said. "See ya sometime. Good luck."

Sara said "thanks" and was gone.

Luke didn't like leaning on Sara's position as a special agent with the FBI, but he had, a time or two, asked for her help. They had some resources that the Department of Fish and Wildlife didn't, and even though the FBI wasn't working on the cases Luke was investigating, he figured they were ultimately on the same team, trying to stop crimes.

CHAPTER 18

Luke was at his desk, just getting ready to shut his computer down, when Stan Hargraves entered.

"Looks like the bird thieves struck again," he said.

"What?"

"I spotted a rope dangling from the rock face up on 410, the one above the highway."

"Dang. I wonder what they got."

"From what I can tell, they didn't get any of the babies. There are two heads sticking up whenever one of the adults brings some food in."

"Weren't there three in that nest?" Luke asked. "I'm pretty sure Lemon said there were three in that nest."

"Yeah, but wasn't that the nest he said had three, but then there were only two, and he thought one might have fallen or been pushed out by the others."

"I thought that was one of the nests up Highway 12."

"I can't remember," Hargraves said. "They're all running together. I guess we should give Lemon a call and see if he remembers. But why would those guys climb all the way up the rock face and not take any of the babies?"

While Hargraves was trying to reach Barrett Lemon, Luke called the FedEx office. The phone rang and rang and rang, about fourteen times, and finally someone answered.

Luke told the employee who he was and asked for Brenda.

"Brenda's not here today," the man said. "It's her day off."

"Okay. Can I talk to whoever works the counter taking in packages?"

"That could be any of us. We're really busy trying to get stuff to the plane. What did you need?"

Luke quickly explained about the guys with the birds and asked if he recognized the man or anyone who might have brought a box in with a bird or live animal.

"Doesn't ring a bell with me," the guy said. "But I'll ask around. What number should I have them call if anyone remembers that package?"

Luke gave the man his number, and, based on the clanging and banging in the hubbub he was hearing in the background, he figured it was a lost cause and he wouldn't hear back from anyone. He made a mental note to run into the FedEx office first thing in the morning.

*

Hargraves talked with Lemon, and the biologist remembered exactly which nest it was and confirmed that there had been three eyas in it when he'd placed the camera near the nest.

"So, they got one," Hargraves said to Luke.

"Why would they go to all that trouble and only take one?" Luke asked.

"Maybe they only had buyers for three falcons, and they needed just one more."

"That's possible. Or maybe they had technical troubles. Did

you see any sign that someone might have fallen?"

"No, but I didn't look real hard. Why would the rope still be up there if someone fell?"

"Good point. I don't know. This whole thing is stupid."

The two men chatted about it for a few more minutes. Then Luke showed Hargraves the photo of the creature that had appeared on Buel Stennett's game camera and the photo of the man at the other falcon's nest.

"That sure looks like a bigfoot to me," Hargraves said. "You think it's real?"

"I have no reason to believe otherwise," Luke said. "I spent a couple hours with the man, and he seems as honest as anyone you'll ever meet. If it's someone in a bigfoot getup, Stennett doesn't know about it."

"But it has to be something like that, doesn't it?" Hargraves asked.

"I don't know. I asked Sara to send the photo to Virginia, or wherever they do all that high-tech photo analysis. Maybe they can spot a zipper on the back or something else that would say it's fake."

"There has to be something they can find," Hargraves said. "I don't think I want to learn that after all these years I've been working around one of these things."

"Probably more than one if it is real," Luke said.

"I'm not going to say a word to my wife," Hargraves said. "She'll freak out and probably make me put in for retirement."

Luke laughed.

"Well, the word is already out," Luke said. "TV, radio, and the newspaper, last night and this morning. It's only going to get worse. And if someone gets ahold of any of the photos of the dead animals, they'll be all over the internet."

Just then, Luke's cell phone started chirping. He looked at the caller ID and said, "Speak of the devil. That reporter from the ABC station is calling."

"Send it to voicemail," Hargraves said as he headed out the door. "You're off-duty."

And that's exactly what Luke did.

*

The next morning, Luke and Sara sat at the kitchen table and watched the morning news shows. Sara's murdered woman case on Yakama Nation land was the top story.

"Got any leads?" Luke asked.

"We know who she was last seen with," Sara said. "But the guy has disappeared."

"That doesn't make him look too guilty," Luke said.

"No, but people don't realize that many Native Americans lead different lifestyles than we do. The guy could have taken off to do some fishing on the Klickitat or Columbia River and didn't tell a soul. Or maybe he is in the mountains hunting deer."

"Well, I hope you find him to at least talk to him."

The next story up was Amber Knight's follow-up report on the dead animals in the trees and the possibility that bigfoot might be involved.

"We have one photo of a dog impaled on a branch in a tree," Knight said. "But we felt it was too gruesome to show on TV."

Knight was a pretty but not beautiful woman of about thirty, Luke thought. She had mousey brown hair that fell in curls to her shoulders. She looked fit and professional in a two-piece dark blue suit over a white blouse.

"I told her that," Luke said to Sara.

"Earlier, I talked with Cliff Upshaw," Knight continued. "He is the president of the Bigfoot Research Institute. I showed Mr. Upshaw the photo of the dog in the tree, and this is what he had to say."

They cut to a man standing with some trees in the background, a microphone stuck in his face. Underneath the man's face were the words: *Cliff Upshow. Presedent, Bigfoot Research Club.*

"They must have a third grader typing up those names," Sara said with a laugh.

Luke hadn't paid attention to that. He was looking at the man on the screen.

"Uh-oh," Luke said. "Heads are going to roll. From my one phone call with Mrs. Knight, she seems to be wound pretty tightly. This will shine badly on her, and she won't like it."

"Well, they should spell the man's name right," Sara said.

". . . we've seen this before," Upshaw was saying on the TV. "According to legends handed down through generations in many of the Indian tribes, there are descriptions of bigfoot, or sasquatch as the native people call him, storing their kills this way to keep the coyotes and other scavengers from stealing them."

The video cut away to Knight as she nodded with a very serious look on her face.

"That's how they do it on the national broadcasts," Luke said.

"It does kind of sound plausible," Sara said. "What the bigfoot guy said about storing their kills in the trees."

"It all sounds plausible," Luke agreed. "Except for the part about where a big hairy creature is the thing that did it."

"There is that," Sara said, standing and kissing Luke on the cheek. "I'm off to work. Good luck with this, whatever it is."

"Thanks," Luke said. "Good luck to you too. Hope you catch the murderer."

Amber Knight was finishing up her story on the tube.

"There are many believers in this creature," she said, looking into the camera, as serious as if she were reporting a mass shooting. "Bigfoot, sasquatch, or whatever you want to call it. The evidence is piling up. We might just have one roaming the woods west of Yakima. For ABC, I'm Amber Knight."

Evidence my ass, Luke thought.

He did get one thing from Knight's interview, though. There was another person he could talk to. He would find Cliff Upshaw today and have a little chat with him.

CHAPTER 19

Brenda with the wild auburn hair was again standing at the corner of the FedEx building smoking a cigarette when Luke pulled in. It made him wonder how smokers ever got anything done if they were always smoking outside of the building.

When Brenda spotted Luke driving in, she took one last big drag off the cigarette, threw the butt into the gravel, ground on it for a second with the toe of her boot, and started walking to Luke's truck.

"I wasn't here," she said. "I told everyone to watch for the Russian dudes shipping birds, but half these guys don't listen, and the other half don't care. They're just in a hurry to get stuff out."

"So, a bird was shipped yesterday?" Luke asked.

"Yep. I looked through the shipping records, and one box, about half the weight of the first one, was sent to the same address in Moscow, Russia."

"Okay. I guess there's nothing we can do about it now that it's gone, but I sure hope you're around if and when the guys come back."

"Me too," Brenda said. "Because I'm sure we can't count on these . . ." She struggled for the right word. ". . . men to do it. Some of them—I don't know how they get dressed in the morning."

Luke chuckled.

"It's not funny," Brenda said. "I deal with this crap day in and day out. I hope we aren't in trouble. I know you said this is serious business."

"That would be up to a judge," Luke said, trying to put a little fear in the woman. "But knowingly shipping federally protected birds, which we believe is what these guys are capturing, could have some pretty serious ramifications."

"Men!" Brenda said. "No offense. You tell them one simple thing. I am so sorry, officer. I'll try to pound it into their child-sized brains."

"Okay, thanks, Brenda," Luke said. "If you see these guys again, please give me a call, day or night. And if anyone sees their vehicle, color, make, that sort of thing, that would help as well."

"I'll do the best I can," Brenda said and turned for the front door.

Luke believed the rest of the crew—all men, he guessed—might be in for a very serious butt-chewing.

He drove to the office to try to run down a phone number for Cliff Upshaw, the bigfoot researcher. He was just looking up information on the organization when Captain Davis plopped down in the visitor chair next to Luke's desk.

"Well, it's happening," he said to Luke.

"What's happening, Cap?"

"This bigfoot thing is exploding, just as we feared. I'm getting calls from national news networks and newspaper reporters from around the country. Everyone wants to talk to someone about it."

"I saw the president of the Bigfoot Research Institute on TV this morning," Luke said. "He looked like he'd just hit the Mega

Millions jackpot. I mean, what could be better for someone like that?"

"Yep, he'll be up for his fifteen minutes of fame. All of this based on fables and ambiguities."

"I'll tell you what," Luke said. "It would explode even faster if the photo and story of the creature that appeared on Buel Stennett's game camera got out there."

The captain hadn't seen the photo, so Luke pulled it up and showed it to him.

"Dang. It sure does look like a bigfoot," Davis said.

"I've asked Sara to send it to their photo lab back east to look at. They should be able to tell if it has been altered in any way."

"I don't believe that Buel would be involved in a hoax like that," Davis said. "Not for a minute."

"I agree," Luke said. "He seems like the least likely person in the state to do something like that. So there must be another explanation."

The captain just sat and looked at the photo.

"You know," Luke said. "I'm not sure why we are pursuing this so hard. Really, the only possible game law broken might be the dead mule deer doe if someone killed it out of season. I'm sorry the people lost their domestic animals, but that's out of our jurisdiction, really."

"The issue is," Davis said, "if it's some other animal that is killing the animals, like a cougar or a wolf, then it *is* our problem."

"I've pretty much ruled that out," Luke said. "So do you want me to keep pushing?"

"Is a bigfoot considered wildlife?" Davis asked.

"I guess in the true sense of the word it is," Luke said.

"There's your answer. I'd say keep working it unless something else pops up that is more important."

"Okay. I'm still helping Hargraves on this deal with the stolen birds being shipped to Russia."

"Help where you can. But if we can figure this bigfoot thing out, it would get a whole barrel full of monkeys out of our hair."

"Will do," Luke said. "I think I'll go talk to the Bigfoot Research guy. That is, if I can find him and he'll fit me into his busy media interview schedule."

*

Luke couldn't find a phone number for Upshaw, so he called the organization's headquarters, but all he got was a recorded message that said the staff was in the field in Washington State.

He thought about it for a minute and then dialed James Dover, the *Yakima Herald* reporter.

"Hi, Luke," Dover said. "Was my story okay yesterday?"

"Just fine, and thanks for leaving me out of it."

"No problem. What can I do for you?"

"You have any idea how I can get in touch with this Cliff Upshaw fella with the Bigfoot Research Center or whatever it is?"

"Funny you should ask," Dover said. "He has called for a press conference at noon today up at Jim Sprick Park. You know where that is?"

"I do," Luke said. "Are you going?"

"Yeah. My editor says I need to hear what the guy has to say."

"Okay. I'll see you there," Luke said. "And thanks again, James."

Luke disconnected from the call and looked at the time. It was a little after ten. He decided he'd drive up to the park now, and maybe he could talk to Upshaw before the media event.

*

When he arrived at the park, which sat next to a district fire station off State Route 410 and featured some old-time buildings like from a TV western, the place was a beehive of activity. Large TV trucks with call letters from Seattle and large satellite dishes on top were parked here and there, and all the local TV vans were already there too. It was still forty minutes until showtime.

Luke parked at the fire station, said hello to three volunteer firefighters, and wandered over to where most of the people were gathered. He saw Amber Knight, dressed like she was going to meet the President of the United States, not the president of a bigfoot research group. He had only talked to the reporter on the phone, so she had no idea what Luke looked like, and he hoped it would stay that way.

After a few minutes, he saw James Dover wander in with a woman who was carrying two cameras looped around her neck. There would be photos in the paper in the morning.

Luke walked over, said hello to James, and introduced himself to the photographer.

"I'm Jen Stephens," the woman said as she shook Luke's hand.

Stephens was slim, almost too slim. Luke guessed she was a marathon runner or swimmer or biker. She wore her dark brown hair short, framing a narrow face with a thin, narrow nose above almost non-existent lips. Luke thought that if she had to, Stephens could slice a piece off a cheese wheel with that nose.

After the introductions, Stephens roamed off into the crowd, and Luke saw her occasionally lift one of the cameras and click off a shot or two.

"So," Dover said, "have you learned anything else since we last talked?"

"Not a thing," Luke fibbed. He wasn't going to say a word about the photo from Buel Stennett's game camera.

"What do you think? Are we in for a dog and pony show?" Dover asked.

"What I think is there are some folks here who are going to play this thing for all it is worth."

"And the media is going to eat it up as fast as it is shoveled to them."

"But you aren't biting?" Luke asked.

"No. I'm still a just-the-facts kind of guy. Sometimes makes for a boring story, but hey, I think our readers deserve it."

"Nice to hear in this sensational news world we live in today," Luke said. "I'll tell you what. Anything else I find out, you'll be the first person I call."

"Cool, thanks," Dover said.

As they were talking, Luke could feel eyes on him. He glanced around and saw Amber Knight boring holes into him.

He turned so she couldn't see his face and said, "Oh crap."

"What?" Dover asked.

"That reporter for ABC over there, I had a very curt phone call with her the other day, and I was hoping I wouldn't have to talk to her."

"Good luck with that," Dover said. "She's marching this way. And I gotta go."

"Chicken," Luke said, then looked up and gave Knight the friendliest smile he could muster.

"Agent McCain," she said. "I'm Amber Knight. We talked on the phone the other day."

"I'm not an agent of anything," Luke said. "You can call me Luke. Yes, I remember our phone call." He wanted to say "vividly" but bit his tongue. "Looks like you got the photo you wanted of the dog in the tree."

"No thanks to you," she said. "Can I get the photos of the deer and the goat?"

"If you're not going to show them on the air, why would you want them?"

"I'd like to see if they are placed in the tree the same way as the dogs."

"Take my word for it—they are," Luke said.

Knight gave a wicked little smile and said, "That's just it, Agent McCain. I don't want to take your word for it."

"What's your deal, Miss Knight?"

"It's Missus," she said with an attitude, holding out her left hand showing a small gold wedding band on her ring finger.

"Is this the story that's going to take you to the big city?" Luke asked.

"I'm just doing my job. This is a story of great interest to our viewers, and evidently to people around the state," she said, waving a hand at the different big television trucks sitting around the park.

"And if it is the story that gets you in front of some of the stations in the bigger markets, all the better, right?"

She smiled again. This time not so wickedly.

"But don't you want it to be right? Factual?" Luke asked.

"This is the 2020s, Agent McCain. The viewers today aren't quite as concerned as some of you older folks about the little things. This is a fantastic story."

Luke ignored the jab about older folks. He was at most twelve years older than her.

"Well, I feel sorry for you, Miss Knight," he said and turned to go someplace, anyplace else.

As he walked away, he heard her say "Missus."

Luke wanted to tell her that she could forget ever getting any information out of him in the future, but he knew it wouldn't do any good.

He spotted Cliff Upshaw a minute later. The man had looked big on TV but was even bigger in real life. He was about Luke's height, around six-foot-five, but probably had Luke by a hundred pounds. He had long gray hair flowing out from under a white Panama hat with a wide black band. Bushy gray mutton chop sideburns rimmed a jowly face that featured a permanent smile. He looked like a happy-go-lucky kind of guy who everyone would like. Luke guessed him to be in his mid-fifties.

Luke walked up to the big man, and Upshaw said, "Cheese it, it's the law!" and let out a laugh that would have made Santa Claus jealous. Then he said with a big, jowly grin, "How can I help you, young man?"

"I'm the officer investigating the dead animals in the trees," Luke said. "Can we talk for a couple of minutes?"

Upshaw looked at an oversized, sparkly gold watch on his left wrist, which Luke thought might be a Rolex or maybe a Breitling, but for what little he knew about high-dollar watches, it could just as easily be a knock-off from India or someplace.

"I have four minutes," the big man said. "Let's go over here."

"I saw you on TV last night," Luke said. "And you said you've seen this before, animals impaled on branches in the trees?"

"Well," he hesitated. "Not exactly that, no. But we've seen things that could only have been done by something big and strong, like a bigfoot."

"Such as?" Luke asked.

"Large animals, like deer and elk, that were killed by having their necks or backs broken. Legs torn right off their bodies. Things like that."

"Were these animals near highways or roads?" Luke asked, thinking about the many dead animals he'd seen over the years that had been killed by vehicles, with broken necks and backs, and limbs missing.

"Some were, and some weren't."

"Did you ever find any footprints nearby that might indicate what kind of creature killed the animals?"

"No, but that's not unusual. I understand there have been no prints near any of the animals in the trees."

"Have you ever seen a bigfoot print?" Luke asked.

"Many times," Upshaw said.

Luke didn't want to get into it with the man, but he had tracked dozens of animals and a few men too, and more times than not, there were always tracks of some kind if you looked hard enough.

"So, what is your plan here?" Luke asked. "Are you going to encourage all the bigfoot hunters of the world to come and make a search?"

"If people want to come and see if they can find bigfoot tracks or some other clues that a bigfoot is roaming around in these mountains, I am not going to discourage them."

"You do that with a herd of elk, and they'll flee to the next county, maybe the next state. Don't you worry that putting that many people in the forests might do the same to a bigfoot?"

"Bigfoot is much smarter than elk," Upshaw said. "They can crawl in a hole or a cave and cover up, and no one will find them."

"Ever search with dogs?" Luke asked. "A dog will find anything with a scent, and my guess is a bigfoot has to give off some kind of an odor with all that hair."

"Dogs can't track bigfoot because the beast gives off sounds that are so high-pitched, they scare the dogs away."

Luke wanted to call horse-pucky on that one but just nodded his head.

"That's how they communicate with each other," Upshaw said. "Sometimes, though, they make sounds that humans can hear."

"Have you ever heard them?" Luke asked.

"Yes, twice. Once down in northern California in the Cascades close to the Oregon border. The other time was over by Mount St. Helens, not long after the mountain blew. I think the bigfoot there was calling for its mate or other sasquatches."

The guy was good, Luke thought. An answer for everything.

"Now I need to go address the media," Upshaw said with a big grin as he shook Luke's hand again. "Thanks for talking to me. I enjoyed it immensely."

As the large man walked away, Luke noticed he had longer-than-normal arms. Put Upshaw in a bigfoot suit and, well, it would be very convincing.

A few minutes later, as Upshaw talked to the media, Luke realized this guy could sell a roast beef sandwich to a vegan. He had the crowd mesmerized with amazing bigfoot stories, and they were believing every word. Luke noticed that even the prim, professional Amber Knight was smiling like she was at a rock concert.

CHAPTER 20

Gregorio Petrov had had a very uncomfortable night. Even with the pain relievers the emergency room doctor had prescribed, every time he moved even slightly his shoulder would throb with pain.

"So, do you think you might be able to climb the tree today?" Sergi Petrov asked his brother. "I have found a source for the shoe spikes."

Gregorio started to laugh, but that made his shoulder hurt even more.

"No," he calmly said to his brother. "Not today, and most likely not tomorrow or the next day. So don't ask."

"I just hate the thought of those young eagles sitting in that nest when we could have them in Russia tomorrow. If we could do that, we would have eighty thousand dollars."

"I can do the math," Gregorio groaned. "But my right arm is useless. There is no way I can climb that tree. I'm not sure I could climb it with two good arms. And after those falcons attacked, I believe the adult eagles would be a much bigger issue. We should forget about them."

His brother wasn't listening.

"They are just sitting there," Sergi said. "I am going to drive up to the nest and see if I can figure out another way to get them."

"Go," Gregorio said. He needed the rest, and with his brother gone, chasing wild dreams, he could get some.

On his way out of town, Sergi pulled into a Jack in the Box to pick up a couple breakfast sandwiches and a cup of coffee for the road. As he went through the drive-through and passed by the main dining area, Emery Hart, who was sitting with a couple of buddies scarfing down Jack's meat lovers breakfast burritos, just happened to look out and see Petrov in the red Jeep Cherokee.

"Hey, hey, you guys!" Hart said excitedly. "That's one of the Russian dudes I was telling you about that came into the store to buy climbing gear to steal those hawks."

"No way, dude," one of the other young men said.

"Yes, way," Hart said. "C'mon, let's follow him. I'm going to call Luke and tell him where he goes."

The boys grabbed their burritos and headed for Hart's Chevy Blazer. He shoved his keys into the hands of one of the other boys and said, "Here, Cam. You drive. I want to be able to talk on the phone. Follow that red Jeep."

As they drove, Hart googled the number for the Department of Fish & Wildlife and called it. But every time he called, the line would buzz and buzz with a busy signal. He didn't know that every bigfoot hunter, media outlet, and person with a missing dog out in the county was also trying to call.

"Dang it. They aren't answering," Hart said. "I think I have the other officer's card somewhere in here."

Hart and the third kid started looking through all the school papers, fast-food wrappers, napkins, and other stuff that was scattered around inside the vehicle.

"Here it is," the third kid, Aiden, said. "Officer Stan Hargraves."

He gave Hart the number, and Hart thumbed it into his cell phone. As he waited for the officer to answer, he looked ahead.

"Don't follow too close," Hart said. "We don't want him to know we're following him."

"I know how to follow a car," Cam said. "I've seen all the *Fast and Furious* movies."

"This is a little different," Aiden said from the back seat.

"Yeah," Cam said. "Like Emery's SUV might have a top speed of sixty-three miles an hour."

"We're not racing," Hart said. "We just need to stay in sight of this dude so we can tell the officer where he's going."

A second later, Hargraves answered.

"Officer Hargraves, this is Emery Hart. I work at the climbing store. I helped Officer McCain retrieve the camera at the hawk's nest the other day."

"Yes, Emery. What's up?"

Hart had the phone on speaker, so the other two guys could hear Hargraves.

"Well, my friends and I were eating breakfast at the Jack in the Box, the one on First Street, not the one on Fortieth. They've got a really good deal on their breakfast burritos. If you buy one, they will give you another one for—"

"Just tell me what I need to know, Emery," Hargraves said.

"Well, we were sitting there eating our burritos, and I looked out the window and I see this guy driving a red SUV going through the drive-up window and I think to myself, I know him from somewhere. Then it dawned on me—it was one of the Russian dudes who came into the store and bought that climbing gear. It wasn't the one with the mustache, but the other one—his brother, I think. They looked like brothers."

"Okay," Hargraves said. "So did you get a license plate?"

"Well, no, but we might be able to get it. Me and my buddies are following him right now. He's driving an older red Jeep, I think. We just got on the highway headed toward Naches. My buddy is driving, and we've told him to not get too close. Do you want us to stay with him?"

"Yes, if you can," Hargraves said.

"He's speeding up," Cam said. "The speed limit here is sixty, and he's up to seventy."

"Did you hear that?" Hart asked into the phone.

"Yes, stay with him, but stay back."

"But we are breaking the speed limit," Cam said. "I already have two speeding tickets on my record, and our insurance agent told my folks that if I got one more ticket they would pull my insurance. My folks will be pissed if that happens."

"Did you hear that?" Hart asked again.

"Yes. Tell him to not worry about a ticket but also to drive carefully."

"Oh God," Cam said. "He's up to seventy-eight. I think he knows we're following him."

"Listen," Hargraves said. "Just let him go. I don't want you boys getting hurt. We know which way he is headed. I'll radio the sheriff and state patrol. I'm sure we can get him. Thanks for your help."

"Okay," said Hart, but it was too late—Hargraves was gone.

"What should we do?" Cam asked.

"Let's follow him for as long as we can without breaking the speed limit too bad," Hart said.

*

Sergi Petrov was just starting into his second breakfast sandwich when he noticed the white SUV behind him. It was the same one that had pulled in front of a city bus to get on the road out of the fast-food place he'd just been at. If he didn't know any better, he might think the car was following him on purpose.

To verify, Petrov started to speed up on the freeway. The white SUV sped up too. Then he slowed, and the white rig slowed. Finally, when he sped up to eighty, he left the white car well behind. When the white car didn't speed up too, he figured he was just imagining things.

Petrov passed through Naches and went on up the highway. Now there were several cars back behind him, including three white vehicles. It was hard for him to tell if one of the white cars was the one he'd seen behind him coming out of Yakima, and he decided not to worry about it. Who would even know who he was or what he was doing?

*

Hart and his buddies stayed far behind the red Jeep. Between Yakima and Naches, they let three vehicles get between them and the Jeep. Then, when they got into Naches, three more vehicles pulled onto the highway at the light. Two of the new rigs were white.

"Let's at least follow him to the Y," Hart said, meaning the junction where State Route 410 and 12 split, one heading to Chinook Pass, the other heading to White Pass. "If we can see which way he goes, we can let the cops know."

The red Jeep stayed straight at the junction, heading up the Naches River on Highway 410.

"You think he's going to try to catch some more hawks?" Cam asked.

"Maybe," Hart said. "But we need to try to stay with him since we've not seen any other cops."

"This is so cool," Aiden said. "Wouldn't it be fun to do this all the time? Maybe I should major in police science in college."

"I thought you were going to be a podiatrist," Cam said.

"I was, but this would be way more fun than looking at bunions and ingrown toenails for the rest of my life," Aiden said. "Besides, it's my dad who wants me to be a podiatrist. He's got bad feet and hates paying for all the doctor bills."

They talked about bunions and other foot ailments for a few minutes, all the while keeping an eye on the red Jeep way in the distance.

"Hope that guy doesn't turn off on one of these side roads when we go around a bend," Hart said. "We'll never see him then."

As they approached Jim Sprick Park, they looked and saw three big TV trucks and a whole bunch of other rigs parked there. Dozens of people were milling around down in the grass near some buildings.

"Wonder what that is all about?" Cam said as he slowed the rig.

"Wait, wait!" Hart said. "That's Officer McCain's truck parked there at the fire station."

By that time, the boys had gone past the entry to the park, so they went up to the next wide spot in the road, turned around, drove back, and pulled in next to Luke's brown Department of Fish and Wildlife Chevy truck.

When the boys got out of Hart's SUV, a woman walked up and asked them if she could help them. She was dressed in jeans, boots, and a Nile Valley Fire Department t-shirt.

"Yeah, we're looking for the officer who came in this truck," Hart said, pointing to Luke's truck. "It's kind of an emergency."

"He's over there in that crowd of people," the woman said, pointing to the group of reporters standing and listening to some guy speak.

"Okay, thanks," Hart said, and all three boys headed that way.

CHAPTER 21

Luke was walking back to his truck and still thinking about his discussion with Cliff Upshaw when he heard someone calling his name. He looked up to see Emery Hart and two other young men headed his way in a hurry.

"It's the guy!" Hart said excitedly before Luke could even say hello. "The hawk guy. The one that is stealing the baby birds."

"Slow down, Emery," Luke said.

"We were following one of the men who came into the store to buy climbing equipment," Hart said, pointing to the highway. "Just now. He's headed that way."

"Okay, okay," Luke said, trying to calm Hart down. "Tell me what happened."

After a lengthy, blow-by-blow explanation starting from ordering the two-for-one Jack's meat lovers breakfast burritos to the time they spotted Luke's truck at the fire station, Luke had a pretty good idea of the situation.

"Let me go call Officer Hargraves to see what happened with the other LEOs," Luke said. "Then we'll go from there."

"LEOs are law enforcement officers," Hart explained to his buddies. "This is so cool."

"Yeah, so cool," Cam said.

"Way better than plantar fasciitis," Aiden said.

Luke called Hargraves on the radio and learned that even though he had put out the information to the Yakima County Sheriff's Office and the Washington State Patrol, there were no officers in the area at the time, and with it being such a low priority, none were coming.

"I'm headed that way," Hargraves said. "But I'm still thirty minutes out. The guy could be anywhere by now."

Luke told him about the boys following the red Jeep and spotting his truck at the news conference at the park and said, "I'll go on up the highway and see what I can see. But like you said, he could be so many places."

"Well, you might get lucky," Hargraves said. He thanked Luke and signed off.

"You want us to go do some more looking too?" Hart asked. "We don't have class until three o'clock this afternoon."

"Naw. You guys have already been a big help," Luke said.

"You sure?" Hart asked. "We could go look up some of these Forest Service roads. My Blazer is four-wheel drive."

"You've helped enough already, Emery. No need to be burning up expensive fuel. You guys go back and get ready for class. I'll call you if I find him."

"You will?" Hart asked.

"Sure," Luke said and told the boys to drive carefully back to Yakima.

Luke watched the three young men get into the Blazer, pull out onto the highway, and head back toward town. Then he looked back at the group of reporters and camera people on the grass and saw Cliff Upshaw speaking to Amber Knight. She had a microphone stuck in the big man's face, and Luke could see the man was very animated as he spoke. The camera was on, and Upshaw was performing. The normally stoic reporter was smiling as the bigfoot hunter talked.

"Hook, line, and sinker," Luke mumbled to himself.

*

After driving up the highway almost to the top of the pass, and then up and down three other Forest Service roads and not seeing anything of the red Jeep Cherokee, Luke decided to give up and head down the mountain.

As he drove, he thought about Cliff Upshaw. Could he be involved in creating all of this with the impaled animals in the trees? Luke had looked at the Bigfoot Research Institute's website and was impressed. It gave an image of complete professionalism and stated that the group was only about seeking the truth when it came to the beast the Native Americans called sasquatch.

The Institute was a non-profit organization that was funded purely by donations from the public. Some publicity like this would probably spur those donations. It would be interesting to know how those funds were being spent, Luke thought. And it would be good to know how much the man who ran the Institute might be paid for his work there. He made a mental note to check into that and then tried to remember the conversation he'd had with Upshaw.

The big man had said that, as he understood it, there were no footprints around the trees where the animals had been found. Luke hadn't told James Dover, the *Yakima Herald* reporter that. And he didn't remember hearing Amber Knight say anything about it on her news story. Had that information been out in the public?

Luke didn't think so, but he also wouldn't know if Jerome Martin or Bill Hoyt would have told anyone about the lack of footprints near where the German shepherd had been found. Maybe Upshaw had talked to Martin about his dog, or April Sommers about her goat. Another thing he would need to check up on.

Upshaw seemed like a nice man, but there was just something about him, Luke thought. He seemed—what was it—slippery. He had all the answers, but he just seemed slippery.

As he drove, he saw a red Jeep CJ-7 coming at him up the highway, and that made Luke think about the rig the boys had seen. They said the man driving was the one without a mustache. Where was the man with the mustache? Emery Hart and Brenda from the FedEx office both had said there were two men that looked like brothers, and one had a dark mustache. The same man Hart had identified in the photos from the falcon's nest. Where was that guy?

Hart may have just made a mistake and thought he saw the other man driving the red Jeep. On the other hand, he was avid and confident that it was one of the two men who had come into the store to buy climbing equipment.

Maybe the men had separated to go scout out more falcon nests. There were about a thousand miles of roads in the Cascades. Two people working on their own could cover way more country and possibly find more nests.

Then he started thinking about the two men. Where had they come from? Both Hart and FedEx Brenda said the men had pretty heavy Russian accents, although Hart wasn't positive what kind of an accent it was. He thought Russian, but he wasn't sure. And they knew the birds had been shipped to Russia, so it made sense that the men were from there.

Luke wondered if the men lived in the area, or had come this way just to look for falcons. He knew there were some populations of newly arrived Russian immigrants on the west side of the state and over around Spokane. And he had checked anglers on the Columbia River with Russian accents that were living down near the Tri-Cities. If these two guys were from someplace else, and here for more than a couple of days, maybe it would be worth checking in with the local motels to see if they had any guests with Russian accents. Maybe he should try showing the photo of the man with the mustache to the front desk staff and see if they recognized him.

He would talk to Hargraves about that. It might be worth the effort.

*

Sergi Petrov spent the afternoon at the eagle's nest. He had worried the white SUV might show up, but the only other people he saw were a young couple who, when they stopped to chat with him as he was walking back to his truck, said they were hunting morel mushrooms.

"We found a bunch of them up in that burned area," the young woman had said. "They're the best eating mushroom there is."

Petrov had never heard of anyone hunting mushrooms, and frankly had never given any thought as to where mushrooms came from. He saw mushrooms in the grocery store and enjoyed eating them on stuff, but he wouldn't know a morel mushroom if it jumped up and bit him.

The young eagles were prime for the picking. Or so it seemed to him. They were testing their wings, flapping and stretching them, but they still couldn't fly.

As he looked at the nest and the tree in which the nest sat, Sergi had worked his way, branch by branch, up the giant pine tree with his eyes and thought it could be climbed. If only Gregorio hadn't broken his shoulder, they would have one or both of the young eagles from the nest, and the birds would be on their way to the oligarch in Russia.

Petrov wasn't going to climb the tree. But he wondered if he could find someone else who would. They would have to pay someone to do so, but with the money they'd make off the young birds, they could afford to pay someone quite nicely.

He thought about the people he knew who they might possibly recruit. He couldn't think of anyone off the top of his head, but Sergi would talk to Gregorio about it tonight when he returned to the motel.

*

"I do not see eagles in bags," Gregorio said when Sergi entered the motel room that evening.

"No, but after watching the birds in the tree, I believe we can get them. The adults leave to hunt and sometimes are gone for an hour or more. If we can find someone willing to climb the tree, I think we can grab at least one and not be harassed by the bigger birds."

"Finding someone willing to climb the tree and fight a young eagle into a bag may be more difficult than the job itself," Gregorio said.

"I have been thinking all the way here about who we might get to help," Sergi said. "We need someone young and agile. Someone like yourself, but with two working arms."

"I think Maxim knows some immigrants here in Washington State," Gregorio said. "Maybe he can give us a name of someone to contact."

"That is a good idea, brother. I will call him now."

Maxim Volkov did know some Russian immigrants in Washington, and he had two names of men who might be willing to climb a tree for a young eagle if they were paid enough. He gave the names and phone numbers to Sergi.

The first man Petrov called was not interested. When he learned what the job would be, he said in Russian, "You must be crazy. Stealing a baby eagle, the bird that is this country's national symbol, would be idiocy. If they catch you, they will throw you in the penitentiary and you will never see American freedom again."

The second man Petrov phoned, a man named Andrei Nikolaev, said he would do it for a price.

"Where are you located?" Petrov asked.

"I am in a town called Burbank, near Pasco."

"Is that close to Yakima?"

"Yes, I believe it is about ninety minutes from Yakima."

"Great. When can you get here?" Petrov asked

"First, we must agree on a price," Nikolaev said.

"How much would you ask?" Petrov asked.

"What is it worth to you?" Nikolaev asked back.

Neither man wanted to start the negotiations on price for fear that they would be too high, or too low. So, they volleyed back and forth for two minutes.

Finally, Petrov offered five thousand dollars. He was willing to go as high as ten but didn't want to get there yet.

"I will do it for no less than twenty thousand dollars," Nikolaev said. "There is risk to my health, and if I were to get caught, I risk going to prison for a long time."

"We are not being paid much more than that," Petrov lied. "And we have great risk as well. I will give you ten thousand dollars and not one ruble more."

When it is was all said and done, Petrov agreed to pay Nikolaev five thousand just for climbing the tree and retrieving the bird and another ten thousand when the young eagle arrived safely in Moscow.

"Just know, I will get my money one way or another if you do not pay as agreed," Nikolaev said. "I have some acquaintances who, for a percentage, will do whatever is necessary to help collect what is owed."

"That will not be necessary," Petrov said. "When can you get here?"

CHAPTER 22

Andrei Nikolaev was not a big man, but he looked like someone not to be messed with. He was shorter than Sergi Petrov by a couple inches, but Petrov could tell the man was strong. He could tell, because Nikolaev was wearing a white t-shirt with the sleeves ripped off, which revealed very large biceps covered in tattoos. A full reddish-brown beard covered Nikolaev's face, with the sideburns running up to the top of his ears where they met a shiny, completely bald head. A tattoo of a king cobra started at the back of Nikolaev's neck and ended with the snake's head, hood flared, staring out of the back of his bald head with evil black eyes.

"What happened to you?" Nikolaev asked when he saw Gregorio Petrov's arm trussed up in a sling.

"Broke my shoulder," Gregorio said.

"Climbing the eagle tree?" Nikolaev asked with a chuckle.

"No, climbing a cliff to capture some young falcons."

"You guys have quite the enterprise going here, eh? Catching all kinds of birds."

"All we need is one young eagle, and we will be done and out of here," Sergi said.

The three men were in the red Jeep Cherokee, headed out of town to where the eagle's nest sat in a huge pine tree next to the Naches River. They had met at the motel where the Petrovs were staying and decided to ride together to the nest.

The Petrovs had received the first payment of twenty thousand dollars for the two young falcons from their cousin the day before, so Sergi had the five thousand dollars ready to pay the scary-looking Nikolaev if he was able to climb the tree and get the young eagles.

"You must be making good money to risk your lives trying to catch wild birds," Nikolaev said.

"Not nearly enough," Sergi said. "But we promised these birds to a relative, and we need to get them for him."

"I will not ask what they will be used for," Nikolaev said.

"Hunting," Gregorio said. "A man wants to train them for hunting."

"I have seen the videos of eagles hunting rabbits and sheep in Mongolia," Nikolaev said.

The men talked about that for a bit and then discussed where in Russia they were born and raised and what other people they might know in common.

*

The morning after Luke had talked with Emery Hart and his buddies up at the park and searched for the red Jeep Cherokee, he talked to Captain Davis and Hargraves about his thoughts on the Russian men possibly staying at a motel in Yakima.

"If they aren't from around here," Luke said, "they gotta be staying somewhere."

"Maybe with friends?" Davis suggested.

"Possibly," Luke said. "But I think it might be worth it to check out some of the motels. It would only take a couple of hours if Stan and I worked it."

They decided they would split up. Luke would go hit the motels at the north end of town, and Hargraves would check the motels on the east side of town. They both had a copy of the photo of the man with the mustache taken at the falcon's nest.

"I'm guessing they are staying in one of the cheaper motels near the Mission," Luke said. "The boys spotted the man in the Jeep at the Jack in the Box not far from there."

"Call if you find them and need some backup," Hargraves said.

"You do the same," Luke said as he headed for his truck.

*

Luke found where the men were staying at the third place he tried. It was a small, mom-and-pop motel not a quarter-mile from the freeway. He called Hargraves and told him where he was. Hargraves said he would be there in ten minutes.

"Yes, this man and another are staying here," the desk clerk, who Luke guessed was also the owner, said when he showed the man the photo. "What do you need them for?"

"We'd just like to talk with them for a few minutes," Luke said. "The other man, does he have a mustache too?"

The clerk thought about it for a few seconds and said, "No, no he doesn't. Did they do something unlawful? We don't allow drugs or anything unlawful here."

"Can you tell me which room they are in?" Luke asked.

"I can tell you, but it won't do any good. They aren't there. I saw them leave about an hour ago with another man."

"Were they in a red Jeep Cherokee?"

"I don't know car brands," the clerk said. "But, yes, it was red. It was not a car, but more like a station wagon."

Luke asked the clerk if he could give him the name of the person who rented the room, and any information on the car, such as license number.

"The license plate is not from Washington," the clerk said. "Or it didn't look like a normal Washington plate. I think it was from Wyoming, maybe."

"Do you have the tag number?"

The clerk dug some paperwork out of a file folder behind the counter. He gave a copy of a receipt to Luke. The man who rented the room was Boris Yeltsin. The license plate number was listed, but there was no information on the state. According to the clerk, the man without the mustache would come in each morning to pay cash for that night's stay.

"Did he pay for tonight?" Luke asked.

"No, not yet. But they didn't pack up their clothes, so I assume they are staying."

Luke thought about what to do next. As he was thinking, the clerk said, "The man with the mustache was injured."

"Injured? How?"

"I don't know how, but when they first showed up, he was fine. Then, the day before yesterday, they came back late in the afternoon, and his right shoulder and arm were all wrapped up."

Luke thought about the nest with only one young falcon missing and the discussion he had had with Hargraves about someone falling from the rope that was still attached near the nest.

"You said there was a third man this morning," Luke said. "Can you tell me what he looked like?"

"He looked like a tough guy," the clerk said. "You know, no sleeves, big muscles, tattoos."

"Any idea how tall he was? Was he fat, thin, facial hair? Can you remember what any of the tattoos looked like?"

The man described Andrei Nikolaev to Luke, including the color of his beard, his completely bald head, and that he was shorter than the other two men.

"And he had one tattoo on the back of his head," the clerk said. "I was too far away to really tell what it was, but it could have been a dragon or one of those Gila monsters."

"Okay, thank you," Luke said when he saw Hargrave's pickup drive in. "We may be back, and please, don't tell the men that we were here looking for them."

"If there is going to be trouble, I want them out of here," the clerk said. "We've had too much trouble here. It drives business away."

Luke tried to assure him there would be no trouble and thanked the man for his time and information. He walked out and met Hargraves in the parking lot and told him what he had learned.

"Wonder who that third guy was?" Hargraves asked after hearing about the 'tough guy.'

Luke thought about it for a minute and said, "Maybe he was coming in to help climb another cliff for more young falcons because the other guy was hurt."

"Could be," Hargraves said. "Or maybe he is buying young birds. By his description, he sounds more like a bird buyer than a rock climber."

The men discussed that for a couple more minutes, and Hargraves asked, "Did you ask the motel guy about video cameras? They've had several shootings around here, and drug deals are happening probably every day nearby. There must be some video surveillance."

"That's the first question I should have asked after he told me they'd left in the red vehicle."

Luke walked back into the office with Hargraves right behind him and asked, "Sorry to bother you again, but do you have security cameras showing the outside of the building?"

The man was at first hesitant but finally said he did have video cameras and took the officers back into a tiny closet-sized room. There was one big TV monitor on the wall with six different pictures displayed on the screen showing various parts of the motel and parking lot. The tiny room served dual purpose, as a couple of mops, a mop bucket, and three or four push brooms were stacked in one corner.

The clerk went to a laptop computer sitting on a small table and started poking keys until he brought up the views on the big monitor of the sidewalk in front of the rooms and the parking lot from two different angles. He started backing the footage up at a speed that was difficult to follow.

"Good thing I don't get seasick," Hargraves said. "All this trying to watch three screens in reverse at sixty miles an hour would probably set it off."

The man slowed the rewind and said, "There they are."

Luke and Hargraves both leaned into the screen and looked at the three men. The video footage was grainy, and the colors only somewhat resembled what they were in real life, but they were able to identify the guy with the mustache, wearing a sling on his right arm, as the man they had photos of at the falcon nest from a few days earlier.

"That's him," Hargraves said. "And what the hell is that on the back of that bald guy's head?"

Both men leaned closer.

"Is that the ghost from Ghostbusters?" Hargraves asked.

"A tough guy like that wouldn't have a movie character on his head," Luke said. "It's got to be a dragon or something."

They let the footage roll and saw all three men climb into an orangish Jeep Cherokee. They couldn't read the tag numbers, but the plates were definitely from out-of-state.

"Could you please save this footage?" Luke asked the manager. "We might need it for evidence."

The man agreed and seemed happy to have the officers out of his back room.

"Wonder what all that was about?" Hargraves said. "He really didn't want us back there."

"Who knows," Luke said. "But as long as he doesn't have a bunch of baby falcons and eagles stored somewhere back there, we really don't care."

"Maybe he secretly has video cameras set up in the rooms," Hargraves said. "I saw where some pervert had about a hundred hours of video of women in various stages of undress taken from secret cameras he had set up in his motel rooms."

"Could be," Luke said, then changed the subject. "Now, what do we do about these guys?"

The two men leaned against the back of Hargraves' truck

and chatted. They decided that trying to find the men up in the mountains was most likely going to be a goose chase, and the best course of action was to do a little stakeout at the motel.

"The manager-owner guy, I guess that is what he is, said the men hadn't taken any luggage out of the room, so they are probably coming back here," Luke said. "One of us can set up here, and the other can watch the FedEx office. If they've gone for more birds, they're likely to go there first."

"That is, if they got any more," Hargraves said.

"I'm guessing that's what they are doing now. Trying to get more."

"The manager keeps watching us. I bet he is up to something."

"I'm sure the city police are on to whatever he's doing," Luke said. "But we'll mention it to the captain, and he can let YPD know that something fishy might be going on."

"I bet he's videoing people in their rooms," Hargraves said.

"You don't know that," Luke said. "Now, let's get going before those guys show up and see us here."

They decided Hargraves would park his truck next to a gas station mini-mart just up and across the road from the motel and watch from there. Luke would go over to the FedEx office and watch there.

While he waited, Hargraves called Davis and asked if he could get a judge to sign off on an arrest warrant for the two men. They had photos of the one man at the nest, which had had young falcons in it the day before and now there were none. And they had eyewitness reports of the men buying climbing gear and shipping birds to Russia.

An hour later, Davis called and said they had the warrant. Hargraves texted Luke that they were good to go on the arrest.

*

When Luke arrived at the FedEx office, he was a little disappointed to not find Brenda standing at the corner of the building sucking on a Marlboro. He parked his truck and walked into the store.

Brenda was behind the counter, talking to a customer about shipping a box of frozen fish to Dallas, Texas.

"Needs to be packed in dry ice," Brenda was explaining. "That's the only way we'll take it."

"Ah geez," the woman who wanted to ship the fish said. "It's frozen good, vacuum-packed, and wrapped in newspaper. I think UPS said they would take it that way."

"I have no idea what UPS does," Brenda said. "We require fish to be packed in dry ice."

"Can't you make an exception just this one time?" the lady asked.

"Ma'am, Dallas is hotter than the hubs of hell right now. This package ends up stuck in some truck out in one of the five thousand suburbs down there and starts to go bad, they'll never get the rotting fish smell out of it. So, NO, we can't make an exception."

"Well," the woman said in a huff, grabbing the box and marching out.

"Lots of privileged stupid people in this world," Brenda said, turning to Luke.

She was rough, but Luke was beginning to like her more and more.

"And, no, the rooskies haven't been back to send more whatever-the-hell kinda birds they are shipping to the motherland."

Luke chuckled, explained what he was doing, and told her he would be watching covertly for the men to arrive from somewhere.

"Go for it," Brenda said. "No skin off my fat ass."

"But just in case I miss them," Luke said.

"I know," Brenda said. "DO NOT ship any more birds to Russia."

"Or fish to Texas without dry ice," Luke said with a smile.

"You got that right," Brenda said. "Now, I need a smoke."

CHAPTER 23

Sergi and Gregorio Petrov and Andrei Nikolaev stood and watched the eagle nest for a while. The adult eagles came and went, and the more Nikolaev watched, the more concerned he was that the adults might cause him severe bodily harm if they caught him robbing the nest.

"You say the adult falcons attacked you and caused you to slip and fall?" Nikolaev asked Gregorio.

"Yep. They were like a bunch of angry bees, buzzing all around me."

Nikolaev looked all the way up the tree at the nest and said, "That would be quite a fall from up there. A person could die."

"We have a safety harness and rope," Sergi said. "That will keep you from falling."

"When will the adults leave for an extended period of time like you said they would?"

"I am not sure," Sergi said. "Yesterday, they were gone for an hour two different times."

They watched for a few more minutes, and Nikolaev said, "Let's get the harness and rope ready. I will go up the tree halfway, and then we will wait for them to leave."

"Good idea," Sergi said. He was already counting the twenty-five thousand dollars that would be coming from Maxim for one young eagle. "All we need is one, but if you could grab them both, it would be really good."

"If I can get the second bird, there would be a bonus in it for me, no?"

"I think we can do that," Sergi said. "How does five thousand dollars sound?"

"Ten thousand sounds better."

"Five thousand per bird," Sergi said. "That adds up to ten."

"I can add," Nikolaev said. "Give me the rope."

The Petrovs watched as Nikolaev climbed from one branch to the next. Sometimes he had to grab a branch over his head and pull himself up to get a knee on it. But the brothers noticed no struggles in his effort to do so.

Soon, Nikolaev was sitting on a branch roughly halfway up the tree.

"Where are the adults?" he asked.

"One has just brought a rabbit to the young ones," Gregorio said. "The other is nowhere in sight."

"Let me know when the one at the nest leaves."

They waited roughly ten minutes before the adult, in full bald eagle colors, with a whiter than white head and almost black body, flapped off the nest and flew up the river out of sight.

"The adult is gone," Sergi said.

As soon as he heard that, Nikolaev started his climb, moving from one branch up to the next. Sometimes he had to work around the trunk of the tree to get the right branch. The higher he climbed, the thinner the branches were.

Almost to the nest, Nikolaev said, "I'm not sure I can get out around the edge of the nest. It is much wider than these small branches."

Sergi and Gregorio watched as the bald man tethered one end of his safety rope to the trunk of the tree and the other to the harness that was around his shoulders and legs.

"Let me see what I can do," Nikolaev said and reached up and out to the edge of the nest.

The young eagles, sensing something was amiss, started to emit loud, high-pitched chirps.

Just then, all three men heard a shrill scream from somewhere above. Nikolaev couldn't see it because he was under the nest, but the Petrovs looked just in time to see an eagle coming in like an F-15 fighter jet in a dog fight.

"Oh shit," Sergi said.

"Look out!" screamed Gregorio.

There was much speculation later, by those who witnessed the attack, and by others who heard about it, as to whether or not the eagle was actually aiming for the king cobra on the back of Nikolaev's head. Intentional or not, that is exactly where the eagle's talons struck when it hit the man trying to climb into the nest.

The impact from the eagle hitting him in the head knocked Nikolaev unconscious, which may have been a good thing because if he had been awake to see the bird coming back for another hit, he might have had a heart attack.

Fortunately for him, the second assault was more of a fly-by, but the damage had already been done. The eagle's sharp talons had ripped into Nikolaev's scalp right at the tattooed snake's face, and the lacerations immediately started to bleed profusely.

"I think he's dead," Gregorio said after watching Nikolaev dangling from his safety rope.

"I hope not," Sergi said. "If he is, we will have to figure out a way to get him down."

A moment later, Nikolaev started moaning and moving around a bit.

"He's alive," Sergi said.

Then to Nikolaev, "You want to try one more time for a baby eagle while you are still up there?"

"He's bleeding like crazy," Gregorio said. "We need to get him some medical attention."

"I think he'll be fine," Sergi said as he looked up into the tree, shading his eyes with one hand to block the sun. "Head wounds bleed a lot, but most of the time they are superficial."

"You can't know that from down here," Gregorio said. "We need to call for help."

"If we call for help, people will know what we were doing."

Gregorio hadn't considered that. "Maybe we call for help, but we disappear before the ambulance gets here."

As they talked, Nikolaev started to become more aware of his situation.

"Are you guys going to help me?" the man in the tree yelled as he pulled himself back into the upright position and got perched on a branch. When he did, the blood started running down his back. "I need help. I may be bleeding to death."

"There is not much we can do from down here," Sergi yelled back. "If you can't climb down on your own, we'll have to call for help."

"That wouldn't be good," Nikolaev said as he tried to stop the bleeding on the back of his head with his hand. "They'll know we were trying to catch an eagle."

"Rip the bottom of your shirt off and tie it around your head," Gregorio said. "That might help slow the bleeding."

Nikolaev worked his way out of the safety harness and then, after several attempts with shaky, bloody hands, he was able to tear the bottom of his t-shirt into a strip. He tied it around his head, gingerly moved off the limb on which he was sitting, and slowly started to climb down.

While all of this was happening, one adult eagle circled just above the nest. The other sat in a tree about seventy yards away, keeping an eye on everything.

"Did I hit a branch or something after the eagle hit me?" Nikolaev asked.

"You hit a couple. Hard," Gregorio said. "Why?"

"I believe I may have lacerated my spleen," Nikolaev said as he moved down to the next branch.

Sergi laughed and said, "How would you know that?"

"Because I have a horrible pain in my guts, right close to where the spleen sits."

"How does he know where his spleen is?" Sergi asked his brother.

"How does he know he has a spleen?" Gregorio asked back. "Do you have a spleen?"

The brothers watched as, very slowly, Nikolaev climbed down the giant pine tree. He did a lot of moaning and groaning and mentioning his spleen along the way down. Gregorio thought that Nikolaev—with his shirt tied around his head and blood on his face—looked a bit like Sylvester Stallone in the first *Rambo* movie. A bald Sylvester Stallone with a full beard that is.

When his feet hit the ground, Nikolaev collapsed. Sergi and Gregorio rushed over to him and helped him up.

"We will get you to the Jeep and take you to the hospital right away," Gregorio said as he put his arm around Nikolaev's back, trying not to get too much blood on himself.

They laid the injured man in the back seat of the Jeep and went as quickly as they could down the highway. As they went, Nikolaev moaned some more, holding his hand on his belly.

"Do you think that eagle ruined my snake tattoo?" Nikolaev said after feeling the back of his head.

"I'm sure it is fine," Sergi said, but he had no experience with tattoos or what affect eagle talons might have on them.

"Good. I paid good money for the tattoo. My ex-girlfriend hated the thing. Said it made me look like a thug. What is this thug? Do you guys know what a thug is?"

"You need to just lay back and rest," Gregorio said. "We're getting you to the hospital as quickly as we can."

*

The emergency room doctor came out to talk to the Petrov brothers about an hour after Nikolaev had been taken back for examination.

"We've stitched up the lacerations at the back of his head," the doctor said. "His tattoo might be messed up a little. What was it anyway?"

"A king cobra," Gregorio said.

"Ohhh," the doctor said. "Once we pieced it back together, we thought it kinda looked like the ghost from *Ghostbusters*. Anyway, he'll recover from that no problem. He has a slight concussion, and he keeps complaining that he injured his spleen, so we've just sent him back for an MRI to see if there are any internal injuries."

The men listened and nodded their heads.

"How did this happen anyway?" the doctor asked. "The cuts on his head were unusual, like something with sharp claws grabbed him."

Sergi had been thinking about what to say if they were asked how Nikolaev had been hurt.

"My brother and I offered up two hundred dollars each to Andrei if he could climb a big pine tree and touch an eagle's nest that sat at the top. Evidently, the eagles did not like him getting so close to the nest and attacked."

"Well, now I really have heard everything," the doctor said, shaking his head.

"How long will our friend need to be here?" Sergi asked.

"If the MRI comes back negative, he can probably go home today. But we won't know that for a while."

When the doctor left, the brothers talked about what to do next.

"Let's go back to the motel and get our clothes," Sergi said. "We will get Andrei's keys, and you can drive his car back here so he has it whenever he gets out. I will pick you up, and we will head back to North Dakota. I have been thinking about the young eagles, and it looks like that will not happen."

"Yes, good," Gregorio said. "But what if we think about going someplace other than North Dakota? How about this Burbank that Andrei speaks of. It sounds like there are many people from our country there. It might be a nice place to live for a change."

Sergi thought about it for a minute and said, "That might not be a bad idea."

CHAPTER 24

After sitting and watching the FedEx office for four hours, Luke was convinced the men were not going to show. During that time, he watched Brenda come out and smoke five cigarettes. She'd noticed where he had parked, and every time she came out for her smoke break, she would give a half wave and twiddle her fingers at him and then, as if she didn't want to give his hideout away, would totally ignore him, looking at her phone while smoking away.

Luke texted Hargraves three times, just to check in and break the boredom. Nothing was happening on his watch either. Hargraves texted back later that he had seen three people, two men and one woman, urinate next to a dumpster, and he had watched a man try to fly a homemade kite in the middle of First Street.

After he looked around and saw there wasn't a breath of air anywhere, Luke texted back and asked how the kite flying went.

Hargraves texted back that it didn't, but it looked like the guy was having fun trying while he dodged traffic.

Luke decided to call it quits and was on his way to the office when Hargraves called.

"They're here," Hargraves said as soon as Luke pushed the Bluetooth answer button on his steering wheel. "Red Jeep Cherokee, North Dakota plates."

"I'm on my way," Luke said.

"I'll get a little closer, and if it looks like they're going to leave, I'll bust them. Otherwise, I'll wait for you."

"Roger that," Luke said and sped up.

As Hargraves watched the men disappear into a room, he pulled around to the end of the building where, if he had to, he could pull in quickly and block the Jeep. When he got there, he watched as the manager of the motel came out of the office and hurried down to the men's room and knocked on the door.

"Crap," Hargraves said to himself. He thought the manager might be telling the brothers that he and Luke had been there asking about them.

After watching the men talk, mostly the manager and the man without the mustache, Hargraves decided their discussion was about something else. The manager seemed to be getting a little upset, becoming more animated as he gestured with his hands. He pointed into the room a couple of times and then held his hand flat palm up and poked at it with the pointer finger of his other hand.

He wants to be paid for the room, Hargraves thought.

A minute later, while the manager and the man in the room were still arguing, Luke pulled in. Instead of waiting at the corner, Luke parked his truck right behind the Jeep. Hargraves pulled his truck alongside the Jeep.

The manager turned to see what was going on, and the man without the mustache quickly closed the door.

*

Sergi saw the trucks with the insignias on the doors pull in behind their rig and knew immediately what was happening. If that damn manager hadn't stood there and argued about getting paid, they might have been loaded up and gone already.

"The police are here," Sergi said to his brother. "They are here for us."

"Do you think the manager called them?" Gregorio asked.

"No, I don't. The writing on their trucks said something about wildlife. They know we took those falcons."

"But how?"

"I do not know. It does not matter now. Besides, the birds are gone, and we have been paid. So, there is nothing they can do about that."

"Except put us in prison," Gregorio said.

Just then there was a knock at the door.

"State police," Hargraves yelled. "Open up!"

He stood to one side of the door, and Luke stood to the other side. They didn't think the men would try to shoot it out, but it was better to be safe than sorry.

The door started to open slowly, and Hargraves said, "Hands where we can see them."

The man with the mustache came out first, one hand in the air, the other still trussed up in the sling. The second man followed.

"Are either of you armed?" Hargraves asked.

Both men shook their heads.

Hargraves directed the men to come out to their car and lean across the hood, arms spread out.

Sergi spread his arms, Gregorio did the best he could with the sling, and Luke checked them for weapons. While Luke was frisking them, Hargraves looked into the Jeep through the windows.

"I see a climbing helmet, ropes like the one left at the nest, and chest waders," he said.

"Let's see some identification," Luke said.

Both men reached into their back pockets and produced North Dakota driver's licenses. Luke looked at them and then passed them to Hargraves.

Luke had the photo printout taken from the camera at the nest, and he compared it to the man with the mustache sitting on the curb. It was the same man, for sure. A small mole on the man's left cheek, seen in the photo and on the man sitting in front of them, was the clincher.

"So," Hargraves said to the men, "you are under arrest for unlawfully obtaining federally protected birds and shipping them out of the country."

They put both men in handcuffs and read them their Miranda rights. Luke put Gregorio in the back seat of his truck, while Hargraves put Sergi into the back seat of his truck.

As they were loading the men into the trucks, the manager of the motel came out.

"You said there would be no trouble," he said to Luke. "This looks like trouble."

"We'll be out of here in a few minutes," Luke said. "We need to get into their room and make sure there are no birds in cages or weapons in there."

"Birds?" the manager asked. "What birds? We have a no-pet policy. If they have pets, they owe me another one hundred and fifty dollars. They signed the form. No pets or pay one hundred and fifty dollars. Plus, they owe me for the room for today. They did not check out in time. I was trying to get them to pay that when you showed up. Can you make them pay for the room and the pet charge?"

"No, we really can't," Luke said. "But I will ask."

Luke went up to the man named Sergi and said, "The manager believes you owe him for one more day's rent. Would you like to pay him?"

"We are not staying there tonight, obviously, so screw him," Sergi said.

Luke turned to the manager and said, "Looks like they are declining your request to be paid. You might take it up with the judge when they are brought before the court on these charges."

"A lot of good that will do," the manager said. "Go look for your guns and birds, and then please leave."

"Yes, sir," Luke said to the man.

And that's what they did, taking the men to the county jail where they were booked on three state and two federal charges, with the possibility of a few more.

*

After they got the Petrov brothers booked, Luke called Emery Hart on his way to the office.

"Hi, Emery," Luke said when the young man answered the phone. "This is Luke McCain."

"I knew it was you," Hart said, "because I now have your number programmed into my phone. I hope that is alright. I mean, who knows, I might see someone doing something wrong and I could just call you. Or that was what I was thinking."

"Well, if you see someone doing something wrong, you should call 911 first," Luke said. "But if it is a fish and wildlife situation, yes, please call."

"That's what I meant," Hart said. "Like if someone shot a deer out of season or was fishing in a closed river, then I could give you a call. My friends and I thought it was so cool to follow that guy who had come into the store and was stealing the hawks, and helping you by climbing that rock and retrieving that camera—that was one of the coolest things I have ever done. I told my mom all about it, and she got all worried that the guy we were following could stop and shoot us or something, but I told her that was crazy, although she read a story about a guy up in Spokane who got shot by some dude just because he made a wrong lane change on the freeway, so you never know."

Finally, Hart took a breath, and Luke said, "That's what I am calling about. I told you I would call when we caught the guys who were robbing the falcon nests, and we did. Grabbed them this afternoon, and the photo from the camera you got off the rock was what sealed the deal. We couldn't have arrested them without that."

"That is so cool," Hart said. "I can't wait to tell the guys and my mom, although she might now worry that those guys found out what I did and come looking for me or something."

"I wouldn't worry about that too much," Luke said. "They'll probably go to jail for a while, and since they are from North Dakota, they most likely will end up going back there when they get out of jail."

"I'll tell my mom, but that won't stop her from worrying. She's a worrier for sure. Man, I wish I had been there when you arrested those guys. That would have been so cool. Did you have to pull your guns or Tasers? Did you put them in handcuffs and read them their rights, like they do on TV? Man, I wish I could have been there. This has been so cool. My one friend, Aiden, was going to be a pediatrician, or whatever a foot doctor is called, but when we followed that guy and started talking about the investigation and how I helped you, he now wants to study to become a police officer. That is if his dad will let him. His dad has issues with his feet and wants Aiden to become a foot doctor so he can get free foot care."

"Well, I hope he does what he wants," Luke said by way of trying to wind down the conversation. "So, anyway, I need to run, but just wanted to say thanks again."

"Oh, man, no problem. It was so cool. The whole thing. My mom did want me to ask about that payment you said you might be able to get, and I told her I didn't want to bug you about it, but she'll be mad if I told her I didn't ask. I'm not worried about it, but she is. My mom is a worrier."

"You should have it in the next couple of days," Luke said. "Thanks again, Emery. Good luck in school and with your climbing."

As Luke was clicking off, he heard Hart start to say something, but it was too late.

"That kid sure can talk," Luke said to himself.

CHAPTER 25

I t had been two weeks since Luke had taken the call about the missing goat up in the North Fork of the Ahtanum. Since then, there had been no other animals found impaled on branches in trees, and the investigation into who, or what, had killed the animals had stalled.

That hadn't stopped the uproar from building about the possibility of bigfoot roaming in the nearby Cascades. National and regional news crews had arrived and talked to everyone from the man on the street in downtown Yakima, to Cliff Upshaw, the director of the Bigfoot Research Institute, about the bigfoot rumors.

Motel and hotel rooms, normally near full-capacity with the other activities going on in the area, were now totally booked with people from all over the country coming in to hunt for bigfoot. Anyone with any kind of house or spare room to rent were getting top dollar for the space. Restaurants were doing record business feeding the masses of people who had arrived at a chance to see the bigfoot.

Luke and Sara didn't watch much television, but if they did catch the news, inevitably the pale fleshy face of Upshaw would be on the tube with his wild hair and long pork chop sideburns and signature Panama hat.

"The TV reporters sure love that guy," Sara said one morning after listening to Upshaw tell one of his bigfoot stories. "He's full of stories and is convinced it was bigfoot who killed those animals and put them in the trees."

"He's full of something," Luke said.

"So, what are you going to do?"

"Not much we can do right now."

"Have you noticed all the folks wearing bigfoot t-shirts now? I'm seeing people wearing them at the grocery store and walking downtown."

"I guess I haven't been paying any attention," Luke said. "But now that I think about it, I have seen some bigfoot decals on cars."

"Yakima's now going to be known for apples, hops, and bigfoot," Sara said.

*

A few days later, Luke finally got the analysis from the wildlife lab in Oregon on the mule deer doe they had sent down there. The techs found nothing unusual on the deer and concluded that it had been struck in the head and neck area, possibly by a falling tree or large limb, or it could have taken a glancing blow from a vehicle.

Luke asked if someone might have hit the deer with something heavy, and the tech said it was a possibility, "but someone or something would have to be very strong to swing it hard enough to break the deer's neck."

The FBI lab in Virginia took a little longer to get to the photo from Buel Stennett's trail camera.

"We can't find anything that shows the photo has been altered," the FBI photo expert told Luke in a phone call.

"Were you able to get close enough to see if there was anything fake about the creature?" Luke asked.

"We looked for snaps, buttons, zippers, seams, and couldn't find anything like that," the woman said. "But the low resolution of the photo makes it impossible to get a very good enlargement."

"Any opinions as to whether the beast is real or not?" Luke asked.

"It looks real to me," the woman said. "But don't quote me. I'm just a city dweller from Arlington, Virginia. I might have come out there for a look-see myself if it wasn't so far away."

*

During that time, Luke and Jack patrolled the region as they normally would. They checked on anglers, and because there were about twenty times the number of people roaming the forests, they checked on them too. Most of the folks he encountered seemed harmless, but there were some obvious fanatics.

One afternoon, he was driving up a Forest Service road off Highway 410 near Gold Creek when a guy stepped out from some brush onto the road and put his hand out for Luke to stop the truck.

"Is there a problem here?" Luke asked as he climbed out of the Chevy.

"No problem," said the man. "We're just stopping all vehicles from advancing up the road."

The man, who was dressed in a ghillie suit, had a bushy red beard and mustache and wore an old infantry helmet. With the beard and helmet, all you could see were two blue eyes peeking out. The man was a few inches shorter than Luke and seemed too thin for the size of his head.

Luke had lowered the back windows of the truck as they were stopping, and now Jack was growling a low, rumbling growl as he looked into the brush off to the side of the road.

"Unfortunately, you don't have the authority to be stopping anyone from driving this road," Luke said. "It's public, and everyone has access."

"I'm part of the bigfoot brigade, and General Foster has put out the orders—no one is to drive past this point."

Oh boy, Luke thought. Jack continued to growl and concentrate on the brush.

"What's your name, soldier?" Luke asked.

"Masters, sir. Corporal Masters."

"And what is the name of your partner standing in the brush?"

Masters glanced that way and said, "I ain't got no partner."

"My dog says otherwise," Luke said, raising his voice so the person in the brush could hear. "Tell whoever is in the brush to come on out. I need to see him, or her, right now."

"I don't take orders from you," Masters said.

"If I have to let my dog out, someone is probably going to get bit," Luke lied. Jack wasn't trained for that and only would attack someone if they were attacking Luke. "It'll most likely be the person hiding in the brush because he knows someone is there, but it might be you. "

Luke could see Masters thinking about it.

"Come on out, with your hands where I can see them," Luke said in the direction of the brush.

It took a minute, but finally a young woman, dressed exactly like Masters, came out of the brush. She was short and slim, had an unbelievably white but pretty face with jet black straight hair falling out of her helmet to her shoulders. The woman, who was in her twenties, had a sheepish look on her lily-white face.

As soon as she came onto the road, Jack stopped growling.

"And you are?" Luke asked.

"Donovan, sir. Would your dog really have bit me? I like dogs, and most of them like me."

"You heard him growling, didn't you?" Luke asked, avoiding her question.

"Yeah, but I don't think he would have bit me. I wasn't doing anything wrong."

"You were hiding where I couldn't see you. Jack didn't like that."

Donovan walked over to the truck and reached through the window to pet Jack. Jack's tail started wagging, thumping the back of the seat.

"See there," Donovan said. "He likes me."

"I'm Officer McCain with the Department of Fish and Wildlife. You think I could talk to your general?"

Luke could see Masters thinking about it, then watched as he reached behind his back to pull something out.

"Easy," Luke said, hand on his pistol in the holster of his utility belt.

Masters slowly brought a radio from behind his back.

"I'm going to call the General," Masters said. Then he turned to Donovan and said, "Leave that dog alone."

"Tell him I am driving up to wherever he is," Luke said as he jumped back into the pickup. He wasn't going to wait for some general's approval.

Donovan stepped away from the truck as Luke started it. He drove around Corporal Masters who stood there with his mouth open, although Luke wasn't positive about that because the bushy red beard was covering it.

He drove a mile up the road and found an encampment of six Army surplus tents. They were all colored tan, probably from Desert Storm, Luke thought.

As he pulled into the camp, he saw several men and women— some dressed in the same ghillie suits as Masters and Donovan, others in desert camo pants and shirts—wandering around. Some were chopping and hauling wood, while others were pounding stakes in the ground around the tents.

Luke looked around and saw a man climb out of a side-by-side UTV and start marching toward him. The man, who Luke assumed was General Foster, was about sixty and looked to be in good shape for a man of his age. He wore a tan shirt with a button-down collar, green Army-style pants with the bottom of the legs tucked into yellow boots. A pistol, possibly a Colt model 1911, sat in a holster on his hip. Aviator sunglasses covered his eyes, and his hair was very short, just gray stubble sticking up from his head.

"How can I help you officer?" the man said, stepping up to Luke after he got out of his truck. The general was maybe five-foot-nine, Luke thought.

"You can help me by giving me some identification," Luke said.

"My corporal told you who I am, did he not?"

"Yes, he did, but until I see a driver's license or some other form of ID, I have no idea who you really are."

"Have I done something wrong?"

"No, but your corporal did. He can't be stopping people from using these Forest Service roads. He said you gave him the orders to do that. So, let me see some identification please."

The man just stood there for a while, staring at Luke, although he couldn't see his eyes. Luke stared right back.

"Listen, officer. We've been training for this for some time down south. We knew eventually there would be a bigfoot sighting, and we're just the group to locate the creature and verify his existence. We don't need a bunch of civilians and amateur bigfoot hunters running around up here chasing the thing up into Canada or someplace."

"First, you're about ten days too late for that," Luke said. "There've been people all over this mountain looking for the sasquatch. And second, nothing short of an act of Congress or a Presidential decree gives you or anyone the right to restrict access to public property. Now, can I please see some ID?"

"Okay," the man said. "I see we've gotten off on the wrong foot. My name is General David Foster. I've done four tours of duty in Iraq and Afghanistan. My little battalion here is made up of former service men and women who are all believers in bigfoot. We just want to be left alone to do what we have trained to do."

Luke was starting to get a little pissed.

"I thank you for your service, general, but until I see some identification, your group won't be doing any looking for bigfoot. And if one of your people tries to stop anyone else from driving this road, he or she will be arrested."

"We have every right to be camping here," Foster said.

"Yes, you do. But you have no right to stop others from doing the same thing. Now, please, give me some identification."

"Why do you need to see my identification? I've told you who I am."

"Yes, you have, but for all I know, you are an escapee from the state penitentiary in Walla Walla, or wanted for murder in who knows where."

"Do I look like a murderer?" Foster said.

"No, but neither did Ted Bundy. Now, ID, or I'll have to arrest you."

"For what?"

"Hindering an investigation, for starters."

"What are you investigating?"

"The killing and mutilation of domestic animals and killing a game animal out of season."

"What? You think a person killed those animals and put them in the trees?"

"Yes, I do," Luke said. "And it was most likely a paramilitary group looking for publicity who did it."

"It certainly wasn't us," Foster said. "It was bigfoot."

"So, what will it be, General? Show me some ID, and I'll get out of your hair."

Again, the man just stood and stared at Luke. Finally, he pulled his wallet out of his back pocket, slid a driver's license out of a slot, and handed it to Luke.

Luke looked at it for a second, saw that the license was for a David Foster of Temecula, California, made sure the photo matched the man in the sunglasses, and then said, "I'll be right back."

He went to his truck and radioed the license information in to dispatch so it could be run for any outstanding warrants. A couple minutes later, Luke received a call back on the radio telling him that there were no warrants. He stepped back out of the truck, walked over to Foster, and handed the man's license back to him.

"Here you go, sir," Luke said. "Now. No more stopping people on this or any roads on public lands. Do you understand?"

"Yes," Foster said. "We'll just have to put up with the looney tunes who have no idea what they are doing."

That was the pot calling the kettle black if Luke had ever heard it.

"I'm not kidding here," Luke said. "We'll be up here checking on you. Everyone needs to just play nicely."

"We're not playing, officer," Foster said. "There is a bigfoot around here someplace, and my group and I intend to find it."

"Well, good luck to you, and just a reminder—you can only camp on Forest Service lands for two weeks. Federal law. So, hope you find it before then."

The general just stared at Luke as he walked back to his truck, fired up the rig, and pulled out of the makeshift campground. During the whole discussion with the general, Luke noticed the rest of the battalion scurried around taking care of getting the tents ready to inhabit.

As Luke drove back down the road, he ran into the red-bearded corporal in the combat helmet and the dog-loving Donovan walking up the road. Luke stopped and rolled his window down.

"You need a lift back to camp?" Luke offered.

"No, sir," Masters said, not even looking at Luke as he kept walking.

Donovan, Luke thought, would have accepted the mile ride back to the camp.

As Luke started to drive away, he was pretty sure he heard the corporal say "asshole."

CHAPTER 26

In the days that followed, the search for bigfoot started losing a little of its luster. People filtered out of the mountains and headed back to wherever they had come from. Either because they had to get back to work after using up all their vacation time or because they were growing weary.

Most of the media members had moved on even earlier. Other stories, like the United States shooting down another Chinese weather balloon with a four-hundred-thousand-dollar sidewinder missile, had become the hot stories. The search for bigfoot was becoming old news.

Maybe by coincidence, or maybe not, another potential bigfoot kill was discovered two days after Luke had had the run-in with General Foster and the bigfoot brigade. A dead coyote was found fifteen feet off the ground, impaled on a tree branch near the boat launch at Clear Lake.

An alert angler at the popular lake near White Pass noticed

some ravens hanging around near the trunk of a pine tree and spotted the coyote stuck on the branch. The angler called 911 who patched the call through to the sheriff's office, who then called the Department of Fish and Wildlife office, who called Luke.

"Got an interesting call for you," said Gloria Hernandez, the receptionist at the Region 3 WDFW office.

"Can't you call Hargraves?" Luke asked, only sort of joking.

"I think you'll want it," Hernandez said. "They've found another potential bigfoot kill."

She told Luke about the call and gave him the contact information for the man who had called it in.

"I know where he is," Luke said. He had been to the boat launch at Clear Lake a thousand times. "Would you mind calling him back and letting him know I'm on the Yakima River, so I won't be there for an hour or more? And ask him to stay away from the tree, and maybe try to keep others away too if he can. I don't need a bunch of footprints around the tree."

"I'll tell him," Hernandez said.

It didn't do any good. When Luke arrived, there were about twenty people standing around the base of the tree, gawking up at the dead coyote skewered on the branch.

"Ah geez," Luke said to himself when he pulled up and saw the crowd of people.

As he was parking, an older gentleman walked up to the truck, and as Luke was getting out of the pickup, the man said, "I'm so sorry, officer. I tried to keep people away, but they just kind of laughed at me and went over there and looked anyway."

"Well, thanks anyway, Mr. . . . ?" Luke said. He hadn't written the man's name down, thinking he would remember it and now he couldn't.

"Nelson. Larry Nelson."

Nelson was maybe eighty, or he could have been ninety, but he was in great shape for however old he was. The man wore a bucket hat over his ears, shading his eyes, and, even though the temperature was pushing seventy degrees, he had a coat on.

"Thanks for trying, Mr. Nelson. I'll go shoo them away. And thanks for calling it in."

As they walked over to the crowd at the tree, Nelson told Luke how he had spotted the coyote. Luke asked the people to move along, and most of them did. A few lingered a short distance away and watched Luke work.

"Did you happen to notice any footprints around when you first walked over here, Mr. Nelson?"

"I really wasn't looking down," Nelson said. "I was looking up at the coyote. It's not every day you see a coyote stuck in a tree like that."

Luke still checked around, but the ground was trampled with footprints of all shapes and sizes. He looked up at the tree to see if anyone might have leaned a ladder against it, possibly leaving some marks, but found none. He searched in a ten-yard circle around the tree and again found nothing.

"Does anyone happen to have a ladder in their rig?" Luke asked the looky-loos.

"I do," a younger man said.

"Can I borrow it for a couple of minutes?" Luke asked.

The man said "sure" and walked over to a white panel van that had **VALLEY PAINTING** in big bold letters on the side with a paintbrush at the bottom of the letter "g" like it was just finishing painting it.

Luke took photos of the coyote on the branch as the painter brought the ladder over to the tree.

"You want me to run up there and get that thing down for ya?" the man asked.

"If you'd like," Luke said.

The man wrestled the ladder into place, ran up the rungs, grabbed the coyote, pulled it off the sharp branch, and dropped it to the ground.

"Thanks a bunch," Luke said as the painter took the ladder down and hauled it back to his van.

The coyote had no visible injuries except for the hole in its side where it had been impaled on the branch. Unlike the other three animals that had been found in the trees, the coyote's neck wasn't broken. At least, Luke didn't think it had been broken.

Had the coyote been alive when it was skewered on the tree? Having a sharp branch run through the vital organs would certainly be enough to kill any animal. But wrestling a live coyote up that high to get it on the branch, with enough power to run the branch into its chest cavity, would be almost impossible. Luke knelt and inspected the animal and shook his head as he thought about what had happened.

"Maybe someone shot it with a high-powered rifle," a different man said from the few people still standing around and watching. "And then used the bullet hole as the place to stick it on the branch."

Luke hadn't thought of that. He rolled the coyote over but found no wound that would indicate the bullet had gone through the animal. Surely, a bullet from a high-powered rifle would pass all the way through.

"No exit wound," Luke said to the man.

"There are bullets that will splinter into pieces upon impact and not leave an exit hole," the guy said.

Luke had read about frangible bullets but had never used them. As he remembered from the magazine article, the bullets had soft lead cores surrounded by thin metal jackets. The design made the bullets incapable of staying in one piece on high-velocity impacts.

"I shoot them at coyotes all the time," the guy said. "Better for selling the hides. There's never an exit wound. There'll be some bullet fragments in the body cavity and meat, but no exit hole."

"Thanks," Luke said to the guy. "We'll do an autopsy, and that should tell us if that's the case."

"I'd bet on it," the guy said. "Otherwise, how would anyone get a live coyote up on that branch? It would be like trying to stuff a wildcat into a gunnysack with all kinds of biting and squirming."

Luke had never tried to put a wildcat in a gunnysack, but he imagined the man was correct. He picked the coyote carcass up by the back legs and carried it to his truck. As he walked past the painter and the bullet expert, Luke thanked them for their help.

"No problem," the bullet guy said. "This was way better than fishing. The trout weren't biting anyway. And now I can tell everyone I saw where bigfoot stuck a coyote in a tree."

"I highly doubt it was bigfoot," Luke said.

"I doubt it too because I have never heard of bigfoot shooting anything," the bullet guy said. "But this will be a good story, and there are a bunch of people out there who will believe this is the work of sasquatch. That dude on TV, Crenshaw somebody, he'll be all over it. And then we'll have the nuts back out here stirring things up again."

"I hope not," Luke said. "But what can you do?"

The bullet guy just shrugged and then said, "It was killed by a frangible bullet."

✳

On his way back into town, Luke stopped at his house, dragged the coyote to a picnic table, threw a piece of plywood on the table, and put the dead canine on it. He wanted to take a quick look inside the animal to see if the bullet guy was right. If the coyote had been shot with a rifle, then it would confirm his and many other people's suspicions that bigfoot had nothing to do with at least this one. Unless, like the man said, bigfoot had become proficient with a hunting rifle and was now shooting animals.

As soon as Luke pulled the coyote into the backyard, Jack wandered over to see what was going on.

"Hey, boy," Luke said. "Sorry to bother you, but I need to get into this coyote and see what killed it."

Jack sniffed the coyote for a minute and then wandered over to a bed that was in the shade and curled up on it.

"Not interested, huh?" Luke said to the yellow dog as he started to make a cut to remove some of the fur and skin around the hole in the coyote's side.

The puncture hole was larger than a rifle bullet hole, but Luke believed the skin could have torn when it was shoved onto the branch. A bullet hole certainly could have been there first and used as a pilot hole.

Next, he cut into the body cavity of the animal and pulled the entrails out. That would give him a clear look at the other side of the hole in the coyote and let him check for bullet splinters. Luke first found a couple metal fragments on the inside of the wound next to a broken rib. Then, as he looked at the coyote's lungs, there were more lead and metal fragments. The coyote had been killed by a rifle shot.

Luke took photos of the places where he'd found the fragments and then bagged up the heart, lungs, liver, and other organs. Then he loaded the carcass and parts back into his truck.

He would send it all to the lab in Oregon, so they could confirm what he found. They would probably be ticked at him for doing what he did, but Luke had to confirm what he, and the coyote hunting bullet guy, suspected.

*

"Another one, huh?" Sara said as they were eating dinner that evening.

It was Luke's turn to cook, and he had barbecued elk burgers from the spike bull he had shot the previous fall.

"Yep, but I know for a fact that bigfoot had nothing to do with the coyote," Luke said.

He explained about getting the call about the animal in the tree and the discussion with the guy at Clear Lake about the coyote being shot with a special bullet.

"He was right," Luke said. "I may have figured that out on my own at some point, but he really made me think."

"You think the other animals died that way?" Sara asked.

"No, I don't. The lab would have found bullet fragments in the doe we sent down there. And the dog and the goat, well, I guess they could have been shot, but why would someone, or something, break their necks too."

"Maybe they were just wounded, and their necks were broken to finish them off."

"Could be, I guess," Luke said. "But I just don't think so. I looked their bodies over pretty closely when I took them down from the trees and I found no other wounds or marks."

"Can you get another look at the goat or dog?"

"If I had to. I know the lady was going to bury her goat on her place. I assume it is still there. I'm not sure what the man did with his dog."

"Could this coyote be some kind of a copycat deal?" Sara asked. "You know, to get some more attention from the media."

"I've been thinking about that," Luke said. "In fact, I'm wondering if all the animals in the trees were staged for just that purpose."

"That would be hard to prove with so little evidence," Sara said. "But if you're still coming down on the side of there not being such a thing as bigfoot, then it has to be a person. So, who benefits?"

"Cliff Upshaw does. He's now a household name from being all over the news. Hargraves said he saw him on *Extra* the other night, and someone said he's been asked to be a guest on the Jimmy Kimmel show."

"I've never met the man," Sara said. "But he doesn't seem like he'd be capable of placing the dead bodies in the trees. Isn't he kind of soft and fleshy?"

"He's a big man, but not in very good shape from what I can tell. Someone like that could hire the dirty work done if he knew it would benefit his cause."

"What about that militia guy you were telling me about that has his force of bigfoot people camping up in the forest?"

"I can't see what would be in it for him. I don't think he's a publicity hound like Upshaw. He's definitely a bit of a kook, but he doesn't seem to be after anything other than commanding a force of followers. Besides, he and his little army showed up as all the hubbub was dying down."

"One of his underlings could have come in here a couple of weeks ago and started the process with the dog and deer."

"Could be," Luke said. "Just doesn't seem like it fits."

"So, what are you going to do?"

"I'll talk to Captain Davis again and see if he has any thoughts. Maybe he wants me to be spending my time on something more productive. I'm not sure what I'll do if he wants me to keep looking."

He looked at Sara. She certainly was beautiful. And smart.

"What would you do?" he asked.

"I'd probably go back to the beginning. Start with the guy who lost his dog and the people you talked with there and see if you missed anything. Run down the birdwatchers, and the goat lady, and even talk to Mr. Stennett. Have another chat with the general. Something might break loose."

"I'm going to talk to the captain first," Luke said. "Now, let's go take Jack for a walk to the river."

CHAPTER 27

Luke was on his way to the office the next morning when he took a call from James Dover, the reporter from *The Yakima Herald*.

"Hey, James," Luke said after prompting the Bluetooth in his truck to answer the call.

"We received a call yesterday about another dead animal, a coyote, found impaled on a branch. Is that true?"

"Yes, up by Clear Lake off Highway 12. Who called you?"

"Person didn't leave a name."

"When did you get the call?"

"Two o'clock, or around there. I didn't get the message until later, and already was on another story, so I couldn't get anything in today's paper."

Luke thought about it for a second. He hadn't gotten the call from dispatch until closer to three-thirty.

"That's weird," Luke said. "I didn't know about it until later than that. Did the person say they were at the lake?"

"Didn't say. Just said there's another bigfoot kill up in the mountains. A coyote in a tree. By the sound of it, you know, the way he said it, he was someplace else. Maybe down here in town."

"We've confirmed that the coyote was killed by a high-power rifle and placed in the tree," Luke said. "So, there is a possibility the caller was the person who did it."

"That's interesting," Dover said. Luke could hear the man typing on a keyboard. "You think the same person killed the other animals?"

"We aren't sure," Luke said. "There's no evidence that the other animals were shot. But the coyote definitely was. And we certainly don't think it was killed by bigfoot—unless the creature has now taken up hunting with a rifle."

Dover laughed as he clicked away on the keyboard and then said, "Wonder what Cliff Upshaw would have to say about that?"

"I'm sure he'd have something to say," Luke said. "Which reminds me—if you are looking for a possible story to go along with all of this bigfoot stuff, you should go talk to a guy who has set up an encampment in the mountains near Gold Creek."

Luke told the reporter about General Foster and what he knew about the bigfoot brigade.

Again, Dover laughed. "I'll talk to my editor, but that does sound interesting. We'll run something in the paper tomorrow about the coyote being a hoax. You wouldn't have any photos, would you?"

"I do," Luke said. "I'll email them to you, though they don't show much. Just a dead coyote stuck in a tree."

"Great, thanks," Dover said. "I'll look at it." And he clicked off.

*

"So, the call could have come from one of the people at the lake after the coyote was discovered," Luke was saying to Bob Davis as the two men sat in Davis's office. "But the timing seems off, and Dover said the caller didn't seem to be at the lake. The guy said the coyote was 'up at Clear Lake' like he was calling from town."

"Well, we know it was killed by someone shooting a rifle," Davis reasoned. "If that person has a hunting license, he's done nothing wrong really, as it's open season all the time on the varmints."

"But if he was the person who killed the mule deer doe, or the domestic animals, then he has broken the law, and maybe more than one."

"What else you got going right now?" Davis asked.

"Just my normal patrols. And, as you know, this is kind of downtime, what with no hunting seasons going on."

"Keep after this bigfoot thing a bit longer," Davis said. "As time allows. It would be nice to figure it out." Then he said quietly, "If that Upshaw fella isn't involved in all of this, I'll eat your hat."

"I kind of think the same thing," Luke said. "But nothing— other than the fact that he shows up out of the blue and becomes the media bigfoot darling—says he is."

"Keep looking," Davis said as he stood up, signifying the discussion was over.

"Will do, Cap," Luke said, heading for the door.

*

After going to his desk and checking his notes to make sure he had contact information for Jerome Martin, the man whose dog was found in the tree; Bill Hoyt, Martin's neighbor; Ruth Rogstad, the leader of the birdwatching group; and April Sommers, the goat lady, Luke headed to his truck.

Since he had no idea where Rogstad lived, he decided he would call her first.

"Hello?" the older woman's voice crackled.

"Ms. Rogstad, this is Officer McCain. I met you up on the trail when you found that deer in the tree."

"Yes, officer," she said. Then Luke heard her quietly shush someone and say, "It's that tall game warden, Lucas McCain." He heard several high-pitched voices and one gravelly low voice all start murmuring. "I'm with the ladies, and we're about to head up to Cleman Mountain and look around. Someone reported seeing a northern saw-whet owl up there, but Mona, who is our resident expert on owls, says it is probably bullshit, pardon my language."

When Rogstad said "bullshit," Luke heard the ladies all start tittering.

"Well, you had better look for yourselves," Luke said. "Because you never know. Listen, I'm headed up that way myself. Do you think I could meet you and the ladies someplace? I just want to ask a few more questions. It will only take a couple minutes."

Rogstad mumbled something to the women, Luke heard a few more titters, and then she was back. "Officer McCain, that would be fine."

They decided they would meet at the café in Naches in half an hour.

Since he was going to be headed that way, Luke called Martin and Hoyt. Martin's phone went right to voicemail. Luke left a short message and then tried Hoyt. He answered on the fourth ring.

"Bill Hoyt," Hoyt said.

"Mr. Hoyt, Luke McCain, with the Department of Fish and Wildlife. We spoke three weeks ago when your neighbor's dog was killed."

"Yes, officer. What can I do for you?"

"If you are at home, I'd like to stop by for a minute. I have a couple more questions about what you heard the night your neighbor's dog disappeared."

"I'm not home now, I'm at work, but I'll be home around six."

"Okay if I stop by then?"

"Sure," Hoyt said. "But I don't know what else I can tell you."

"I tried to call Mr. Martin, but he's not answering. Have you seen him around at all?"

"I don't really pay attention to what he's up to. But I can tell you that I haven't heard his other dog howling at night. Maybe he's gone somewhere."

"Did his other dog show up?"

"I assumed it was his other dog. I've heard some barking once in a while over that way."

"Okay, thank you. I'll see you at six."

✱

When he pulled into the café parking lot, Luke spotted the black Chevy Suburban that had been parked at the trailhead up on Bethel Ridge. He looked through the window and saw the four members of the birdwatchers hiking group sitting at a round table. He parked, shut the truck off, climbed out, and walked in.

"Hello, officer," Doris Engle, the woman with the low gravelly voice, said to Luke. "Come sit down."

Luke took a seat, and the tall woman with the dyed red hair, Rogstad, said, "Can we buy you a cold drink?"

"No, I'm fine, thanks," Luke said. "I just have a couple of questions."

The questions Luke asked were the same he had asked when they had met on the trail. He almost felt stupid asking them again. Sara had suggested talking to everyone again, so that was what he was doing. He had nothing else.

The questions were the same, and the answers the same. The ladies had seen no one else on the trail, no cars parked near the trailhead, and they hadn't heard anything except for squirrels chattering and birds chirping, including the call of the mountain chickadee on their hike.

When he couldn't think of anything else, he paused and started to tell the ladies thanks when the small, white-haired Betty Harris said, "Aren't you going to ask if we've ever seen the bigfoot? That's what this whole thing is about, right?"

"Well, yes, some people believe it was bigfoot who killed that deer and put it in the tree."

"And you don't?" Harris asked.

"Well, let's just say I'm skeptical. So, have you ladies seen a bigfoot?"

"Three of us did," croaked Engle. "We were driving down from a hike we took up by Dog Lake."

"We were up there looking for a Townsend's solitaire," Rogstad interrupted.

"And a lazuli bunting," Mona Sands said.

"Anyway," Engle growled, "it was just starting to get dark, and this creature ran across the road in front of us."

"He was big and hairy," Sands said. "Running on two legs."

"Looked like a sasquatch to us," said Rogstad.

"What about you, Ms. Harris?" Luke asked.

"I was in the back seat, and Ruth's big head was in the way, so I missed it," Harris said.

The two women who weren't Ruth Rogstad tried to stifle laughs into their hands.

"When was this?" Luke asked.

The ladies looked at each other and started talking all at once. The consensus was that it had been three months ago, or somewhere in there.

"Did you call anyone to tell them about it?"

"I called Gerti Davidson," Engle growled. "But she didn't believe me."

"No, I mean the authorities. The sheriff's department, for instance."

"Like they'd believe us," Sands said. "We may have mentioned it to a few friends, but they all thought we'd been drinking."

"And were you?" Luke asked.

"Maybe a little," Sands said with an innocent grin.

"I wasn't!" Rogstad exclaimed. "I was driving. I was as sober as a priest."

"I think you mean a judge," Harris said. "It is sober as a judge. Priests are always hitting the sacrificial wine."

"Yeah, like judges are sober," Rogstad said. "Old Walt Ferguson is in the bottle by ten o'clock. And if he drinks his lunch, which happens quite often, they have to cancel court in the afternoon. And besides that, it's sacramental wine, not sacrificial wine."

"It doesn't matter where it comes from," Harris said. "They

make some good wines in Sacramento but—"

"Okay," Luke interrupted, although he had heard the same thing about Judge Ferguson and about the wines from northern California. "We're a little off-topic."

He tried to nail down just where the ladies had seen the creature and asked the obvious questions about maybe it being a bear or something else that would explain it.

As the ladies chattered and argued about everything, Luke wondered how they stayed friends. By the time he walked out of the café, his head was spinning and starting to hurt.

"Goodbye, Officer McCain," Rogstad said as he was leaving. The ladies were all looking at him, and as soon as he said "goodbye," they turned to each other and tittered like a bunch of school girls.

CHAPTER 28

Luke arrived at Bill Hoyt's house at a little before six and saw the man's truck parked in the driveway. He drove up the drive and watched Hoyt come out on the front porch, a Bale Breaker beer in his hand.

"So, what's up with the hunt for bigfoot?" Hoyt asked after Luke got out of his truck.

"Pretty much the same as it is always," Luke said. "Chasing moonbeams and rumors. But I would like to find out what happened to your neighbor's dog and the other animals."

"I've thought a lot about it," Hoyt said. "And it is still a mystery to me. I definitely heard something heavy running out through the back forty there. But nothing else has come to mind."

Luke told him about the coyote in the tree and how it had died.

"Do you remember hearing any kind of gunshot or even the thump of something that could have been a rifle with a suppressor on it?"

Hoyt looked up into the sky, like he was running the whole thing through his mind again, and finally said, "No, sir. I didn't hear a thing right before the dogs went silent. They were going crazy barking one second, and the next they were not."

"Okay," Luke said. "I really don't think the other animals were shot by a rifle, but I wanted to ask."

"They had to die somehow," Hoyt said.

"We're still thinking they died from the broken necks," Luke said.

"That would be a difficult task," Hoyt said. "Unless the dogs were sedated somehow."

Luke thought about that for a few seconds. He guessed something like that might be possible.

"Hmmm," Luke said. "Now you've given me something else to think about."

Luke thanked Hoyt for his time and walked to his truck while thinking about the dog and goat bodies. He wished he had also sent them to Oregon for analysis. Maybe they could have detected some kind of sedative in the dead animals.

*

He hadn't been able to raise Jerome Martin on the phone, so Luke drove to his house. When he got there, the place was quiet. There were no cars in front of the house and no lights on or noise coming from inside.

Luke walked up to the door, knocked, and got the hollow sound of an empty house. It was so hollow, he had to look in the window to see if the furniture was still there. It was.

He walked around the back of the house, thinking he might see the German shepherd that hadn't been skewered in the tree. Buster, Luke thought. Or was it Brutus? He couldn't remember. He whistled and said, "Here, boy." But no dogs appeared.

Since he was there, Luke walked out to the back. The gate had been securely affixed back in the fence. He knew he would find nothing, but he walked all the way out to the tree where the dog had been anyway.

He looked around the tree and then scanned a full circle for as far as the landscape allowed. Over in some brush, toward Hoyt's house, he saw a flat piece of cardboard. Luke walked over and picked it up. Had it been there the day they'd found the dog? He didn't remember seeing it, but maybe a piece of cardboard wouldn't be noticed.

The cardboard was thick, like from one of those big boxes a refrigerator or some other large appliance might come in. Luke estimated it was four feet by four feet. He started thinking and walked back over to the tree and placed the cardboard right below the branch that had held the dead dog.

Luke stepped on the cardboard and then off and pulled it away. His footprints, which were obvious in the dirt a few feet away, were non-existent where he had stepped on the cardboard.

He put the cardboard back down and jumped on it, then slid it away. Still no prints. So, someone or some ones, could have stood here and left no prints. Pretty simple and definitely effective. Why hadn't he thought about that earlier?

With the cardboard in hand, he headed back to his truck. He wanted to get out to April Sommers' place and see if there were any discarded pieces of cardboard there. Unfortunately, by the time he got there, it would be dark. He'd have to leave that until morning.

When Luke jumped back into his truck, he was pumped. Maybe he was finally getting somewhere. Sara had been right. Go back to the start and work the problem again. He didn't know if the cardboard was the answer to the question of how there were no footprints around the trees where the animals had been placed, but the more he thought about it, he believed it was.

He drove off down the highway, thinking about the cardboard. Unfortunately, it was just one piece of the puzzle. How had someone been able to kill the dog and the goat by breaking their necks and then get them fifteen feet up into the tree?

Hoyt might have been on to something with the idea that sedation may have been used. He would have to check on that tomorrow too. He would call Jack's veterinarian in the morning and see what light he might shed on the situation.

Luke looked at his phone. He had enough service to call Sara.

"How's it going?" she asked when she answered.

"Great!" Luke said.

He told her about finding the cardboard and the footprints and the thought about the sedation.

"Wow, that's great. Now you need to figure out who is doing this and why."

"Bob Davis said to me this morning that if Cliff Upshaw wasn't somehow involved, he would eat my hat."

"Which one?" Sara asked. "You've got some pretty skanky hats."

"They're not that bad. But I kind of agree with him. Upshaw has to be part of this somehow."

"Well, there you go. Figure it out."

"Working on it. I'm about twenty minutes out and I'm starved. Your night to cook. Hope it is something good."

"Oh, it is," she said. "I'm taking you out!"

*

They ended up at Outback Steakhouse because their favorite place, Sea Galley, had closed. Luke wasn't wild about the spices Outback put on their steaks, but he did like their Bloomin' Onion thing. He ordered a center cut sirloin without spices, and Sara had filet mignon.

"So, you're making some headway," Sara said as they waited for their dinner.

"Yep," Luke said. "Still have some questions that need to be answered. I think I'll push on Cliff Upshaw a little and see if I can figure out how he fits into this deal. I wanted to do some looking into his organization but just haven't had the time. Is that something that maybe I could coerce Yakima's hottest FBI agent into doing for me?"

"Flattery will get you everywhere," Sara said. "I'll do some snooping around."

Their salads arrived, and then their steaks, and the conversation wandered around to other things.

"Did I tell you that the ladies of the Weekly Walking Warblers have seen a bigfoot?" Luke asked.

"Who?"

"The birdwatcher ladies. I talked to them today just to confirm they hadn't heard or seen anything else when they spotted that deer in the tree."

"That's a cute name," Sara said. "Do all hiking or birdwatcher groups have names?"

"Evidently," Luke said.

"So, what about spotting a bigfoot?"

Luke told Sara the story, leaving out some of the unnecessary details the ladies had shared.

"What do you think?" she asked.

"I'm not convinced it was a bigfoot, but they certainly were. Or, at least, three of them were. The fourth, a little lady with short white hair who was sitting in the back missed it because a much taller lady with big red hair was blocking her view."

Sara laughed at the thought of that.

"I'm sure it was just a bear. I've seen them many times stand on two legs and look around. The ladies probably saw the flash of something going across the road, and when they spotted it in the trees, it was standing on its hind legs to look back at them over a stump or something."

"Their eyesight is probably not all that good anyway," Sara said.

"And they admitted that they'd had a snort or two after their hike," Luke said.

Sara laughed again. Luke loved her laugh.

"Speaking of," Luke said. "Have you ever heard that Judge

Ferguson might have a little drinking problem?"

"Not specifically, but he has canceled several court dates and meetings that were supposed to happen in the afternoon. Why?"

"Just a rumor going around," Luke said. "None of my business really."

Luke saved a couple bites of his steak for Jack and asked for a doggie bag when the waiter came to take their plates.

"You spoil that dog," Sara said.

"And you don't?" Luke said.

"I'm just thanking him for saving you from real trouble a few times," Sara said as she pulled a napkin with a few bites of her own steak out of her lap.

*

Driving home from dinner, Sara asked if Luke would stop by the grocery store. She needed to pick something up for work the next morning. He parked, she ran in, and he stayed in the truck.

A couple of minutes after he parked, he saw Frank Dugdale come out of the store. Luke wondered if Jim Kingsbury was with him. He rarely saw one without the other. He watched as Dugdale got closer, but Kingsbury did not appear.

Luke rolled the truck window down and said, "Hey, Frank. Where's that partner of yours?"

Dugdale looked around, saw Luke, and walked over to the truck. Luke noticed the man was wearing a tan t-shirt with a big black silhouette drawing of a bigfoot on it. The creature's feet were abnormally big. Under the drawing of the sasquatch were the words, YOU KNOW WHAT THEY SAY ABOUT MALES WITH BIG FEET.

"He's playing Bingo tonight. I hate Bingo. Most boring game in the world. If I never hear another 'I seventeen,' it will be too soon."

Luke chuckled and said, "Okay. Nice shirt by the way. Looks like something Jim would wear."

"It's not esoteric enough for him. Or so he said when he saw me wearing it. Plus, you see them all over now. He likes to be original."

"Where'd you get it?" Luke asked.

"That new store there in Naches that opened next to the woodworking place a while back. They have about every bigfoot souvenir you can think of. They're doing a land-office business. Good timing on their part, huh?"

"I guess so," Luke said, thinking back to the stuff he saw being moved into the empty store in the little group of businesses right off the highway running through Naches. When was that? He would have to try to remember.

"Hearing about any good fishing?" Dugdale asked.

"I checked some guys at Rimrock the other day. They had their limits of silvers, but they are pretty small."

"Always are," Dugdale said. "But smoke 'em up, and they're danged good on a cracker. Might have to grab Kingsbury and give it a shot. Thanks."

With that, the man with three first names and a bigfoot shirt was headed to his rig. Luke wondered if the store selling bigfoot stuff would still be open. He looked at his phone. It was three minutes to eight. No, he thought, they probably wouldn't be. That would be another place for him to check out tomorrow.

CHAPTER 29

Maybe it was from eating almost a whole Bloomin' Onion, he didn't know, but Luke had awakened in the middle of the night and couldn't go back to sleep. His subconscious had been working as he digested the big meal. Then, when he was awake, his conscious mind was going hard at it too.

He tried to remember if the bigfoot store had opened before or after the first couple animals had been found in the trees. If it was before, well, someone might have had a little advance knowledge that this was all going to explode. If it was after, then some entrepreneur was smart enough and quick enough to cash in.

Luke didn't know much about the way the supply chain worked in the retail world, but even if the store had opened a week after the whole bigfoot thing started gaining traction, could they really get enough stuff shipped in for sale that quickly?

Then he started to think about the cardboard he'd found in the field behind Jerome Martin's house. Was it really that simple?

He started second-guessing himself. He would head to the goat lady's house first thing. If he found something there, or if she had found something after he had been there, then maybe he was on to something.

And he started thinking more about the big, affable Cliff Upshaw. Behind that awe-shucks exterior was there some kind of mastermind at work? He was glad Sara said she would do a little research on him and his organization.

Somewhere along the line, Luke fell back asleep, and Sara woke him as she was headed to work.

"Better get up," she said as she was walking out the door. "You have a case to solve. I'll call you if I find out anything on Upshaw."

*

Luke called April Sommers first thing. She said she would be around her place all day and he could swing by anytime. He told her he would be there in the next hour or so, loaded Jack into the back of the truck, and headed her way.

From his house, he had to go all the way across the valley and then west for twenty miles. He got caught up in what little rush hour traffic was around—people headed to work, talking on their phones, women doing their eye makeup while stopped at lights. He had lived in bigger cities, and although the traffic was getting worse around central Washington, it was nothing like in Seattle or Portland. He wondered how people who lived in those cities put up with it.

Luke did understand why folks liked living way out in the country, but he still questioned the thought process in bringing a bunch of goats out where coyotes, mountain lions, bears, and if not now, soon, wolves would be roaming around looking for something to eat. It hadn't seemed to deter Sommers.

When he pulled into her driveway, she was hauling a load of something, maybe manure, in a wheelbarrow to a big pile of lawn clippings and pulled weeds.

When she saw him, she stopped, wiped her forehead with the

back of her shirtsleeve, took some leather gloves off, and walked his way. She was wearing blue bib overalls and had her blonde hair tied back with a red bandana.

Luke climbed out, and Sommers said, "Officer McCain. Have you figured out what happened to my goat?"

"Not yet, but I think I'm getting closer to knowing who killed Sam, and why."

Sommers looked surprised that Luke had remembered her goat's name. "So, you don't think it was a sasquatch or whatever?"

"No, ma'am, I don't."

"Please, call me April," Sommers said.

"Only if you will call me Luke," Luke said as he turned and pointed to his truck. "I have my spoiled yellow Lab with me. You mind if I let him out?"

"No . . . I mean, yes. I love dogs."

Jack piled out of the truck and ran right over to Sommers. Somehow, Jack, and most other dogs and animals of all kinds, Luke believed, seemed to instantly know a good person from a bad. Within seconds, the woman was on her knees, loving on the big yellow dog.

"I know all about you," Sommers said to Jack as she scratched his belly. "You're a hero."

"Now, now, please. I have a hard enough time living with him as it is."

She wrestled and loved on Jack for another minute, and he sat there smiling with his tongue hanging out, looking at Luke as if to say, "neener, neener."

"So, my first question is, have you had any other issues with your goats? Any others gone missing?"

"None missing," Sommers said. "I've had a couple of cougars come through during the night, but as soon as the goats raise a ruckus, I turn the lights on and get out there with my rifle. They just seem to go away. The next day, I'll find their tracks out behind the pen."

"That's good," Luke said. "When I was last here, you said you were going to bury Sam. Did you do that?"

She looked at him with a strange look and said, "Yesss."

Luke told her why he was asking, about the coyote that was shot with the rifle loaded with a fragmenting bullet and the thought that maybe her goat and the one dog had possibly been sedated before they were killed.

"You want to dig him up?" she asked.

"No, not right now. But we might, at some point, need to send his remains to the federal wildlife crime lab in Oregon to see if he was sedated or shot before he was placed in the tree."

"I sure didn't hear a shot," Sommers said. "I think I would have, don't you?"

"I would think so, but some rifles now can be equipped with suppressors that knock the noise down considerably. If the goats were making a lot of noise, it might have come across as just a muffled pop or thud."

She thought about it for a minute and said, "Boy, I sure don't remember hearing anything like that."

"Okay," Luke said. "You mind if Jack and I go have another look around where we found Sam in the tree?"

"Be my guest," Sommers said.

"Did you happen to find a square piece of heavy cardboard out there after I left the last time?" Luke asked as they started walking toward the back of the place.

Another strange look. "Noooo, why?"

"It's nothing. We'll go take a look. C'mon, Jack."

He and Jack wandered around out past the goat pen and into the trees where he had found the goat impaled on the tree branch. Jack did what Jack always did. He searched around and sniffed brush, grass, tree trunks, old fence posts.

At one point, the yellow dog stopped and sniffed for some time not far from the goats. Luke went over and looked for whatever had grabbed Jack's attention and saw a very fresh cougar track in the dirt. Sommers was right—the cats were coming through this area.

Luke saw nothing unusual or out of place, but he still kicked around. Jack stopped in some knee-high grass and again kept sniffing the area. Luke assumed he'd found more cat tracks.

"Whatcha got there, boy?" Luke asked as he got close enough to see in the grass.

He looked down and saw a square piece of carpet, beige in color, maybe the indoor-outdoor kind. The carpet was soiled, but it didn't look sunbeaten or all raggedy like it would if it had spent months outdoors.

Luke picked the carpet up, carried it over to the tree where the goat had been found, grabbed a fir bow, brushed all his and Jack's tracks out of the dirt, plopped the carpet down, and stepped on it. When he pulled the carpet up, there were no tracks.

As he had done with the cardboard at the other place, he plopped the carpet down again and jumped on it with both feet. Still no footprints when he pulled the carpet away.

"Interesting," Luke said.

Jack, who was standing a few feet away looked up at Luke and, ears forward, tilted his head, trying to figure out what Luke had said.

They spent a few more minutes looking around and then walked back to Sommers' house. She was working again around the pile of debris, stirring it with a rake.

"Composting," she said when she saw Luke. "Makes for good garden fertilizer. What's that in your hand?"

"A piece of carpet."

"You found it back there?"

"Yep. Not far from the stand of trees where we found Sam."

"Huh," she said. "I'm out there with my goats fairly regularly and have never seen it before."

Luke told her about his theory that whoever had killed the dog and her goat had used the carpet and cardboard to cover their tracks.

"Who would think of that?" she asked.

"Not me," Luke said. "Or not until I found the cardboard, and now this piece of carpet."

"So, I guess that eliminates bigfoot," Sommers said. "Unless he's got access to some carpet samples."

Sommers offered Luke some iced tea, which he passed on, and they talked for a few more minutes. She asked about needing Sam's body, and Luke again said he didn't think they would need it. She told him she would hate to dig him up, but if it meant catching whoever killed him, she would go along with it.

Luke thanked her for her time and said he would call her if he learned anything new. Then he whistled for Jack, who was nosing around the goat pen. He came running and jumped into the back of the pickup when Luke opened the door. Luke climbed in the driver's seat and started the truck.

"Thanks again, April," he said out the driver's window.

She just waved, then walked over and started stirring the manure into the compost pile.

*

On the way back to town, Luke called Captain Davis and told him about the cardboard at Martin's house and the carpet they had found at Sommers' place, along with his theory on how they had been used to mask the tracks where the bodies of the animals had been found.

"That's interesting," Davis said. "At least now we know some aberration wasn't floating in and out of these places. Now we need to figure out how the other animals were killed."

"And who killed them," Luke said. "If I can figure out the who, we might also learn the how."

Luke told the captain he was still trying to find Martin to question him again, and he was planning on talking with Cliff Upshaw again too. Luke told Davis about Sara's offer to help do some background checking on the head of the Bigfoot Research Institute.

"That's great," Davis said. "The guy seems slippery, so will be hard to nail down is my guess."

"We'll get it figured out," Luke said. "I'll keep in touch."

He was headed up to Martin's place, and he also planned to go talk to the general at the bigfoot brigade camp, but his first stop was going to be at the store in Naches selling the bigfoot shirts. During his bout with insomnia, Luke was pretty sure he remembered seeing the merchandise or equipment being moved into the building just a day or two after Martin's shepherd was found in the tree.

Very weird timing. Convenient, for sure. Possibly a coincidence. Probably not.

Luke pulled into the little strip of businesses and saw that there were people coming and going from the store. The business was so new there was no permanent lighted sign on the front, only a big vinyl banner stretched across the façade above the door that read: BIGFOOT CENTRAL. In the window, smaller banners read: T-SHIRTS, TOYS, GAMES AND MORE!

He parked his truck in one of only a couple open spaces in the second row, got out, and looked around. He didn't recognize any of the vehicles parked around the place, so he went into the store.

The business was loaded with t-shirts, sweatshirts, and hats. Luke saw the shirt that Frank Dugdale had been wearing the previous night in a pile of folded t-shirts on a table. Over on one wall were two shelves full of what Luke thought were giant, hairy slippers, complete with big hairy toes. Stuffed sasquatches of different sizes were stacked in a corner, and there were racks of other shirts of various colors in the middle of the store.

A twenty-something woman with purple hair and a nose ring walked past Luke carrying a long nightshirt with the same bigfoot drawing that was on Dugdale's shirt but with the words: I SLEPT WITH BIGFOOT.

Luke looked behind the sales counter to see if he might recognize anyone. All he saw were two girls, college-age maybe, ringing up happy customers. He wandered over and interrupted one of the girls, a strawberry blonde with about a million freckles on her face, as she was selling a ball cap with the black bigfoot silhouette on the front to a fat man in a giant pair of shorts that went almost to his calf-high dark socks and an even bigger stained white t-shirt.

"Excuse me," Luke said. "Is the owner around?"

"No, he's gone to Yakima," the girl, whose name tag read Shade said. And then to the fat man, "That'll be twenty-seven dollars."

"Do you know when he will be back?" Luke asked. He wanted to call the girl Shade, like in the thing you put on a lamp, but figured her name must be pronounced Shaw-day or something, so he didn't risk it.

"No idea," said Shade, who was now handing the fat man change for a fifty.

"Can you tell me his name?" Luke asked.

The fat man turned and gave Luke an angry look.

"Jason. His name is Jason."

"Do you know his last name?"

"Geez, dude," the fat man said. "Kinda rude."

Luke ignored him, but as he looked at the guy, he wondered how he was going to get his fat head into the cap.

The freckle-faced girl was thinking about it. "I actually don't know his last name. Don't think I've ever heard it. All I know is everyone calls him Jason."

Luke thanked her, took another look at the fat guy who was still giving Luke the evil eyeball, and walked back out to his truck. There were only about five thousand Jasons around, so that didn't help. He was hoping the girl would say the owner's name was Cliff Upshaw. But that would have been too easy. He'd just come back later and hopefully catch this Jason fella.

He climbed into his truck and was watching the customers come and go from Bigfoot Central when Luke noticed a man sitting on a handmade bench in front of the woodworking place, just down from the Bigfoot store. He was a thin man with dark hair, wearing a leather apron over jeans and a striped shirt like most of the loggers around wore.

Luke climbed back out of the truck and walked over to the man.

"Pretty crazy, huh?" Luke said.

"Oh, this is nothing," the man on the bench said, still watching the bigfoot store. "You should have seen it two weeks ago right after all the national news about the bigfoot hit. I couldn't find a place to park at my own damn business."

"I'm Luke McCain," Luke said.

"Trent Scott," the man said while standing up and shaking Luke's hand.

Luke said, "Pretty amazing timing, having a bigfoot store pop up at the same time that all this bigfoot stuff got out on the news."

"Nothing amazing about it," Scott said. "I've been doing some thinking on it. This guy opens up the store with who knows how many thousands of dollars of inventory two days after a bigfoot supposedly starts killing animals and hanging them in trees."

Scott paused, still watching the store and shaking his head.

"There's no way in hell that someone can rent store space and get that much inventory ordered and delivered in that short of time. No way in hell!"

"I was kind of wondering about that myself," Luke said. "Say, do you know who Cliff Upshaw is?"

"Who doesn't," Scott said. "The guy is on TV more than that tight end for the Kansas City Chiefs who is dating that pop star chick."

"So, have you seen him at the store?" Luke asked.

"Yeah, a couple of times," Scott said. "But I'm not watching the place all the time. I'm trying to make a living too. And frankly, just having that many people coming through town hasn't hurt my business. I sold an oak bed frame and chest of drawers yesterday to some people who drove all the way here from Utah just for the chance to see the bigfoot."

"I'm wondering if Upshaw has an investment in the store," Luke said.

"I wouldn't know. I see this one dude coming and going who seems to be running the outfit, but I've never talked to him," Scott said. "I do know one thing, though."

"What's that?" Luke asked.

"Whoever owns the place is making a shit-ton of money."

CHAPTER 30

On his way up the highway to Jerome Martin's place, Luke thought about what Trent Scott had said. The bigfoot store was making a lot of money. The fat man had paid twenty-seven dollars for a twelve-dollar hat. Luke hadn't looked at the prices of the other merchandise, but the markup on the items in the store had to be incredible.

And, as Scott had indicated, there was no way the store just popped up in a few days. There had to be some planning for it all to happen like it did. Maybe months' worth. Luke was now convinced that whoever owned the store either killed the animals and put them in the trees or knew who did it and when it was going to happen.

As Luke drove west on Highway 12, he decided he would talk to Upshaw sooner rather than later. But he didn't know how to get in touch with the man. So, as he had done before, he called James Dover, the reporter at *The Yakima Herald*.

"Hey, Luke," Dover said. "Figure out who killed those animals?"

"Not yet, but I'm getting closer. You happen to know how I could get in touch with Cliff Upshaw?"

"You think he's involved?"

"Let's just say we're not ruling anyone out. In fact, did you do it?"

Dover laughed. "No, my wife has to come kill the spiders in the bathroom. I can't kill a bug, let alone a dog or someone's goat."

"There you go. I've ruled one person out. So, is Upshaw still around?"

"I'm not sure. Supposedly, he went to L.A. to do some TV stuff. I have his cell number, though."

Dover gave the number to Luke and said, "If something breaks, let me know will ya? I'd hate to think those Mensa candidates over at the TV stations would have the story before me."

Luke told him he would and thanked him for the number.

As soon as he was off the phone with Dover, Luke dialed Upshaw. The phone rang five times and went to voicemail. Luke left a message asking if Upshaw could call him back, saying he had some bigfoot questions for him.

*

Jerome Martin still wasn't home, and the house didn't look like a thing had changed since the day before. Luke again went to the back and whistled for the other shepherd, but it was quickly evident that no one was home.

Luke remembered meeting Martin's cousin or brother-in-law—some relative—the day the dog went missing, but he couldn't remember his name. He looked through his notepad where he kept names and phone numbers and couldn't find where he had written down the relative's name. He had tried to call Martin on the way up to his house, but it had gone to voicemail again. Luke hadn't left a message.

Luke started thinking. Would Martin actually kill his own dog to create all of this? If he had, it would be pretty cold. He had to think about that one some more.

Coming down from Goose Prairie, he hit the road above Gold Creek and went in search of General Foster and his troop of bigfoot hunters. Fortunately for them, none of the soldiers in the bigfoot brigade tried to stop him from driving up the road, and when he got to the camp, he saw that half of the tents were down, and people were working on dismantling the others.

Luke parked his truck and looked around to see if he could find Foster. In a minute, he spotted the man, sitting at a table, talking to the red-bearded corporal, Masters, and another man.

Luke jumped out of his truck and started toward the men when he heard a female voice say, "Where's that yellow dog of yours?"

What was the girl's name, Luke thought. Donovan. That was it.

"Hey, Donovan. What's happening here?" Luke asked as he turned to the young woman standing by some big boxes. She was in desert camo fatigues and her jet-black hair sat around her face in long, straight strands like one of those magazine models.

"We're bugging out," she said.

"I see that. How come?"

"Don't know. Just following orders to get this stuff packed up by two o'clock because we are bugging out."

"I'll go talk to the general," Luke said.

"How is your dog?" she asked. "He seems way too nice to be biting people. He wouldn't have bit me, would he?"

"No, he doesn't bite nice people, and you seem pretty nice. Jack's a good judge of character."

That made Donovan smile, and when she did, two big dimples appeared in her cheeks.

"Officer McCain," Foster barked. "How can I help you?"

Luke walked over to the general, who dismissed Masters and the other guy. Luke again thought he heard Masters say "asshole" under his breath as he walked away, but he let it go.

"Just stopped by to check and see how you all are doing and to let you know we think we know who killed those animals and put them in the trees. I am sorry to tell you that it was a person, not sasquatch."

"I've heard it all before," Foster said, waving his hand like he was shooing a fly. "That doesn't mean there isn't a bigfoot in the area."

"So, why then are you bugging out?" Luke asked.

"Because, as I feared, there have been so many people out here stirring things up, there is no way to find a track or any other clues."

Luke wanted to remind the man that he had told him that very thing the other day, but he decided against it.

"So, it's off to the next rumored sighting?" Luke asked.

"Well, yes. There was a report late yesterday of a bigfoot being seen in the Rocky Mountains near Lincoln, Montana. We're headed that way tonight."

Luke wished the general good luck, said goodbye to Donovan, and told her good luck as well. When he saw Masters, the man was staring daggers at him. He might have also mouthed the words "asshole," but his big, bushy red beard covered his mouth, so Luke couldn't tell.

*

As he was driving down the mountain, Luke started thinking about the dark-haired Donovan. She was pretty and seemed nice. What was she doing with Foster's bunch? He would have liked to spend a little time with her just to find out what her story was.

Some people might have described the bigfoot brigade as a cult. But it seemed more harmless than any cult Luke had ever heard of. At least Foster's people were outdoors, doing something they believed in. It took all kinds.

As he drove by on the highway through Naches, Luke started to pull into Bigfoot Central to see if Jason the owner had returned, but the parking lot was packed, and people were coming out with bags full of stuff. He decided he'd try to run down Jason a little later when the store wasn't so busy.

It was lunch time, so Luke went into town and stopped at the little sandwich shop. They made a really good turkey and cheese on sourdough, and today he had a hankering for it. The sandwich came with a big dill pickle and some unusual brand of potato chips that were quite good.

Luke ordered his sandwich with a Pepsi and was just sitting down when in walked Jim Kingsbury and Frank Dugdale. Kingsbury's shirt of the day was black and read in big white letters: SAVE THE MAGPIES.

"How was Bingo last night?" Luke asked.

"Pretty good. I won two regular games, one with four corners, and was one number away on the black out."

Dugdale was shaking his head.

"How much did you win?" Luke asked.

"Seven dollars," Kingsbury said. "Better than a kick in the teeth."

"I would've taken the kick to not have to sit through five minutes of that stupidity," Dugdale said. "Gawd, what a dumb game."

"What's up with the shirt?" Luke asked, nodding at Kingsbury.

"Well, it seems everyone hates magpies," Kingsbury said. "They're always trying to shoot them or trap them. I figured someone should be in their corner."

"So that's you?" Luke asked.

"At least for today," Kingsbury said with a smile.

The men asked Luke what was up with the investigation on the bigfoot killings, and he told them they were making some headway.

"I can't tell you what we know right now, for fear of running the suspects out of the country, but we are now positive it wasn't bigfoot that killed the animals and put them in the trees."

"I coulda told you that," Dugdale said.

"Yeah, but what about the story about the sasquatch that ate Tuffy Spellman's hamburger when we were elk hunting up by Kloochman Rock?" Kingsbury asked.

"That's all it is," Dugdale said. "A story."

"Well, I believe it," Kingsbury said.

About that time, the lady brought Luke's sandwich and soda over to him.

"Gee, that looks good," Kingsbury said and turned to the woman. "I'll have one just like it."

"Me too," Dugdale said. "And since you are so flush after that dynamite game of Bingo last night, you can buy for all three of us."

∗

Luke was just about back to the office when his phone rang. He looked at the caller ID and saw it was the Yakima County Sheriff's Office.

"This is Luke," Luke said after accepting the call.

"Hey, Luke. Garcia here."

"Yeah, Paul. What's up?"

"We just got a very interesting call."

"Okay . . ."

"You know that Jerome Martin guy, whose house we were at when I called you about the dog stuck in the tree."

"Yeah, I was just up at his house this morning. I've tried to reach him a few times and can't get ahold of him."

"That's just it. His mother called. She's very worried about him. She hasn't heard from him in five days, and she says he's one of those sons that calls her every night to check on her. And he didn't come to Sunday dinner, which he never misses, she says."

"That's weird. His house definitely looked like he hadn't been there in a while. What are you going to do?"

"We're going to try to ping his cell phone and see if we can get a location. Run his credit card to see if he's used it someplace."

"Maybe he's running," Luke said. "We are pretty sure someone killed his dog and the other animals to create this huge interest in bigfoot so they could sell a bunch of t-shirts and hats. He might be involved."

"Wow, killing your own dog, though," Garcia said. "That's pretty messed up."

"You remember his cousin or nephew or uncle that was there with him, helping to look for his dog?" Luke asked.

"Yeah, what about him?" Garcia said.

213

"Maybe he has a line on Martin. You remember his name?"

"Ah, geez," Garcia said. "Wasn't it Jacob or Justin? Something with a J. Maybe Jason?"

"That's it!" Luke said. "It was Jason. Jason Ball."

Luke told Garcia about the theory he'd been developing that the animals were killed to make it look like bigfoot was involved to create a media storm, bringing people here to look for the creature.

"The person or persons who killed the animals are likely the same who opened the bigfoot store in Naches. The guy who works next door said it has been crazy busy since the day they opened."

"I saw the crowded parking lot there the other day and wondered when that store opened," Garcia said.

"Here's the deal," Luke said. "I haven't talked to the owner of the store yet, but one of the sales clerks told me the name of the owner is Jason. She didn't know his last name."

"Could be him, I guess," Garcia said. "But there are Jasons everywhere. I had four on my son's little league team a few years ago. Jason B, Jason L, Jason G, and Jason P."

"Well, I intend to find out here very soon," Luke said.

"You know," Garcia said. "As I think about it, wasn't he the one who told the story about his old grandpappy finding the dead animals in the trees and the Indians told him it was the work of sasquatch? Martin said he'd never heard the story, and Ball was quick to say it was his other grandfather."

"That's right. And we sat there and bought it—hook, line, and sinker," Luke said.

"I guess his grandfather could have told him the story," Garcia said. "And Ball used the premise to spark the bigfoot explosion."

"I wonder where Martin fits into this?" Luke said. "We need to find him too."

"We're working on it," Garcia said. "When we find him, I'll let you know."

"And if Jason Ball is the owner of the bigfoot store, I'll let you know."

CHAPTER 31

A s soon as Luke arrived at the office, he went right into Davis's office and told him everything he had discovered, including his phone conversation with Garcia.

"If I was a betting man, I would say the store owner is the cousin, Jason Ball," Luke said.

"You're probably right," Davis said. "But my gut says that Cliff Upshaw is still involved in this somehow."

"I've placed a call to him but haven't heard back. The *Yakima Herald* reporter I was talking to thinks Upshaw is doing television in L.A."

"Well, if this thing blows up, and he's still down there, we'll never see him again."

"No, but I think we can pretty much destroy his image and his business if we find out he is involved. These bigfoot people are pretty serious, some of them anyway, and would hate it that a slickster like Upshaw made all of this up just for publicity and the mighty dollar."

"Any thoughts on where Martin might be?" Davis asked.

"Mexico? Miami? Someplace like that is my guess," Luke said.

"Still, wouldn't he call his poor old mother?" Davis asked.

"You'd think so," Luke said. "If he knows something about all this, he might be gone for good. Garcia said the sheriff's department is trying to track him down."

"Well, I hope they find him."

The two officers talked for a few more minutes, and then Luke headed to his desk to take care of some emails and reports. He wanted to wait until close to five to run back out to the bigfoot store. While he was at the computer, he looked up the driver's license for Jason Ball. There were seven in the Washington State Department of Licensing database. He found a Jason Ball with an address in Tieton and brought it up. The license photo showed the face of the man he had met a few weeks ago at Jerome Martin's house.

Luke made an enlarged copy of the driver's license, folded it, and put it in his shirt pocket.

*

At four-thirty, Luke's phone rang. There was no caller ID, but he recognized it as the number he had called for Cliff Upshaw.

"Officer McCain, this is Cliff Upshaw," a jovial voice boomed over the phone. "Your message said you had some bigfoot questions for me?"

"I do, but I also have a pretty interesting photo I would like to show you. Is there somewhere we could meet sometime soon?"

Luke really wanted to see Upshaw in person, and maybe the carrot of the photo that he had from Buel Stennett's trail camera would be enough.

"You do, huh?" Upshaw said. "Is it of a bigfoot?"

"As a matter of fact, it is," Luke said. "From a game trail camera. Special police photo experts say it is as real as can be."

"Interesting," Upshaw said. "I'm down in Southern California right now but plan to be back up in Washington day after tomorrow. Can we meet then?"

"That would be fine," Luke said. "I'll call you then."

"Did you want to ask me the bigfoot questions?" Upshaw asked.

"They can wait until we meet," Luke said. He thanked him for calling and clicked off.

*

The clock on his dash showed five o'clock exactly when he pulled into the parking lot of Bigfoot Central. The open sign was still flashing in the window, so Luke hustled out of the truck and to the door just in case they closed at five.

As he walked into the store, he saw there were a few people still shopping, and the same two young women were tending to the cash registers. When Shade, the blonde with all the freckles spotted Luke, she smiled and walked his way.

"I told Jason you were here earlier and wanted to talk to him," Shade said.

"What did he have to say to that?" Luke asked as he pulled the photo of Jason Ball out of his shirt pocket.

"Not much, but he only stayed a few minutes and hasn't been back."

"Is that usual for him?" Luke asked.

"Well, no, he usually is here by now, so he can take care of the money in the cash register and make sure everything is locked up."

"So, you think he'll be back?"

"I would think so, but I don't know. He said for us to just lock up at six—that's our closing time—if he's not back."

Luke unfolded the enlarged printout of Ball's driver's license photo and showed it to the young woman. "Is this the Jason you work for?"

Shade looked at it for a few seconds and said, "Yep, that's him. Looks a little older now, but that's Jason."

"Thank you, ah, I'm sorry, but how do you say your name?" Luke asked.

"It's Shaw-day. My mom thought she was being cool and spelled it this way," she said as she pointed at her name tag. "So most people just call me shade, like a lamp shade."

"Ok, well, thanks Shaw-day. If you see Jason, would you tell him I would really like to talk to him?" Luke said as he handed her his card.

"Will do," she said as she looked at his card. "Luke, or is it Loo-kay?" Then she giggled.

Luke thought it was funny too and said, "Call me whatever you'd like, but most everyone calls me Luke."

When he left the store, Luke called Garcia.

"I have a positive ID from the girl in the bigfoot store. Jason Ball is the manager of the store. And might be the owner. He wasn't there. The girl said he took off as soon as he heard I was there asking for him and hasn't returned."

"I'd really like to talk to him about where Jerome Martin might be," Garcia said.

"I ran Ball's information through the state and got an address," Luke said. "He lives in Tieton. I'm going to run out there and see if he's there."

"Holler if you find him," Garcia said. "I think I'll jump into my personal car and find a place to sit and watch the bigfoot store, see if he shows up this evening."

On the way over the hill to Tieton, Luke called Sara. "Looks like I'm going to be late getting home. So no dinner for me."

"That means no dinner for me either," Sara said with a laugh. "It's your night to cook."

Sara asked what he was up to, and he told her the full story—about Martin's mother calling, Jason Ball, his theory about the timing of the dead animals in the trees, and the bigfoot store.

"Sounds about right to me," Sara said. "I wonder where Martin is and why he would have disappeared."

"Who knows?" Luke said. "But we really need to find Ball and talk to him. He's the key to this whole deal."

"Good luck," Sara said. "Oh, I'm still checking on Cliff Upshaw, but I should have all the information you wanted by tomorrow."

Luke thanked her, apologized for the dinner situation, and told her he would be home as soon as possible.

*

It took him a couple of tries down some gravel driveways that wound through apple orchards, but Luke finally found Jason Ball's house. There were no vehicles there, and when Luke knocked on the door, it sounded as empty as Martin's house had.

Luke looked through the window. An odd assortment of furniture, nothing matching the other, sat in the living room. It barely looked lived in. He wandered around the back of the place and looked around. The lawn hadn't been mowed in a while, as some of it was eight inches high and going to seed. If he had to guess, Luke thought Ball had lived here at one time but had abandoned the place and hadn't been back.

Out past the overgrown backyard was a small wooden shed. There had been a door on the building at one time, but it was gone now. Since it was open, Luke went and stuck his head in the door. A rusty rake, two shovels, a pitchfork, and an old lawn edger sat in one corner. An old reel mower, the push kind that Luke hated to use as a kid, sat in another corner. On nails in the studs hung a garden hose, an extension cord, and a coiled-up length of yellow nylon rope.

On the lone shelf in the shed sat some assorted cans of stuff—wasp spray, rose dust, spray paint, and garden herbicides. In the middle of the bottles and cans sat a newish brown bottle of something that Luke couldn't identify. The name on the bottle's label was acepromazine.

Luke pulled his phone out, googled the name, and quickly learned that it was used by veterinarians and wildlife biologists to tranquilize animals. Learning that, he looked around the shed for a dart gun or syringes. He found none.

He took photos of the bottle of tranquilizer on the shelf and went around the outside of the small building to see what else he might find. After a five-minute search, seeing nothing more of interest, Luke went back to his truck.

If someone had used the drugs on Martin's dog and April Sommers' goat, that would answer how they were easily moved out of the yard or pen to be killed and impaled on a branch in the trees where they were found. If it was Ball doing all of this, why had he picked Sommers' goat Sam as his victim? He sat in his truck and called Sommers.

"Hello?" she answered.

"Hi, April. This is Luke McCain."

"I never get calls, so I wondered who was calling. Did you catch the guy?"

"No, but I am getting darned close. Do you know a man by the name of Jason Ball?"

There was a pause and she said, "That son-of-a-bitch. You think he did this?"

"We don't know, but from your response, I take it you know Mr. Ball."

"I dated him for a few months a couple years ago. I let him move in, and pretty soon he acted like he owned this place, and me. He was like this really nice guy, but he had a mean streak in him. I came home one time and found him out there kicking one of my goats. Said the thing head-butted him, and he was teaching it a lesson. When I finally figured out he was stealing money from me, I booted him."

"So, were you at the same place when he lived with you?" Luke asked, just to verify Ball knew where she lived.

"Yes, sir." She paused again and then said, almost to herself, "That son-of-a-bitch. You know, I almost told you about him the first time you came out and found Sam in the tree. He's the first person I thought of that could've done something like that."

"Well, we're pretty sure he's involved in this somewhere along the line," Luke said. "Let me ask you this—was he ever around when you doctored any of your goats?"

"Yes, several times. I had him hold goats for me when we needed to give them shots and stuff."

"Did you ever have to sedate them?"

"Once. One of my nannies got tangled up in a bunch of barbed wire. She was going crazy. I had some tranquilizer here, so I quickly gave her a shot, she settled down, and we were able to get her free without any more damage. I still had to take her to the vet to get her stitched up in a few places."

"Was Ball there for that?"

"Yes, he was. I don't know if I could have done that one on my own."

"Do you own a tranquilizer gun?"

"No. Never have had the need for one. You think he shot Sam with a tranquilizer gun?"

"I'm just guessing he did, but I don't know. I'm convinced now that Sam and the other guy's dog were sedated somehow." Then he asked, "Have you ever used, let me get my note here, the tranquilizer acepromazine?"

"Yes, sir. I have a bottle out in the goat shed."

"When we're done here, would you mind going out to see if that bottle is still there and shoot me a text to let me know?"

"Will do," Sommers said. And then again, quieter, to herself, "That son-of-a-bitch."

*

On his way home, Luke called Garcia and told him that it looked like Ball hadn't been home in days and that he had found some more evidence that he was involved in killing the animals. Garcia said he was going to stay and watch the bigfoot store for a couple more hours, but so far there had been no activity there.

"We need to find him," Luke said.

"We will," Garcia said.

A few minutes later, Luke received a text from Sommers.

Bottle of tranquilizer is gone. Last used two months ago. Was three quarters full then.

Luke texted back: *Thanks. I'll let you know what happens.*

A second later, Luke's phone buzzed again.

Catch that son-of-a-bitch!!!!!!!

Luke counted the seven exclamation points and thought, she is pissed.

CHAPTER 32

Garcia stayed on stakeout until ten o'clock. If he had stayed twenty-three minutes longer, he would have caught Jason Ball.

Ball drove up right in front of the store, jumped out of his Honda CRV, unlocked the door, went in and grabbed the daily receipts, and was back out in four minutes. He hopped into the small SUV and drove off into the night.

Shade had told him earlier that day that some big game warden dude had come into the store looking for him. He wasn't quite sure how they'd figured out he was involved in the death of his cousin's dog or April Sommers' goat, but they had, and now he needed to be careful.

He had been staying at his girlfriend's place for the last month, and that's where he headed now. As he thought about it, he wondered just what kind of evidence they could have on him. He had left no footprints or fingerprints.

When he'd left the game warden and the sheriff's deputy at Jerome's place the day after he'd put the German shepherd in the tree, he thought he'd been pretty convincing on the whole bigfoot story. Luckily, with a few anonymous tips to the TV stations, the bigfoot rumors took on a life of their own.

It was perfect timing for the opening of their store.

On his way to his girlfriend's, Ball called his partner.

"How'd we do today?" the man said after he answered.

"Another five-thousand-dollar day," Ball said. "Not as good as two weeks ago, but not bad."

"Maybe we need to put another animal in a tree, a sheep or something. Stir it up again," the man said.

"I don't know. That game warden figured out the coyote pretty quickly," Ball said. "And now he is snooping around the store. He was in there twice today looking for me."

"He's got nothing on any of us," the man said. "We somehow need to keep this rolling. I'm thinking it might be time to pull the suit out. Get some folks to actually see a sasquatch."

"I'm not getting in that suit," Ball said. "I have the store to run, and besides, I'm not big enough for the suit."

"I think I can find someone. We'll have to pay him. But he'll do it for enough money."

"Okay, let's think about it," Ball said.

The two men talked a while longer, and Ball said, "I think they are looking for you too. Are you coming back?"

"At some point," the voice on the phone said. "You know where some sheep might be? A sheep would be good."

"I'll think about it," Ball said and hung up.

✳

Luke was waiting at Bigfoot Central at nine o'clock when Shade and the other girl who worked behind the counter showed up for work.

Shade pulled some keys out of her purse, unlocked the door, turned on the lights and the open sign, and walked to the counter.

Luke walked in a minute later.

"Hey Loo-kay," she said with a giggle when she saw him. "What's up today? Still looking for Jason?"

"Yes, we REALLY need to talk to him," Luke said. "Did he come back last night?"

"Let me check," Shade said as she opened the small safe bolted to the floor underneath the counter. "Money's gone from yesterday, so yep, he came through here at some point."

Luke saw her open an envelope full of ones, fives, tens, and twenties. She pulled the bills out, split them in half, and put them in the two registers on the counter.

"Looks like you're all set for the day," Luke said. And then he leaned in closer to the young woman and said, "You mind if I ask kind of a personal question?"

Shade giggled, and it looked to Luke like all the freckles on her face went just a little darker red. He guessed it was her way of blushing.

"Any idea how much money this place is making?" he asked quietly.

Luke could see a flash of disappointment on her face. Like she was thinking he was going to ask her out for drinks. Then, just like that, the look was gone.

"I can't really say," she said. "Jason would kill me."

"I won't tell a soul where it came from," Luke said. "It's just for me."

She thought about it for a few seconds and then leaned even closer to Luke and started to whisper. "I counted the receipts last night. Jason always has me do it on nights when I close. There was just over four thousand nine hundred dollars in sales yesterday."

"Wow!" Luke feigned disbelief.

Shade looked left and then right, like someone might be hiding in the pile of stuffed bigfoots and trying to listen in, and said, "That's nothing. When the news of the bigfoot first came out, we had several days over fifteen thousand."

"No! Really?" Luke said.

"Really," Shade said.

Luke thanked the young woman for her time and repeated that they desperately needed to talk to her boss as soon as possible.

"Has someone died or something?" Shade asked.

"No, nothing like that," Luke said as he was walking out the door.

Back in his truck, Luke called Garcia and told him that Ball had shown up at some point in the night and collected the money from the bigfoot store.

"Dang it," Garcia said. "I should have stayed longer."

"You going to watch the store tonight?" Luke asked.

"I can't," Garcia said. "I'm supposed to be in Seattle later today for some medical tests."

"You okay?" Luke asked.

"Yeah, my family has this deal that hits some of the Garcia clan but not others. The University of Washington wants to hook me up to a bunch of machines to see what's going on."

"Let's hope they don't do a brain scan—they might not find much there," Luke said.

"Very funny," Garcia said. "So, you want to watch the store, or should I get Williams or one of the other deputies to do it?"

"Don't get Williams," Luke said. "He can't even stay awake during the daytime. He'd fall asleep, for sure, and we'd miss Ball again. I'll plan on doing it tonight."

"Okay," Garcia said. "Unless they find that I'm dying or something, I can do it tomorrow night."

"Good luck with the tests," Luke said. "I'll let you know if I catch up with Ball."

Luke left the bigfoot store and walked over to the grocery store. He bought a bottle of Coke, a bottle of 7-Up, a bottle of water, and a bottle of Pepsi. He would never admit it to anyone, but he also bought a pack of Hostess cupcakes. It was the junkiest of junk foods, but sometimes he just needed something like that. He'd done his workout this morning—he could afford the calories.

As he drove back out to Jason Ball's house, Luke ate the cupcakes and drank the Pepsi. He had other plans for the Coke, 7-Up, and water.

He had no idea if Ball would try to sedate another animal, but it wasn't beyond the realm of possibility, especially if the bigfoot craze started to wane. Luke thought he might save some poor animal's life if he switched out the brownish-colored acepromazine with a mixture of sodas that matched the drug's color.

When he arrived at the house, he again checked for any sign of life around the place. Finding none, he went back to the shed, put rubber gloves on, dumped the water out of the water bottle, and poured the acepromazine into the empty water bottle. Then he shook up the bottles of Coke and 7-Up and opened the lids slowly to let the carbonation out. He poured some of each soda into the brown medicine bottle. The concoction wasn't a perfect match in color, but it was close enough. Someone in a hurry, working in the dark, would never tell the difference.

That done, Luke set all the bottles down on a cement block he found nearby and took some photos to document what he had done. When he grabbed the block, he noticed the imprint in the grass where another block had recently been removed.

After taking some photos, Luke carefully placed the brown medicine bottle filled with soda pop back on the shelf, picked up the other bottles, and headed to the truck.

Back on the road, on his way to the office, Luke called Sara and told her that she wouldn't have to fix dinner because he was going to be watching the bigfoot store. He was going to stay all night if he had to.

"I have some information on Cliff Upshaw," Sara said.

"And?" Luke asked.

"He is six years behind in paying his federal income taxes. Some years he has claimed no income at all. His organization seems to be funded totally by donations. Not surprisingly, he made a ten-thousand-dollar payment just two days ago to the IRS to cover some of the taxes and penalties. If he hadn't paid them by the end of the month, he would have been headed to prison."

"Isn't that convenient?" Luke said. "Wonder where that money came from?"

"Oh, I'm sure some of the news shows paid for his appearances," Sara said. "So you can't say he got the money from the store. On the other hand, he sure could have."

Luke told her about his talk with Shade, the bigfoot store clerk, regarding the money the store had made during the last month.

"But other than the neighbor seeing Upshaw walk into the store a couple times," Luke said, "there is no real connection between him and Ball."

Luke decided not to tell her about his little change-out with the tranquillizer, or his breakfast of a Pepsi and Hostess cupcakes.

✳

Back at the office, Luke again met with his captain to bring him up to speed.

After Luke explained everything, Davis said, "I think we have enough to get an arrest warrant for Ball. It's not enough for Upshaw, though."

Luke agreed. He was happy the captain wanted to try to get the warrant for Ball.

"I'll send it over to the judge right away. I'm guessing we'll have the warrant by this afternoon."

Luke wondered if the judge Davis was contacting was Judge Ferguson but didn't say anything.

"Sounds good," Luke said. "If we could get approval to get into Ball's phone and computer, we might be able to figure out if he conspired with Upshaw to make all of this happen."

"I'll ask," Davis said. "And I'll let you know as soon as we have the warrant."

"I'm going to be watching the bigfoot store from my Toyota tonight," Luke said. "He'll come for the cash receipts at some point."

Luke told the captain about setting up the meeting with

Upshaw for the next day.

"If we have Ball by then, maybe we can get him to turn on Upshaw for leniency."

"We'll see how it goes," Davis said. "Good luck tonight."

CHAPTER 33

The body of Jerome Martin was found about the time Luke and Davis were meeting. Martin's bloated body had floated into the bay where the Yakima Valley Boat Club has their marina on Rimrock Lake. A couple of anglers were headed out of the marina to try for some kokanee and spotted something big floating near the shoreline. As soon as they saw it was a body, they called 911.

It took an hour for the deputies and EMT crews to get the body to shore. When they did, they pulled the wallet out of Martin's back pocket and figured out there had been a missing person alert out on him. One of the deputies knew Garcia had been helping to find the man and called him.

Garcia told them he was in Seattle and to expect to see Officer McCain from the Department of Fish and Wildife. "He's working a case, and Jerome Martin was involved in it somehow," Garcia told the deputy.

Garcia hung up and then called Luke.

"You'll never guess who washed up on shore at Rimrock Lake?"

"I don't know . . . bigfoot?"

"No. Jerome Martin."

"What? How'd he die?"

"Not sure. I guess they're thinking drowning right now, but they haven't really looked at the body."

"I'm headed that way now," Luke said. "Tell them I'm coming."

"Already did," Garcia said. "How weird is this?"

"It's weird," Luke said. "Hey, did they find your brain?"

Garcia hung up on him.

Luke ran in, told the captain what Garcia had just told him, and said he was on his way up there.

*

Luke rarely went anywhere with his lights flashing and siren blaring, but this called for a little extra speed, so he ran with lights and noise. As he drove, he wondered who would want Martin dead. And why. It must have something to do with the bigfoot sightings, Jason Ball, the store, and Cliff Upshaw. It was too much of a coincidence to not be connected.

Martin could have committed suicide. But how likely was it he would do it by jumping into Rimrock Lake? He had to have been murdered. And if that was the case, Ball and/or Upshaw had to be the prime suspects.

If he was right in his belief that Ball was killing the animals to set all this up, could it be that far of a stretch to think he might kill his cousin? April Sommers said Ball had a mean streak in him. But if Martin found out his cousin had killed his dog and confronted him about it, and was threatening that he was going to turn him in to the sheriff, would that be enough for Ball to kill him?

Had Ball been turned in and gone to jail for the crimes he'd committed to set up the bigfoot hoax, he'd lose the big sales income from the store. Many people had killed for less.

The same could be said for Upshaw. He would lose fame and

whatever fortune he was making off all this. Well, Luke thought, Upshaw would still probably be famous, but for all the wrong things.

Now they really needed to find Ball.

*

When Luke arrived at the marina, the EMTs were just putting the body of Jerome Martin on a gurney to roll it into the back of the ambulance.

Luke spotted Mark Williams, one of the longest-tenured deputies in the sheriff's office, standing near the body and EMTs.

"Hey, it's the rifleman," Williams said when he saw Luke.

Luke had asked Williams a dozen times not to call him that, but it never did any good, so Luke now just ignored him.

"Can I get a look at the body?" Luke asked.

"Sure," Williams said. "We found a bullet hole in the middle of his back, so he either died from that or was wounded so badly he couldn't swim and drowned. The coroner will have to make that call."

Luke went over to the body. He remembered Martin standing on the front porch of his house, wanting to know what killed his one dog and where his other dog might be.

Luke asked the EMTs if they could roll the body over. It was hard to tell in the wet shirt Martin had on, but the bullet hole looked small. To Luke, it looked like it was a smaller-caliber rifle.

"Probably a .223," Williams said. "Or maybe a .22-250. There was no exit, so the bullet is still in there somewhere."

"I wouldn't count on it," Luke said. "At least not an intact bullet."

"What do you mean?" Williams asked.

Luke told him about the coyote they'd found in the tree near the boat launch at Clear Lake and how the animal had been killed by a high-powered rifle, probably a .223. He explained how the frangible bullet had broken up at the point of entry, sending tiny shards into the canine's lungs and other vital organs.

"You think that's what happened here?" Williams said, pointing at the body.

"I'd bet on it," Luke said. "But, like you said, we're going to need the coroner to determine that."

He really wanted to take three minutes and dig into the hole in Martin's back to see if he could find any fragments, but doing something like that would get him severely reprimanded and maybe fired. He would just have to wait.

That didn't mean he couldn't use the information on Jason Ball when the time came.

The EMTs were just pushing the gurney into the ambulance when Luke noticed something sticking out of the leg of Martin's pants.

"Hold on," Luke said and walked back over to the body on the gurney. "What's that?"

Williams asked one of the other deputies there who was wearing rubber gloves to come over to lift the pant leg. Around Martin's ankle was a small length of yellow nylon rope. A frayed end was just poking out of the hem of the dead man's pant leg.

"I'll be damned," Williams said.

"If you are going to sink a body with a leg tied to a concrete block, you'd best use some quality rope," Luke said, pointing to the end of the rope.

He immediately thought of the concrete block he had found in the back of Ball's house, the one he had used to set the bottles on for the evidence photo. Then he remembered the imprint of the recently missing block.

As Luke thought about the stuff in Ball's shed, he was certain he had seen a coil of yellow nylon rope hanging on the nail there. He couldn't match the block pattern, if it was a concrete block that had been tied to Jerome Martin, because it was now at the bottom of Rimrock Lake. But he believed a good forensic scientist could match two pieces of nylon rope. Ball's house would be his next stop.

Luke stood with Williams and watched the ambulance pull out of the marina and drive off down the road.

"Such a stupid thing to die over," Williams said. "All this bigfoot stuff."

"It's more than bigfoot," Luke said. "It's all about the money."

"Probably," Williams said. "It usually is."

*

As Luke drove back to Yakima, this time obeying the speed limits with no lights or sirens, he thought about everything. The pieces were falling into place. He believed he had figured out how the animals had been sedated. And he thought he knew how whoever killed the animals had left them in the trees without leaving any prints. But he had yet to figure out how the animals got placed so high in the trees.

There were only two logical answers, Luke thought. The person had either taken a ladder with him, or there were two people, one sitting on the shoulders of the other to lift the animal into the tree.

He tried to picture that scenario. If it had happened that way, the bottom person would have to be big. Really big. Someone of at least Luke's height, and strong enough to lift a man on his shoulders along with the weight of a ninety-pound animal.

The first person who came to mind was Cliff Upshaw. The bigfoot expert was at least as tall as Luke and weighed 350 pounds, maybe more.

Put a man of Jason Ball's size up on Upshaw's shoulders, and that person could definitely reach fifteen feet up into the tree. Lifting ninety pounds dead weight that high still would be a heck of a feat.

Luke tried to picture the chain of events the night Martin's German shepherd had ended up dead in the tree. Ball, who knew the layout of the house and the backyard, along with Upshaw, came in with a dart gun loaded with a syringe carrying a dose of acepromazine appropriate for a big dog. The dogs started barking, and although they were most likely familiar with Ball, they had never seen Upshaw before, and they got riled up.

Ball or Upshaw, probably Ball, shot the dog, and as soon as he started going down under sedation, Upshaw tore the gate off the post and then kicked the other dog to make it run off. That would have been the yelp Bill Hoyt heard. They grabbed Brutus, or Buster, whichever one it was, and dragged his limp body out to the tree. One of the men then hit the dog with something heavy, maybe a piece of steel, to break its neck.

Luke tried to picture Ball putting the dog over his shoulder and then climbing up on Upshaw's shoulders. That didn't seem right. Then he thought about the years he and his dad had shot bucks up in the Cascades. When they got one close enough to the road that they could drag the carcass to the truck and haul it to camp, they would use a block and tackle to lift the deer high enough on the meat pole so it could be skinned.

With no more ruckus coming from the dogs, the men would have plenty of time to throw a rope over a branch and rig a block and tackle to lift the weight of the dead dog. Then, after cutting a small pilot hole in the dog's side, Ball could swing the dog on the rope, and jam it on the sharp branch while sitting on Upshaw's shoulders.

That worked.

Luke thought some more. Hoyt said he'd heard heavy footsteps run by near the fence between his place and Martin's. Could that have been Upshaw running back to his truck for the block and tackle? Seemed logical.

Something similar probably happened with the goat at April Sommers' place. Ball knew the setup and could have just shot into the herd with the dart gun, and the goat that fell was the unlucky one to be carried to the tree.

The deer that the lady birdwatchers found was probably easier for whoever did it. Luke had always thought the doe had most likely been hit by a vehicle. One of the men probably found it next to the road, saw it wasn't too skinned up, and took it up the trail. A block and tackle would work there too, or even a ladder. A ladder could sit on a piece of carpet and not leave any marks in the ground.

In a way, it was unusual the deer had been found. Luke guessed that more than a few hikers had walked right by the dead deer in the tree. People are like most animals and don't look up for danger. But birdwatchers look up into the trees frequently.

Thinking about it, Luke wondered how many other deer or coyotes—animals that wouldn't be missing from a yard or farm—were skewered into trees around the area. Placed there in hopes someone would see them to help build the fervor over the bigfoot. He guessed there were more that had yet to be found. Some might never be found. They would just be a skeleton of bones stuck on a branch forever.

Then he started thinking about Martin. What had happened? Luke could come up with at least three scenarios where Ball could have shot his cousin. Ball may have owed him money, and Martin wanted to be paid back. Or Martin found out Ball killed his dog and was going to turn him into the authorities. Or Martin was having an affair with Ball's lady. He could probably come up with a few others if he thought about it a little longer.

Luke could only think of one reason that Upshaw would have killed Martin. If Martin found out that the bigfoot expert was a fraud, and he was going to let the media or cops know about it, Upshaw might have shot him.

When Garcia returned from Seattle, he would chat with him. The murder of Martin was not Luke's investigation. All Luke needed to do was figure out who had killed and mutilated the domestic animals and killed the deer and coyote. There could be some other charges, such as wasting game meat and a couple of others, but he wasn't trying to find the murderer.

CHAPTER 34

On his way home, Luke made one more stop at Bigfoot Central and chatted with Shade for a few minutes. She told Luke she had not seen Jason all day, but he had called.

"Did he ask if I had been in looking for him again?" Luke asked.

"Why, yes, he did. What's his deal with that?" she asked. "You seem like a perfectly nice guy."

"Most people think so," Luke said, smiling.

"I told him you just needed to talk to him, you know. Like it's no big deal."

"Well, thanks for that," Luke said. "Do you happen to know what kind of a car Jason drives?"

"Yeah, it's a gray Honda," Shade said. "Like a smaller one. A XKG or a CJ5 or something like that."

"A CRV?" Luke asked.

"Yeah, that's it. I think. It's a little one. I rode in it once. Not very big."

"Okay, thanks Shaw-day," Luke said. "I guess I will just keep coming by to see if I can catch up with him."

"Looking forward to it," she said with a smile, then turned to help a lady who had an armful of shirts and hats.

If he didn't know any better, he might get the idea that the cute, young Shade was flirting with him. Luke was old enough to be her . . . what? Not her father. But certainly, a much older brother. He'd have to think about whether to tell Sara. She'd once threatened to shoot a woman with romantic intentions who had taken a bus from Portland to find Luke.

*

Luke's plan was to run home, grab a cooler with some drinks and a few granola bars, roust Jack, load the dog, drinks, and food into his personal Toyota Tundra, and park someplace across the highway from the bigfoot store to watch. His hope was that sometime after the store closed, Ball would come in to collect the daily receipts from the safe, and Luke would grab him.

Luke was loading the stuff into the truck when Davis called.

"We got the warrant for Ball," Davis said. "But it is just for the animal deaths. If you think he's the guy who killed Martin, that'll have to come from YSO."

"I'd say it's probably eighty percent Ball did Martin," Luke said.

He told the captain about finding the yellow rope around the dead man's ankle and the same yellow rope and missing concrete block from Ball's house. And he mentioned his thoughts about the bullet hole in Ball's back and how there was no exit wound, just like the coyote in the tree at Clear Lake. If it was a frangible bullet that killed Ball, there should be forensic evidence that matched the two.

"That's all good," Davis said. "I assume you're talking to Garcia or someone from YSO about all of this."

"Yes, sir," Luke said. "If we can arrest Ball and hold him,

then the sheriff and the county prosecutor can figure out if there's enough to pursue murder charges."

The captain told Luke to be safe and stay in touch and then rang off.

Next, he called Sara, who decided to work late after she found out Luke was going to be on a stakeout. She had heard something about a dead guy found at Rimrock Lake but hadn't known it was one of the people who'd had their animal killed and placed in the tree.

"That's not good," Sara said after Luke told her all about it. "You think this Ball could be the murderer too?"

"Probably is. Or maybe Upshaw. One of them did it is my guess."

"I'm not sure I want you out there by yourself in the middle of the night with this guy if he is a murderer," Sara said.

"I won't be by myself. Jack is coming with me. He's always good company."

"That makes me feel a little better," Sara said. "You know, I could come sit with you. I have a gun and everything."

"I'll be fine," Luke said. "This Ball is kind of a little weasel. I'm pretty sure I can handle him. And if not, Jack will back me up."

"Jack can't do anything if you are shot dead with one of those frangible bullets."

"He might bite him," Luke said. "That would show him."

"Not funny," Sara said. "I'm serious. You need to be careful."

"I'm wearing my vest," Luke said. "We'll be fine."

They agreed that Luke would text her every half hour to let her know what was going on. He decided not to mention the pretty, freckle-faced Shade. He'd do that later. Maybe.

*

It was about half past six, and Luke had just settled in across from the bigfoot store for what he figured would be at least a five-hour watch when his phone rang. He looked at the caller ID and saw it was Dover from *The Yakima Herald*.

239

"Hey, James," Luke said. "What's happening?"

"I was just going to ask you the same thing," Dover said. "I talked to the sheriff's office, and they have identified the dead man pulled out of Rimrock as Jerome Martin. They wouldn't say, but I have to assume it is the same Jerome Martin who had his dog killed, supposedly by bigfoot. That seems a little fishy."

"Don't quote me," Luke said. "But yes, it is the same Jerome Martin. And it is more than fishy. Did they tell you Martin had been shot in the back?"

"No, they wouldn't say how he died. They just said his death was suspicious. Which in sheriff speak means he didn't drown while taking a swim."

"I don't know for sure that is what actually killed him, but a bullet in the back has to be high on the list of things that might have," Luke said.

"So, it has to be related to the bigfoot deal, right?"

"I really can't say," Luke said. "But you're a smart guy. Smart people might come to that conclusion."

"Are you looking at anyone as the murderer?" Dover asked.

"I'm not doing anything on the murder investigation," Luke said. "I'm trying to find who has been killing pets, barnyard animals, and wildlife and hanging them in the trees."

"And that wouldn't be bigfoot?"

"We've pretty much ruled him out," Luke said. "So he's free to go about his business and do whatever it is that bigfoots do. Or is that bigfeet? Anyway, he doesn't need to worry about being hassled by the law."

"Can I quote you on that?" Dover asked.

"Sure. Just keep my name out of anything to do with the murder and the body at Rimrock. You need to talk to the sheriff's department folks about that."

"Did you ever get in touch with Upshaw?" Dover asked.

"Yes, thanks again for the phone number. I'm meeting with him tomorrow."

"Good luck with that," Dover said. "He kind of strikes me as slippery."

"Slipperier than a frog in a gully-washer," Luke said.

Then Luke, again off the record, told Dover about the troubles Upshaw was having with the IRS and said he might want to look into all that.

"It's pretty interesting," Luke said.

"Geez, thanks," Dover said. "I will. This is the kind of story that might get my byline in the national news."

"Just remember," Luke said. "You didn't hear it from me."

Luke's phone buzzed. He looked at it. Sara: *Where's my half hour text? Are you okay?*

While he was wrapping up the conversation with Dover, Luke texted: *I'm fine. On the phone with James Dover. Text you later.*

"Thanks again," Dover said after a little more chit-chat and hung up.

Seven minutes later, Garcia called.

"How's the stakeout going?"

"Just getting started. How'd the tests go?"

"Good. They didn't find anything, although I guess they have to do some more blood analysis. I feel fine. They just wanted to look to see if this whatever-the-hell-it-is-called is sitting in there waiting to get me. A cousin, my uncle, and my great-uncle, all on my old man's side, died from it."

"Well, that's good . . . er, I mean not good."

Since he had Garcia on the phone, Luke shared his thoughts on everything, including who might have killed Martin and why. He told him about all the evidence he had, most of it admittedly circumstantial, from Ball's shed.

"I've got the warrant to arrest him for killing the animals," Luke said. "If I can corral him tonight, you guys will have him to seriously look at for the murder."

"What about that Upshaw guy?" Garcia asked.

"We're pretty sure he's somehow involved in the animal killings, but he's been in California for several days. He may not have even been in the area when Martin was killed. I'm going to meet with him tomorrow and get a read on him."

"I've heard him talk," Garcia said. "He could sell sand to an Arabian."

"Yeah, he's got a gift," Luke said. "That's for sure."

"I'm finally out of all that Seattle traffic," Garcia said. "Should be home in a couple hours. Holler if you need me."

"Will do," Luke said. "Drive carefully."

After he ended the call with Garcia, Luke opened a bag of Doritos and a Pepsi and sat back to watch. He heard Jack's tail thumping in the back seat.

"Sure," Luke said. "Sleep away back there, but the second there is food, you're wide awake."

Jack moved forward, put his nose between the two front seats, and looked at Luke with sad, brown eyes.

"You are pitiful," Luke said, slipping the dog a chip.

*

Jason Ball, driving an older Honda CRV, pulled into the parking lot in front of Bigfoot Central at a quarter to midnight. Luke saw the car coming down the highway and watched it swing into the lot.

"Okay," Luke said to Jack. "Here we go."

Jack had been with Luke on a few of these and had intuitively learned by the tone of Luke's voice that something exciting might be about to happen. He was awake and ready to work.

As soon as he saw Ball go inside the store, Luke started the truck and pulled across the highway. He kept his headlights off so as not to alert Ball of his arrival. He parked out of sight of the windows, climbed out, let Jack out, and walked to the door.

*

Ball unlocked the door to the store and walked to the counter. He knelt, pressed the digital combination into the keypad on the safe, and opened the door. He was just starting to count the money when he thought he heard a vehicle pull up outside.

He listened for a minute and heard a car door close. Ball peeked up over the counter and saw a man walking up to the door of the store.

"Shit," Ball mumbled to himself. He reached around behind the safe and pulled out the pistol he had placed there just for this occasion. If someone was coming to steal the store money, the thief was going to have to fight for it.

*

Luke slowly walked up to the glass door of the store and started to open it.

"Get the hell out of here!" Ball's voice came from somewhere in the dark.

"State police," Luke said. "I need to talk to you, Mr. Ball."

"I don't want to talk to you," Ball said. "Get the hell out of here."

Luke's eyes were adjusting to the dark, but he still couldn't see Ball. The voice was coming from back by the sales counter, where the safe was. He slowly and quietly slipped through the door, keeping Jack at his side.

"I have a warrant for your arrest," Luke said. "Come on out."

*

"Shit," Ball mumbled again.

They were going to arrest him? For what, he wondered. Surely, they hadn't found Martin's body. He was swimming with the fishes, tied to a block at the bottom of Rimrock Lake. Must be for the animals. He thought of April Sommers. She was just smart enough and vengeful enough to point the cops at him. He'd deal with that bitch later. He had to think.

There was a back door to the store, but as far as he knew, it hadn't been used since they'd opened the business.

"Come on out," the cop said again.

If he could get to the door and slip out the back into the darkness, he could call for a ride and be gone.

243

"Stand up and show me your hands," the cop said.

That ain't happening, Ball thought.

He really didn't want to kill a cop. That never ended well for the killer. But he needed a few seconds to get into the storage room and out the back door. So he quickly stood and fired in the direction of the cop's voice. Then he ran for the back door.

CHAPTER 35

The bullet hit Luke in the chest at the same instant he saw the flash of the gunfire. He went down hard. In his subconscious he heard footsteps running, and then he heard Jack take off, growling as he went.

His chest was on fire. And he couldn't breathe.

He heard a door slam somewhere in the back, and then he heard nothing. Luke pulled his pistol and waited, struggling to breathe.

No time to panic. He had to think it through. Yes, he remembered putting his body armor on. But the pain. Had the bullet pierced it? He felt for blood. There was none. But why the hell couldn't he breathe?

A second later, Jack was back. He came in and licked Luke's face. Then he ran back toward the back of the store.

Luke remembered feeling this way once before during a high school football game. He'd taken a helmet to the solar plexus from a tackler on an interception runback, and it had knocked the wind out of him.

He relaxed just slightly. He was realizing he wasn't mortally injured. Maybe he had a broken rib. He needed his body to reset and get some air back into his lungs. Finally, after what seemed like minutes but was only probably twenty seconds, he took a small breath. He slowly exhaled, and two seconds later he took a bigger breath.

Luke wanted to get up and run after Ball, but he thought better of it. He grabbed the radio mic on his shoulder and said, "Wildlife 148, requesting assistance. Shots fired. Bigfoot Central store off Highway 12 in Naches."

He gave information on Ball as the shooter and a description of the man. Luke didn't mention he'd been hit. He was feeling better by the minute.

"Roger, 148. Backup is on the way," the dispatcher's voice crackled over the radio.

Jack once again came back to Luke, who was now sitting up. Then Jack ran to the back of the store.

Luke got up, felt a searing pain in his chest, and slowly walked toward the back, looking for Jack. He kept his pistol ready, though he figured that if Ball was still in the store, Jack would be barking or growling, and Ball might have tried to shoot the dog. He had killed his cousin's dog—what would stop him from shooting another?

When he got to the back, Jack was sitting at the door. He looked the same as when he had to go outside to pee at home. He just sat and stared at the doorknob.

"Okay, hold on here a minute," Luke said.

If he opened the door, and Jack took off after Ball, he knew he couldn't keep up. Luke had always been able to slow Jack down when they were hunting and he got on the hot scent of a running pheasant. He hoped he could control Jack the same way now and opened the back door.

*

After he'd fired into the dark, Ball headed for the storage room, went through the back door, and ran out into the night. He ran straight away from the building until he hit some railroad tracks. If he turned to the right, it would take him toward Yakima. Left would take him toward the mountains. Other cops would inevitably be coming from Yakima, so he turned left and ran as fast as he could up the tracks.

When he had run as far as he could before he finally had to stop and catch his breath, he pulled out his phone, saw the last number he had called, and hit it. The phone started ringing. After four rings, a tired voice said, "What is it?"

"I'm in deep shit," Ball said breathlessly. "I need some help. Right away."

"What happened?"

"That wildlife cop showed up at the store. The same one that has been hounding me. Said he had a warrant for my arrest. I didn't know what to do, so I took a shot at him and ran out the back door."

"What? How stupid are you? If you killed that cop, you'll be hunted down like a dog, and they'll probably kill you!"

"I know," Ball said. "That's why I need help."

"Where are you?"

"On the railroad tracks running west out of Naches. I think I can get to some orchards, and then they'll have trouble finding me. Can you come this way, and I'll call in a while to guide you in to where I am?"

"Okay," the voice said and hung up.

Ball looked back down the tracks and listened. So far, the cop wasn't following him. That was good. Or maybe it wasn't. Maybe he was dead. That wouldn't be good at all.

He could hear sirens in the distance. He had to get going. He started running again, tripped on the raised edge of a railroad tie, fell face first into some rocks, hit his chin, and felt blood start pouring from a cut. He used a few more times, put his hand on his lacerated chin, got up, and started running some more.

*

The man who took the call from Ball hung up and stared at his phone for a few seconds. What an idiot, the man thought. Then he shut his phone off, rolled over, pulled the blankets up over his shoulders, and went back to sleep.

*

Jack headed out the door but didn't quite know which way to go. The pavement behind the store didn't hold much scent, so Jack was sniffing in circles, trying to catch something that would tell him which direction to run.

Luke looked around, remembered there were some railroad tracks running thirty yards behind the store, and headed that way. His breathing was getting easier, but his chest was throbbing with each step he took.

"This way, boy," he said to Jack and led him to the tracks.

Jack did some sniffing around and then started up the tracks headed west. Luke pulled the flashlight off his utility belt and scanned the dirt next to the railroad ties. He found fresh shoe tracks and figured those had to be Ball's. Jack was on them.

Luke could tell the dog really wanted to run after the hot scent, but whenever he got more than thirty yards ahead, Luke would say Jack's name, and the dog would stop until Luke caught up.

They were about two hundred yards up the tracks when Jack stopped and started circling around in a small area in the dead center of the railroad bed. Luke again pulled his flashlight and immediately saw blood in the dirt and gravel.

Luke pointed the flashlight ahead and could see drops of blood continuing in the direction Ball had run. Ball, he thought, must have cut himself good. That was fine with Luke. It would make it easier to track him, although he knew Jack was all over the trail too.

As he was looking at the drops of blood, Luke heard sirens in the distance.

"Wildlife 148," Luke said to the dispatcher. "I'm on the railroad tracks running through Naches, headed west, about three hundred yards west of the store."

"Roger, Wildlife 148. I'll inform backup."

A second later, the dispatcher was back. "Wildlife 148, backup will be there in two minutes."

The sirens were getting louder. They were coming fast up Highway 12.

"Roger. 148 out."

*

Ball was walking up the tracks now. He couldn't run anymore. He was exhausted. His chin was still bleeding but not quite as badly. It hurt like hell.

The sirens were getting closer, and his only hope was that the cops wouldn't know which way he'd gone when he left the store. He hadn't seen the wildlife cop following him, so he decided his best bet now was to move over to the highway. His ride should be getting close. He'd call, tell him where he was, jump in the rig, and they would be outta there.

Ball was holding the pistol with one hand, the cut on his chin with the other. He stuck the pistol in the waist band of his pants and pulled his phone out of his pocket. His hands were bloody and sticky, but he was able to get the number up on his phone again and press send. He put the phone to his ear and listened. It rang once, twice, three times.

"Come on," Ball said, almost yelling at the phone.

After the sixth ring, it clicked over to an automated message about leaving a name and number.

He looked at the number. It was the right number, so he pushed it to redial. The phone again rang six times, then went to voicemail.

Now Ball could see blue lights in the distance. The sirens were getting louder, and the lights were coming fast. Where the hell was his ride? Why wasn't he answering his phone? What was he going to do?

Luke was having to hold Jack back from charging ahead almost constantly now. They had to be getting close. Instead of rushing into the dark to face an armed man, Luke decided it would be best to wait another thirty seconds until the other officers arrived.

He told Jack to sit, and they waited in the middle of the tracks. The first officer to arrive was a young sheriff's deputy Luke had only met once. Garrett was his name, Luke remembered. But he couldn't remember if it was his first or last name. The deputy had parked fifty yards down the tracks on a siding road that ended there and had come running the rest of the way up the tracks.

"What's the situation?" Garrett asked breathing heavily.

Another sheriff's rig pulled in behind Garrett's, and the officer got out. Luke saw that it was Williams. It took the older deputy a little longer to run the fifty yards. He waited to give both men the sitrep.

"Whatta we got going here?" Williams asked.

Luke gave the deputies a brief recap of what had taken place.

"Geez," Garrett said after Luke told them he'd been hit in the chest. "You sure you're okay?"

"He's fine," Williams said. "Let's go find this dirtbag."

"Ball is bleeding," Luke said, shining his flashlight on the blood drops in the gravel. "But I have no idea how badly he's hurt. He's definitely armed, and he's shown he is willing to shoot a cop. So let's take it easy."

Luke could see Garrett was getting amped up. Maybe too amped up. The kid started to almost hyperventilate.

"You going to be okay?" Williams asked Garrett.

"Yeah, let's go," the young deputy said.

Both deputies had drawn their sidearms and held them at the ready as they started to move forward, three abreast, with Luke in the middle, following Jack.

*

Ball had moved off the tracks into some long grass. Somehow, the cops had figured out which way he was headed. He could see the light of a flashlight swinging back and forth a couple hundred yards behind him. At least one cop was coming up the tracks toward him. Two cop cars, blue lights flashing in the night, were parked next to the railroad tracks farther back. Two cop cars meant at least two cops.

At one point, he thought he saw a dog in the lights. Maybe that's how they were tracking him.

He pulled his phone out again and tried the number, with the same aggravating result. He'd done all the dirty work and made that guy a bunch of money. Now, he was leaving him out in the wind to hang.

There were two options, Ball figured. One was to wait until the cops got close and just give up. He'd most likely not get shot to death in that scenario unless the wildlife cop had died back at the store. Then the other cops just might be pissed enough to seek revenge.

Or, he thought, he could try an ambush. He wasn't a great shot with the pistol, but if he let them get close enough, he figured he could hit two of them before they got a shot off. If there were three or more, well, then he might be cooked.

One way, he was going to prison, for sure. Maybe for a long time. The other way, well, it gave him a chance. Ball backed into the grass a little farther and looked down the tracks. The flashlight was getting closer. He figured when he saw a cop's head over the top of the grass, that's when he would jump up and shoot.

CHAPTER 36

The three officers moved slowly up the railroad tracks. Luke kept the flashlight on and checked for blood. The drops were becoming more sporadic, but he'd find one here and there. Jack was definitely on Ball's scent, and even though he wanted to go, Luke held the yellow dog back to stay ten yards ahead of them. They kept three abreast, Luke and Jack in the middle of the tracks, pistols at the ready.

Suddenly, Jack froze and started with a low growl from deep inside his chest. Luke recognized it instantly. It had saved him from bears and cougars and men who wanted to do him harm. He stopped and held his left fist above his shoulder. It was dark, but both deputies caught it and stopped in their tracks.

Luke looked at Williams and nodded his head into the grass on the side of the tracks Garrett was walking, where Jack was looking. Garrett saw what was happening and started to breathe faster.

"Easy," Luke whispered to the young deputy.

"Ball! We know you're there in the grass," Luke said. "Come on outta there with your hands above your head. If you still have that pistol, throw it out ahead of you onto the railroad tracks."

Out of the corner of his eye, Luke could see Williams move slightly around to his left to have a better view of the grass. Garrett saw Williams move and started moving forward too.

Luke wanted to tell the young deputy to stop, but it was too late.

*

How, Ball wondered, did they know he was there in the grass? They were surely ready for him, so his ambush plans were going down the shitter just like everything else. He was about to give up and throw his pistol out onto the tracks when he caught motion above the grass.

There was the cop, moving up. The cop couldn't see him. It was his chance. Ball slowly came up just enough to see the cop's body, put the front sights on him, and pulled the trigger.

He saw the cop start to fall, and then everything went black. There wasn't even enough time to panic. Ball thought he was dying, and then there were no more thoughts.

*

Luke caught the motion in the grass and started to turn toward it. Then he saw the flash from Ball's pistol muzzle. That was all he needed. He pulled down on Ball and started squeezing the trigger. He was only vaguely aware that Williams was shooting at the man too.

The shooting was over in an instant. While it was happening, it seemed like everything was moving slowly, but all-in-all, from the time Ball shot Garrett to the time Ball fell backward into the grass, it was probably only three seconds.

Williams moved slowly forward to check on Ball. Jack, who hadn't moved during the shooting, moved closer and was growling at the man he'd been tracking. Luke turned to see where Garrett had been hit.

"Ball's dead," Williams called a few seconds later from the grass.

"Garrett's still breathing, but we need to get him help right away," Luke said.

Williams radioed dispatch to send an ambulance, and to hurry.

The two officers tended to the young deputy the best they could. It looked to Luke like the bullet had hit Garrett in the upper arm and had gone through it into his chest, probably breaking bone on the way. Garrett was wearing body armor, but it didn't cover his armpit, and that's where the bullet had entered.

The blood coming out of the wound was bright red and frothy, telling Luke that the bullet, or maybe bone particles, had hit at least one of Garrett's lungs. He quickly pulled rubber gloves from one of his utility belt pockets, put them on, and tried the best he could to cover the wound under Garrett's arm.

It took fifteen minutes for the ambulance to arrive, while Luke and Williams took turns pressing on the wound. Garrett was struggling to breathe, but he was breathing, which meant that only one of his lungs was not working.

The EMTs took over as soon as they arrived, coming over to the tracks from the highway. As they were loading Garrett onto the gurney to get him to the ambulance and back to the hospital in Yakima, one of the EMTs, a tall and athletic woman dressed all in black, told the officers that they had most likely saved Garrett's life.

"Stupid kid," Williams said after the ambulance had gone.

"We were all not very smart when we first started," Luke reminded him.

"I know," Williams said. "But as the senior officer, I should have kept him out of the way."

"Don't beat yourself up," Luke said.

They spent a couple minutes going over the whole thing again and looked at Ball. He'd been hit once in the head, just above the left eye, and it looked to Luke like he had at least two more bullet holes in his chest.

"What was he thinking?" Williams asked after a minute. "Did

he really think he had a chance?"

"Who knows," Luke said. "Maybe he was thinking he had killed me, and this was his only way out."

Two state patrol officers arrived shortly after the ambulance left.

"Your captain called," one of the officers said. "He wants us to take over the scene."

"It's all yours," Williams said. Both he and Luke knew there would be an investigation into the shootings, and the state patrol would be handling it.

"Come on, Jack," Luke said as he and Williams started to walk back down the railroad tracks to their rigs.

As he was walking, Luke felt his pocket vibrate. He pulled his phone out and saw he had four missed calls and fourteen text messages.

Instead of reading all the messages, which he assumed were from Sara, he called her.

"What the hell?" she said, obviously pissed.

"Listen," Luke said. Then all the emotions of the last hour hit him, and he started to shake, almost uncontrollably. "I can't talk right now. Just know that Jack and I are fine. Can you come up to the bigfoot store and get us?"

Sara could hear the emotion in his voice. She thought he might be ready to cry.

"What? What happened?" Now she didn't sound pissed but scared.

"I'll tell you everything when you get here. We're fine. See you soon."

"This might not go well," Luke said to Williams after he ended the call with Sara.

"Can you blame her?" Williams said. "Geez, you get shot, then you shoot the guy who shot you?"

"I don't think it was me who shot him," Luke said. "I can't hit a refrigerator at twenty yards with a pistol."

They didn't talk any more about it. Ball was dead. He'd been killed in a situation of kill or be killed for the officers. It didn't matter who fired the killing shot. If there ever was a justifiable shooting, this was it.

*

There were plenty of tears when Sara showed up at the bigfoot store. Most of them were hers, but Luke shed a few too. It was dawning on him just how close he had come to being killed, not once, but twice.

"That's why I wanted to be here with you," she said. "You needed backup."

He wasn't going to argue with her.

Another ambulance had been called, and the medics checked Luke out. After doing some pushing and prodding, which hurt like hell, one EMT told Luke he most likely had one broken rib, maybe two, and he'd have a contusion that might eventually run from his groin to just below his larynx.

"That'll be something to see," said Garcia, who had rushed up to the store as soon as he'd heard on his radio what was going on.

The medic recommended Luke get to the hospital sooner rather than later for x-rays and to get treated.

"You'll definitely want some prescription pain pills," the medic said. "Or you'll never get any sleep."

They asked Luke one more time if he would like to have them take him to the hospital, and again he declined. The EMTs loaded up and took off.

Over the next two hours, Luke told the story of what had transpired to a state patrol investigator, Captain Davis, and to Garcia, all of whom had shown up at the store.

Someone eventually noticed Jack sitting by the side of Luke's pickup and asked Luke what the dog wanted.

"He wants in the truck," Luke said. "Could you please let him in?"

The guy opened the door, and Jack jumped into the back seat and promptly went to sleep.

Sara was wanting Luke to go to the hospital, and they were just about to head that way when in walked Shade.

"Hey Loo-kay," she said with a giggle. "Someone called and said there were a bunch of cops and ambulances here at the store. I thought I better come check it out."

Sara gave Luke a sideways glance when she heard the cute blonde with about a million freckles talk to Luke like they were best friends.

Luke started to move and winced at the pain. Sara came over and lifted his arm over her shoulder to help him walk.

"You may be out of a job, Shaw-day," Luke said. "One of the deputies can tell you everything that happened."

"That's a bummer," Shade said, giving Sara a good once over. "Where's Jason?"

"The deputy will tell you all about it," Luke said as he and Sara walked slowly to Luke's truck.

Sara put Luke into the passenger seat and climbed in to drive.

"Can you just take me home?" Luke asked.

"Absolutely not, Loo-kay," she said. "We're going to the hospital."

Luke just groaned.

CHAPTER 37

It had been three days since the shootout in Naches. Luke spent almost all of that time on the couch, taking pain pills as needed. As was the case with every officer-involved shooting in Washington State, both he and Williams had been put on paid administrative leave until the investigation into the shooting was completed.

Because Jason Ball was dead, the county didn't push very hard on the investigation into the dead animals in the trees. Davis had shared all of Luke's findings, and after deputies discovered a .223-caliber rifle loaded with frangible bullets in Ball's vehicle, everyone assumed he was the man who had perpetrated the bigfoot hoax.

They also eventually came to the conclusion that Ball had killed his cousin. The coroner had found bullet fragments in the dead man's lungs and heart that matched the metallurgy of the bullets found in Ball's rifle. And forensics matched the yellow rope in Ball's shed to the rope that was tied around Jerome Martin's ankle.

Investigators never determined the reason for Ball killing his cousin.

*

The morning after the shooting, James Dover called Luke and got all the details about the events that had taken place at the bigfoot store and on the railroad tracks in Naches. Luke again asked to remain anonymous, and the story in the next day's paper, which wasn't really a paper but an online edition, said the information came from an unnamed source close to the investigation.

When the story came out, Garcia called Luke and said, "You should have let that reporter use your name. Everyone around here knows you were the unnamed source."

"I have no idea what you are talking about," Luke said.

"How's that contusion coming along?" Garcia asked. "I really want to see it when it goes full bloom."

It hurt too much for Luke to laugh, so he just ignored him

Garcia told Luke that Deputy Garrett, whose last name was Ketcham, would survive the gunshot wound. He had required nine hours of surgery to remove the bullet and bone fragments from his right lung. He also needed bone grafts in his upper humerus, and there was a chance the young deputy might still lose the arm.

"They say you and Williams saved his life," Garcia said.

The two men talked for a few more minutes, then Garcia said he had to go and rang off.

*

Amber Knight, the over-professional reporter from the local ABC affiliate, called Luke after the story in the digital newspaper ran.

"Agent McCain, this is Amber Knight. I'm doing a follow-up on the shootout in Naches and how it was related to the bigfoot sightings around the area. Could I get an interview with you today?"

"As I've told you before, I am not an agent, Mrs. Knight," Luke said. "And since the doctor has ordered me to stay immobile for the next several days, I won't be available for any interviews."

"We could do it over the phone," she said, but Luke had already disconnected.

*

Luke also received a call from Cliff Upshaw the day after the shooting.

"Officer McCain, I guess we aren't going to be able to meet after all," Upshaw said.

"Why is that?" Luke asked.

"I understand you were shot last night, so I figured you wouldn't be up for it."

"Only six people other than me know that I got shot last night, so tell me Mr. Upshaw, how did you know?"

"Oh, you know how news travels," Upshaw said in his most jovial voice.

"No, I don't," Luke said. "But yes, I would still like to meet with you today. I have a whole bunch of questions for you."

There was a long pause, so Luke jumped back in.

"We have Jason Ball's phone, and right now the detectives are tracking the number he called numerous times right before he died. We're thinking he had a partner, and that person left Ball out there to take a bullet. Any idea who that person might be?"

"Oh, uh, I wouldn't know anything about that," Upshaw said.

"Well, here's something you probably don't know," Luke said. "I have it on good authority that the payment you made last week to the IRS to cover some back taxes and penalties has been revoked because there is evidence that the funds you used to pay them were acquired through fraud."

"That's a lie. How do you know that?"

"Oh, you know, news travels," Luke said. "In fact, you might be looking over your shoulder because federal officials are searching for you right now. They have some warrants in hand. You are going to prison, Mr. Upshaw."

"You can't scare me with your bullshit accusations," Upshaw said.

"It's all true," Luke said. "So, tell me. How long had you and Ball been planning this whole bigfoot scam? Months? A year? It was a good one, for sure. But you guys were way too greedy. Opening the store two days after the rumors got rolling was just too soon. Nobody can get the merchandise that quickly. Not even Walmart."

"Since you have no idea where I am right now," Upshaw finally said, "I'll tell you. Ball screwed up. He was supposed to order the stuff and open the store six months ago. But when we found out the merchandise was going to arrive, we decided to go for it. You fouled the whole thing up. We thought nobody would find those animals for weeks or even months. When you did, I had to get up there and convince the world that bigfoot was on the loose."

"Do you know why Ball shot his cousin?"

"It was because of the dog. He found out that Ball had killed his dog and was going to turn us in."

"What about the photo of the bigfoot on the game camera?" Luke asked. "That was you in the suit, wasn't it?"

Upshaw laughed.

"You probably won't believe me, but I have no idea what you are talking about. That's why I was so interested to see the photo you had. If your photo experts say it is real, I guess you should believe them."

"Why don't I believe you?" Luke asked.

"I've just told you the truth about everything else," Upshaw said. "Why would I lie to you about that?"

Luke started to ask another question, but he heard a click, and Upshaw was gone.

He sat and thought about the conversation for a few minutes. Upshaw had confirmed pretty much everything Luke thought he knew about the case. He didn't have a chance to ask how they had gotten the animals in the trees, but it didn't matter really. He now knew for a fact that Upshaw and Ball were in this all along. Sooner or later, Upshaw would be caught.

Then he thought about what Captain Davis had said. The man was slippery.

*

Two days later, Luke was headed into the hospital to visit Garrett Ketcham. He walked by a man being pushed to the front door in a wheelchair. Luke thought he knew the guy from somewhere, but he couldn't place him.

The man had a full beard, was wearing a white t-shirt with the arms torn out, had large tattooed biceps, and as Luke looked at him going away, he could see a tattoo of some kind of beast coming up the man's neck and onto the back of his bald head. The tattoo was covered in a big square bandage taped to his skin.

Where, Luke thought, had he seen that guy?

He waited for the orderly to come back in with the empty wheelchair and said, "Excuse me. Do you know what that gentleman you just wheeled out of here was in for?"

"Funny story," the young man said. "He said he was climbing a tree to get into an eagle's nest, and the eagle attacked him, trying to grab the king cobra tattooed on his head. It made him fall, and he thought he'd ruptured his spleen. They did tests, and his spleen was fine. Then, two days ago, his appendix ruptured, and they had to do emergency surgery for that. The doctors think he was having appendicitis all along."

As soon as he heard the orderly mention the eagle nest, Luke remembered where he had seen the man. He was the third guy with the Russians in the security footage at the motel on North First Street.

Luke tried to hustle as fast as he could, which was about as fast as an 87-year-old man with one leg, to try to catch up to the guy with the tattoos, but he was too late. He was nowhere to be seen.

The orderly was right, Luke thought. It was a funny story. He'd have to remember to tell Sara about it tonight when she got home.

That is, if she was talking to him yet. She was still mad that he hadn't let her come along to see him get shot, or he guessed that's what it was. And, for some reason she was still calling him Loo-kay.

He had stopped trying to figure women out a long time ago. She would come around in a few days, he figured.

And she did.

A week later, Luke was looking at the photo of the bigfoot from Buel Stennett's trail camera. Sara came over and looked at it again too.

"I just can't figure this out," Luke said. "Your photo expert says the picture has not been doctored, and the creature looks real. Upshaw said he had nothing to do with it, and I kind of believe him. So how do you explain it?"

"There is only one explanation," Sara said.

Luke looked at her and waited.

"Bigfoot is real," she said matter-of-factly. "And he's running around out there right now."

ACKNOWLEDGMENTS

Once again, I would like to thank retired Washington State Fish and Wildlife police officer Gene Beireis for his assistance and patience answering my emails and phone calls, helping to make sure Luke is handling the situations in this book as they would happen in real life.

ABOUT THE AUTHOR

Rob is an award-winning outdoor writer and author of the bestselling and critically acclaimed Luke McCain mystery series set in the wilderness of Eastern Washington and featuring a fish & wildlife officer and his yellow Lab, Jack.

Rob and his wife, Terri, live in Yakima, Washington with their very spoiled Labrador retriever.